soft power
a failure in 46 parts

by matt segur

Ghostweed Press ✝ Chicago

Copyright © 2002 by Matt Segur

All rights reserved. No part of this publication may be reproduced or transmitted in any form or by any means, electronic or mechanical, including photocopy, recording, or any information storage and retrieval system, without permission in writing from the publisher.

Published in the United States by Ghostweed Press, Chicago.

www.ghostweed.com

Publisher's Cataloging-in-Publication Data
Segur, Matt, 1977–.
Soft power/by Matt Segur—1st ed.
p. cm.
ISBN 0-9718252-0-3
I. Title.
PS3569.E459 S6 2002
813'.54—dc21   2002090568
CIP

Printed in Canada

Publisher's Note

The first complete and corrected proof of soft power *was destroyed in an industrial accident. This reconstruction was compiled from the writer's original holograph manuscript and the early galley proofs with the generous and diligent assistance of his widow and now stands as the definitive edition.*

soft power

soft power

1. *sony robot dog*

A moment deleted from Stanley's life. Just a brief one. He might have used it to read a sign, admire a color, or exclaim in anger. No great loss.

He was walking to work, crossing a street: looked carelessly right instead of left, stepped forward. He saw his own foot below him. His foot marked the start of the deleted scene of Stanley Rollick.

Clap.

Then just as suddenly the glitch corrected and he was on all fours, palms bloody by the sharp sidewalk concrete. It took no time at all to deduce, from the squeal of the car tires and from the pain, what had happened. His suspicions confirmed as a nearby adolescent looked on admiringly and said "Wicked!" by instinct, and doubly confirmed by the ministrations, apologies, and admonishments of the big, American car's driver. Still, the fact that he couldn't fathom how he must have flown to end up exactly there made him worry: he had missed something important. What if he were routinely missing moments—bits and pieces of time—and only the side-effects had brought this one fugue to his attention?

But he went on his way, brushing off the anxiety, like the grit in his palms, with the hypothesis that catastrophes often feel that way. He kept walking, barely registering the thing, because he was expected at work, where he went after sleep.

He got there soon enough, pushed his way in the door, still shaking a little, and didn't speak to the guy coming off the last shift: just waited for him to stand up and took the chair. He sat in the chair, now comfortably and appropriately at work, waited for the car vibrations to subside, and thought about what had happened.

Stanley Rollick, 21, fantasizer, theorizer, and nervous walker, right wall follower, nonparticipant, progenitor of countless uncomfortable pauses, eavesdropper and eyeroller, amateur, klutz, and above all a neglector of vital immediacies, found nothing novel in the event itself, only in his fuzzy reaction. Being pushed around was his M.O.

He worked at a storage company, which suited him because he could be paid to sit and read. He looked in on half a million cubic feet of people's things partitioned into numbered crates that stood, resoundingly silent, under the buzzing fluorescent warehouse lights. Every so often a truck came to deliver a new, anonymous crate or take an old one away. Aside from that it was only Stanley and the oppressive mass of all the neglected things. The mass of a rectangular solid—for example one of the regimented storage crates that this company provided—is its length times its width times its height times its density, and all those multiplications add and add and add so that the mass is oppressive indeed. He tried not to think about it, instead thinking about being paid to sit and read.

By now his routine consisted almost entirely of being paid to sit, read, or doze at work; not being paid to do those same things at home; and, in between, taking exploratory walks in expectation of—or intending to put himself in the way of—unspecified events that subsequently failed to transpire. He felt he was missing those more than anything: events. And if accidents with cars weren't what you woke up hoping for, they were something at least.

Maybe that car knocked his brain around a little. When the morning hours drifted by, slowly bending the light in the grim little lobby toward darkness, Stanley eventually relaxed into the chair and began to doze, every so often pulled back to the orange desk and the greenish light by some sound or other. He had strange dreams—unpleasant dreams—that mostly slipped from his consciousness with the same fragility as his flight above the car, but one episode refused so to dissipate:

The dream was about work. Many of his dreams while at work were about work, which raised troubling questions about the efficacy of sleep as a means of escape in that setting. Stanley—or somebody, the eye—was exploring the warehouse, up and down the rows upon rows of crates. He was trying to localize something that irritated him: an insistent, powerful, low-frequency hum. He traversed the aisles again and again, searching for a pattern as the strength of the sound rose and fell in response to his movements. He couldn't find it; it was impossibly difficult; he wanted to cry in frustration at his incompetence to perform the simple task. He had no choice; he had to continue until he found it, that sound. The sound was dangerous, and it was hiding. He walked and walked, and always it slipped around behind him. Finally, after a dream-eternity, he stumbled as if by accident upon the crate that seemed to broadcast the hum. Though the crates were of standard proportions, this one was bigger: weirdly foreshortened, its corners sweeping outward with angular, cubist menace. It contained Something. Even if he'd been capable of unlocking the crate he was afraid to, but by inaction he felt lax in his duty as an employee. He stood, paralyzed by this dilemma, flooding with panic. Just before he shook awake he caught sight of the lot number: 1588.

2. cold storage

Stanley's routine had stagnated since he dropped out of school two years early, insolvent without his ROTC scholarship. He wasn't the sort to fit in, but never did he stick out so jaggedly as during his tenure with ROTC. Not that he'd expected to like it: just to be able to tolerate it, as means to the end of a college education. Which seemed like the natural sequel to a high school where his teachers suggested that, while nothing special, he was not an abject waste of their time.

The incompatibility was there from the start, when he arrived at the first informational meeting for ROTC recruits and sat off to the side in typical fashion. The officer—the voice of the authority—was congenial enough, but Stanley had worried at the contrast between himself and his peers. Everywhere he looked were thick, adolescent muscles, still soft but eager to learn. Stanley had no such muscles but only the softness. He was nervous and uncertain where the rest were assured, easy.

The organizations that process the young have a thing for making them wait, probably because it needs the long lesson to inculcate the understanding that they're less important than the apparatus. While the ROTC recruits were made to wait one of the others—a hulking boy but with warm eyes that weren't unkind—walked over and settled himself into the folding chair next to Stanley's. The chair squeaked against the gleaming urethane gymnasium floor, the sound reverberating, embarrassing.

"Tom," he said.

Stanley smiled in response, awkward. Briefly he was paralyzed for want of something to say but finally it came to him: he swallowed and then muttered, tripping over his tongue, "I'm Stanley."

Charitably and good-naturedly, Tom laughed, probably assuming Stanley to be a "late bloomer." "Do you play any sports?" His hair was very short, already in ROTC style, down to the mysterious oily sheen that Stanley never would learn to display, the slicked surface and the clay-like, alien protuberance above the shining forehead.

"Um..."

Again Tom laughed, understanding. "Ok, do you watch any sports? Help me out."

"Um..."

"Alright." Tom thought for a while. "I was in a military junior college before this. I can probably help you out if you have any problems. You'll figure it out. A lot of these guys can be real pricks but if you follow the rules nobody will bother you much."

That had turned out, by and large, to be the truth. Stanley's conversations might never have gone much deeper than this one with Tom, but he was able to keep his head down so that nobody bothered him, much. There's no story of chronic humiliation or of martyrdom here, those fates reserved for the kids who couldn't lay low the way Stanley could. Instead, his falling out with ROTC was to be slow and inward.

The first thing, superficial or not, was that he hated getting out of bed at four am. Every morning he tore himself out of sleep and into a cold, dark regimen of physical demands, and every morning he couldn't stand it. He talked to other recruits about it, and all he could figure was that they fought off the pain by staying up even later than necessary—as if to deprive their oppressor of that control—and by drinking—beer, mostly. Stanley did these things too, but without the therapeutic effects that the others seemed to enjoy. His window to the world fogged with perpetual exhaustion. His lectures were like the muted talking in an adjacent room: he couldn't make it out, and he did poorly. He had no friends aside from other boys in ROTC who tolerated his innocuous presence, and he had little time outside class, drills, and sleep. What time he did have he spent sitting around with said boys drinking said beer.

This crystallized the second thing: his strict, inviolate separation from all those around him. The other recruits could have been mute, capable only of guttural squeals and grunts, pawing at each other and at him, and the level of genuine intercourse between their now-piggish forms and his own would not have changed for the worse. He'd spend time with them, and when asked a question he'd supply the answer he supposed was expected, but sooner or later someone would say something to make him feel alone.

"I miss my girlfriend."

"Yeah, It's so hard to talk to the girls here."

And then, inevitably, some awful punch line:

"Yeah well they wouldn't need to talk if they'd just..."

These things weren't said entirely without irony, but close enough. And it wasn't that they offended him or that he felt himself better than them; he just couldn't empathize.

Stanley had read about the puzzles of consciousness, and he knew the standard argument. He knew that he was conscious. He couldn't know whether those around him were conscious, but he could infer consciousness when they did or said things that his own consciousness might have led him to do or say. So that whenever he found himself in one of these dialogues he'd suddenly become preoccupied by the image of himself sitting in a resonant old Victorian drawing room somewhere, hands on nervous knees, coughing and glancing around at the other seats where sat inanimate, hastily constructed wooden figures, fully dressed, with faces as two bottle caps nailed on for eyes and one for a mouth and with mechanistic innards made by a child eager to convey an

soft power

impression of functionality, simplistic noises irregularly piercing the silence like a grandfather clock's whir and click. Stanley hated ROTC.

He wasn't the type to fight his way out of situations that he could suffer through, so he stuck with it for two years until it wore him out. Quitting school, or anyway his hazy dream of school, hadn't felt like much of a loss ultimately, and before long he'd ended up at the storage company, dozing, dreaming about lot #1588.

He was not inexperienced with troubling dreams; he had a recurring nightmare. In the nightmare he sat, leisurely, in a very governmental public place of some sort—a subway station or post office, where nobody would actually spend leisure time, but Stanley found himself there doing exactly that. He heard a shriek and turned to see a woman holding her hands to her cheeks in movie-horror at what she—and now Stanley with her—was witnessing. Two passersby, both women, stood, facing each other, strangely close together. Were they hugging? They grappled frenziedly but it was without affection. Stanley looked closer and tried to make sense of what he was seeing, and it was this: no heads. Atop one woman's neck, just at the spot where her head ought to be, was instead a formless lump leading immediately down the other woman's neck, as if they'd both been decapitated and the holes sewn together, but judging by the shrieking and the pathetic, collapsed writhing of the two disconcerted bodies, this was nothing deliberate or gradual. Quantum mechanics had reared its ugly head and done one of the innumerable things it was always threatening in textbooks. These women walking in opposite directions had bumped into one another, but instead of a bruise and a curse—the more probable outcome of such an encounter—their heads had passed through and become enmeshed. Stanley would spring away from his pillow with a start, trying to sort reality from the dream, and for ten incoherent minutes be unable to free himself of the notion that this could happen to him at any moment. The next day he'd always find it funny, having reassured himself that Planck's bark was worse than his bite. But the humming of that crate stayed with him.

✝

3. purity girl

Pure like whiskey was Audrey Livingston's rage. She evaporated and condensed it, distilling gross injustice from minor annoyance. She moonshined outrage for its bitter immediacy, because the sour taste of whiskey lets you know you're still there. She played with her anger, let it thicken. She savored it, guarded it like a locket note, held it against her chest and knew she could open it whenever she liked and take comfort from that purity. She wasn't reckless. She wasn't a servant to it. It was an amusement. It was ironic. Still, harsh talking could beget harsh feeling, and sometimes she amplified a tirade for the fun of it into a rage she couldn't quite stop.

The grist of the anger this time was two men in her bookstore, talking. The bookstore where she worked—*The End of Books*, it was called—enjoyed a reputation among a small crowd of refugees fleeing the brightness of chain stores. The stacks, dusty in the slats of light from the occasional window, had the odor of age and experience—a complicated flavor, strong tea. And beyond a broad selection of cheap used books it offered the pleasant ambiance of the owner's music collection, which he told the employees to play to keep themselves amused. You could stay there a week and not hear the same thing twice. Audrey was proud of the place, proud to work there.

She'd gotten the job after she arrived in town from her native New York, visiting a college friend who was too busy working to give her much time. Nonetheless, arriving there without her parents in Susan's apartment, feeling the cold polish of its glistening orange wood floors against her toes and wandering alone through the dirty city streets during Susan's workday, she felt as though she'd suddenly been introduced to authentic life hiding behind the contrivances that her life in the care of her parents and then her university had been. The city offered an inexhaustible treasure hunt: *suffer through my ugliness, my sameness, the dull regularity of my businesses, the spatial rhythm of my supermarkets. Turn the other cheek to all of this, and I may present you with a trinket: an unassuming restaurant with a talented chef, a back alley grocer selling weird, pungent spices in unremarkable baggies. And once you've found it it's yours to keep.* She'd become addicted. Intending to stay for a week she'd instead found herself an apartment and cancelled her plane ticket home, 'home' having changed its meaning just as easily as 'today' or 'here'. *The End of Books* had been one of her treasures. She'd walked in and sat cross-legged beneath the cover of the shelves basking in the density of it for an hour—novels, histories, cookbooks, and records she'd never heard of but that she immediately liked. She'd asked for a job—and gotten one—on the spot.

Sitting, then, listening to something quiet, droning, and pretty, reading an old pulp biography of Mary Shelley, she'd had a premonition of her annoyance when she felt the rush of cool air as the door opened and the two men entered. They both wore beige dockers with brown leather belts and button-down shirts—red and blue respectively—tucked into them. One was about forty, the other about ten years older, both gesticulating boldly and talking loudly of shop:

"I think what we need to do is sit down and come up with a solution that we're both happy with that we can take to them and..."

She read at them, jolted by irritation each time she noticed that she'd been distracted from the page.

"The big thing is that I don't want to be... without talking to you and without us together having the same in-game in mind. We haven't had a chance to talk about that. I mean, that puts you in an awkward spot. I'm sensitive about that because you're... to me you really are the project. I view my role as being a facilitator and administrator. You are the one that knows the situation. You are the living project."

She twisted the music up a notch.

"I agree with that. My concern is that, without talking to them, is about our priorities in getting people on board. I've tried to get Kevin and Jerry and the CFOs on our side, and I'm concerned that we're losing sight of our agenda here."

Audrey had a gauge for people's conversations which related their inanity to the number of minutes that went by before a specific was mentioned. At times like this she'd watch the clock making its slow progress while the conversation stultified its way through solutions, synergy, burn rates, proactivity, sports metaphors, rules of thumb, and all kinds of meta-discussion. She got angrier, the longer they talked, wanting to admonish them: "Say something real!"

But she was professional. By the time they left, still chattering back and forth in a cyclic dialogue that knew no beginning or end,

soft power

she was digging her nails into her palms and quite intent on closing early, and she did.

She turned out the lights, tallied the register, locked up, and walked toward the train still hovering on the magic carpet of her rage. Audrey was short but even when calm strode with such urgency and apparent aggression that people visibly made a path for her. Something about her mode of dress was taken as a warning. Today she wore a men's short-sleeved plaid collared shirt in a dated palette of oranges and greens, jeans and black boots. Her hair, though, was the main thing. She didn't like the face in the mirror, and if she couldn't make herself look good, she could make herself look bad. Volition counted for something. Her hair, since she'd been sixteen, had been where her frustration went—genuine anger now, not the affectation—in order to get it out into the world and be done with it. When it came, she channeled it into an urge to buy the thickest, most abrasive, most chemical hair treatment she could find, slathering the awful stuff onto her head and leaving it in twice as long as the little foil pouch said. Her hair would change color as often as the weather but was consistently dry and straggly, with the weary listlessness of those oppressed. She kept it short, each hair displaying in a few inches the recent strata of her moods.

On the train was a pretty normal collection of bombed-out boat people, everyone still except for their eyes. The eyes went this way and that, saying, "Look at me," or, "Don't look at me," or, "I'm tired," or, "I'm lonely," but most often, "I don't want to be here." Audrey didn't want to be there either, not across from the tobacco-chewing kid, round and Aryan, the skin on his pisiform head seeming to drag just a moment behind the rest of him. He kept spitting on the floor, as if the designers of the train had put it there for the express purpose of storing the viscous strands of his stained spittle. Inevitably he eventually missed, arcing a tremulous wad squarely onto Audrey's boot. She stared at him, wordlessly.

He laughed, then said, "Sorry."

Somewhere in the tangle of her responses to this there was joy as the tension overmatched the strength of her restraint in an instant. "You're not sorry! You're a slug! You just sit there dripping and being fat and disgusting! And then somebody expects you to restrain your dripping and you say, 'Sorry. Don't blame me. I'm a slug. I'm disgusting.' You're pathetic."

Heads slowly turned to get a glimpse of the action because anything to relieve the sense of time lost in transit. "Hey!" was all the slug could protest when Audrey smeared her spittled boot against his pant leg and stomped off the train.

And then? Purity.

4. i could be so

Forbidding manner aside, when you weren't spitting on her shoe Audrey was as gentle as you could imagine. People liked Audrey because Audrey did things and prodded them into doing things. It was Tuesday, and on Tuesday she got together with a few friends and they ate dinner together. It had started eighteen months earlier, on a Monday. She'd called Susan:

"Hello?"

"What's tomorrow?"

"What?"

Like a battle cry: "Food club!"

"What?'

"Come over at eight. Bring food." Then, whispering, "This week's theme is *Cajun Extravagance. Cajun Extravagance.*"

And it had worked. She made blackened shrimp and beignets. Susan brought enormous, amorphous, soft biscuits. Simone and Oliver brought grits and string beans. Everybody liked it so long as Audrey kept the themes interesting: *Secrets of Nippon. Underwater Food. Weirdest Sandwich Contest. Indian Buffet. Things that are Red. Food Wrapped in Other Food.* They rotated through hosts. They'd do the advance preparations at home and then cook and assemble whatever it was at whoever's house it was. Learning to cook is about adding things to your bag of tricks and getting new ideas; they'd argue about the best way to mince garlic, season a fish, skin a cucumber, or whatever. Simone had started dressing in the mode of the theme, and that had caught on too.

When she got home, calmer to be there, Audrey began putting together a pastry with cinnamon, sugar, and ground beef for *Moroccan Speakeasy.* She couldn't afford a belly-dancing outfit. No doubt Simone already owned something appropriate.

It was funny the way envy hung in the hair around Simone and Oliver. Audrey felt it sometimes, but usually she was able to look past it and enjoy their company, which turned out to be mortal once you got to know them. They'd been a couple since she'd known them; some sort of ideal in her mind of conjugal bliss. The first time she'd met them, she'd been captivated, imagining the details that she didn't know. They had this shroud of exoticism, and she'd expected that if she followed them home she'd find out they lived in space or underground or in some carefully concealed neighborhood where it was still 1940 and always cool and mysterious out. Audrey made a point of never asking Simone where she got the clothes. Magnificent clothes. Not expensive; anyone with a budget could have that, and Simone didn't even have the budget. Her clothes looked like they might have been cheap if you only knew where to get them, but that was presumably in some other country that wasn't on Audrey's map. Not like it would have helped her to get there, because the clothes were always draped so as to accentuate Simone's blessed thinness, tallness, shapelessness. The sort of good looks you couldn't aspire to but only have or not. Audrey had not, and usually was comfortable with that, but Simone and Oliver, they had. Her skin self-tanned and unplaceably asian, dark eyes, hair usually covered by a handkerchief, veil, shroud, sari, or the equivalent. He a dagger with chiseled, angular features and strong and steady, the bushy tuft of hair humbly unkempt, walking into a place and rearranging it in an instant with sheer presence.

They brought lamb with mint honey sauce. Nobody else could make it that night, so just the three of them sat on Audrey's back porch watching the luminous summer dusk, inhaling alternately the cool breeze and the warm, rich smoke of Simone's cigarettes. Along with the lamb, Oliver had gotten a good price on four unmarked bottles of sweet dark beer from a guy he knew. Audrey held her knees to her chest and dazed at the big bottle—wet with condensation—that Simone's small hand gripped loosely by the lip. She told them about "Spitty."

Oliver, with his kind laugh: "We'll teach him a lesson, later."

"I hate men," said Simone, poking Oliver in the stomach. He slapped at her hand.

"Really." Audrey moaned with feigned unctuousness, "I was this close to lesbianism."

"I'm in if you are. Let's go buy tanktops and cats!" As with the clothes, Simone rejoiced in any kind of attitude that she could

soft power

model. They all laughed, and through the brickwork of the alley the sound and then its echoes subsided and were replaced by an aftershock of laughter that spread first through Audrey, then Oliver and Simone in turn. Finally, though, those last spasms died out and the silence and the relaxation of Audrey's diaphragm made her piercingly aware of the alley's empty stillness, and she, too, felt very still.

"I'll be home late tomorrow. I have to eat dinner with Sean," Simone seemed to remember to Oliver, just then.

"It's so awful", he imitated her voice, "I have to be taken to dinner tomorrow by my handsome and fabulously successful boss, and I just hate that."

"Shut up!"

"I see how you're going to be. I'll just go out binge drinking with all the sexy young things."

Audrey braced herself against the awful weight of their glares and the argument to come but to her surprise they were content to glare. On that note, they left, taking their tenseness with them. Goodbyes were exchanged, and Audrey washed the dishes, savoring the searing heat of the water against her wrists for the hope that its energy might seep into her. Though she enjoyed the gatherings, she had to fight off the feeling of emptiness when everyone went home, leaving her alone with the quiet of her apartment, not yet ready for sleep but too exhausted to do much beyond the immediate chores. She slapped off the faucet and with a metallic shudder the spasm of the water abruptly stopped, the impulse echoed a moment later by the sound of the light switch as she turned it off and the creaking of the floorboards beneath her footsteps. She walked to the window and looked out onto the darkened, empty street punctuated by the low wails of somebody crying, somewhere, until she felt she could sleep.

※

5. analgesic

Stanley stared at #1588 and felt ill. It was where the computer had said it would be in the warehouse. Nothing was really amiss; it looked like the identical crates that surrounded it. It made the same sound when he kicked it—deep and hollow and resonant—but he didn't feel reassured. According to the plan, looking at the box was supposed to reassure him.

He had felt fully awake for the first time that morning as he looked out the train window at the angles of buildings crossing each other, those nearby passing up those in the distance. Vertical lines stay vertical; lines into the distance twist across the window.

He had worried about the dream all night. It had kept him up, away from other dreams. He decided, looking out at the brown buildings and the grey sky, that going out into the warehouse, finding #1588, and examining it would set his mind at ease. He'd gone out into the warehouse, feeling exposed and small below the high, dirty fluorescents. He'd found #1588. He'd examined it. His mind was not at ease.

It smelled. He scolded himself for imagining things but kept sniffing and little by little convinced himself that it really did smell. Like his apartment when he neglected to take out the trash. Like carrion. And he couldn't look away from it. When he'd tried to walk away, he'd turned and then felt, immediately, it sitting there: immobile, inanimate, yet malodorous and somehow a threat. He stopped, spun around, and sighed at its static silence. So he backed away, down the aisle, slowly retreating, watching it; this superstition was ridiculous. The side of #1588 that he could see shrunk in the distance to a fine line and then he turned and ran, panicked, to the entryway. The door locked behind him made him feel safe, like the blanket covering to the neck against the night or the lamp restraining the burglars to the darkness at the edge of the room.

He made himself pick up his book and read, and he started thinking about something mentioned in it: thermostats. He'd studied the thermostat in his apartment—a brushed metallic hemisphere on the wall, the prototype for more devices of the kind than he cared to imagine.

Inside the rounded ersatz bronze cover, a rolled up strip of metal coils around itself, clockwise, six times. Attached to the end of the coil, held horizontal above it, is a glass vial filled with mercury. The mercury has nothing to do with measuring the temperature; it acts as a level. When the tube is tilted counterclockwise, the two metal contacts inside the vial are suspended above the mercury so the circuit is broken. When Stanley turns up the temperature control, coil and vial twist clockwise, bathing the contacts in mercury, completing the circuit, igniting the furnace. The coil is two strips made from two different metals pressed and glued tightly together. The two metals have different properties, in particular expanding at different rates when subjected to heat. When the coil heats up, each material wants to get longer at its own pace but considering their unnatural marriage something has to give; the strip bends ever so slightly. The length of the coil magnifies minute variations in temperature into a pitch of a few degrees to the orientation of the vial. The furnace heats the room, the coil unwinds, the vial twists counterclockwise, the circuit breaks, the furnace is extinguished.

The interesting thing about the thermostat is it's mercury, glass, metal and wires—simple enough to build, a stupid little contraption—but to the naive observer it appears to *want* something: it wants to keep the temperature of the room constant. The thermostat can replace a man who stands next to the furnace and runs it for a while whenever he feels cold. The thermostat is not like the man; it doesn't really want anything. But these two, the man and the machine, respond to information analogously. Someone (Johnny Thermostat?) meant to complete that analogy when he invented the thing.

Johnny Thermostat would have been an engineer. Conceiving an arrangement of parts with a particular logical property was once the domain of engineers. Engineers built machines, and machines were analogies. In the Second World War, the German engineers at Mittelwerk had to figure out how to guide a rocket along the thousand-mile arc to London. No remote control—the rocket had to *want* to hit London. They had no way for the rocket to measure its absolute position in the skies above Europe, and without a road to spin against you can't build an odometer. What they had was an accelerometer—a weight on the end of a spring, pushed toward that spring when the rocket accelerated, deforming the spring in proportion to that acceleration, generating current in proportion to that deformation. And there's a relationship between how you've accelerated and how far you've gone. Isaac Newton figured out in the sixteenth century that the integral of acceleration is velocity, and the integral of velocity is position. And here's where the German engineer completed the analogy: a capacitor generates an opposing voltage in proportion to its charge, and its charge is the integral of the current applied to it. The current proportional to acceleration coming into the capacitor causes a voltage proportional to velocity coming out. A second capacitor reaches zero voltage at the moment its charge—proportional to distance—reaches a preset value—say, half the distance to London. The spring and weight reflecting acceleration connects to the capacitors analogous to double integration, and in the physical world as in the analogous world of mathematics the compound is a device that measures position—the rocket knows when it's gone far enough to turn off the engines. It was elaborate, but Stanley suspected that the people in London living beneath the silent shadow of the V2 could have attested that it worked. The ones that weren't blown up, anyway.

Stanley liked this stuff—thought it clever—but it wasn't what his book was about. It was about Alan Turing, the mathematician. Five years before the War, he'd figured out how to put the engineers out of business, or at least irrevocably change that business.

Alan Turing, like Stanley, had thought about *thought*. He'd thought about the sorts of things people do when they think—they way they draw figures, make notations, keep records, and follow instructions—and he'd tried to imagine a machine that could do those things. His machine had a paper tape for keeping notes. It could move the tape forward or backward. It could write a symbol on the tape. It could erase the symbol on the tape. It had some number of "states of mind." Each state of mind told it, contingent on the symbol written on the tape, what to do with the tape and what state of mind to adopt next. He described a vacillating sort of machine that wrote "01010101..."; it switched between two states, one that wrote "0" and another that preferred "1." He described a counting machine that wrote "01," then "011," then "0111," and so on.

If you spent the time, you could devise one of these machines—called Turing Machines now—to do just about anything.

But Turing himself had broader ambitions. He wrote out the states for a Turing machine that he called the *universal* machine—that word, 'universal', whether in physics, mathematics, or literature, seeming to be the sign of a sure thing. The universal machine first read off the tape a description of *another* Turing machine, then performed whatever operations that machine would have. He demonstrated that if you solved the analogy problem once and built the universal machine, you never had to do it again. From then on, you merely had to tell the universal machine, by way of all those marks on the tape, what kind of machine you wanted it to be: thermostat or V2 or *Pong*. He hadn't stopped there; he'd said that the human mind must be a Turing machine. So there sat Stanley, thinking, wondering if his *want* was so different from the *want* of his thermostat after all, or the *want* of a bomb using its jets to drop neatly onto an invisible X on a building, somewhere.

Stanley wanted someone to come in wanting storage services and realize that they wanted to talk to him instead. He wanted something to hurry towards when he left work in a hurry. He wanted to think he wasn't just wasting time getting older.

Why all these wants? Stanley was shy, of course. He couldn't talk to anyone, least of all to "girls." As if that weren't enough (it was enough), Stanley felt uneasy about the whole alleged process. To meet somebody, he knew, he was expected to "hit on" some "girl." Even the vocabulary made him feel guilty; it all sounded so nasty. What would he say if he did this and the response was an unlikely "Are you hitting on me?"

"No?" That would be a lie.

"Yes?" "Yes, I am *hitting on* you?" No! Better to keep as he was than to face the prospect of having to make that admission, the

soft power

sound of it unconscionable. So he kept as he was, wanting people, wanting events.

Wanting, after his night of tossing and turning, to fall asleep, as he finally did there at work. Sitting back in his slippery vinyl swivel-chair, his eyelids pulled slowly but inexorably shut. Then a sudden, panicky jerk back awake—the sign that you're falling asleep. A warning of things to come, because Stanley had another bad dream. No surprise that it was about a girl, considering his recent line of thought. The scary thing was that she was suspended in amber. Crouched, fetal, naked but not alluring, lost, silent, still. Suspended in that murky, refractive block of amber through which Stanley's eye seemed to move freely. That was it; no story, no dialogue. Just a slow pan through the amber, staring, terrified, into the girl's closed eyes—she sleeping or dead, deprived of volition by the encasing prison. When he started from this second nightmare, Stanley didn't know which way was up. He fell out of his chair. Where was he? Was he in amber? Was he her? Who was he? A few minutes later he was more sure but no less frightened.

He anxiously waited out the clock until he could leave, then got on the train to take him home, feeling paranoiac and jittery. And it was on the train that he got the genuine event he'd been waiting for. The ride began in the ordinary fashion. A man was delivering a spoken performance for money; it was less interesting than he appeared to think. Stanley watched the woman in the seat in front of him as she dug a scuffed, outdated polaroid camera from her bag, focused on the man, pushed, and the photo churned slowly but steadily out from the bottom of the camera. She removed it and placed it against her book. The indistinct grey globules of emulsion simmered and stewed but at first seemed unwilling to alter their doings to suit the image the woman had seen fit to photograph. But slowly, then, a few at a time, they grudgingly relented and a ghostly image of the train emerged on the glossy paper. The photo was so brazenly awful that Stanley wondered if perhaps there was something wrong with her; the top of the subject's head peeked inconspicuously out from the bottom of the frame; dead center, twisted slightly, was an air-vent in the ceiling of the train; the colors were dull, lifeless. It was the sort of photo that only a very small child or a crazy person would take, and this woman wasn't one of those to look at her.

Puzzled as he was by the photographer, he almost failed to notice when the door opened and the girl of his dream walked through it and sat down across from him, but notice he did. She was small. Her smallness, her short, messy hair, her sharp features, and her darting, aggressive eyes made her boyish, but it was a brash, feminine boyishness that nearly dared you to mistake her for a boy. It was confidence that she didn't need to convince you with long hair, bright makeup, wide bosom. Old, careless clothes subtly hinted at her form; her boots were big and black and intimidating. That was it: she was fierce. The sort that Stanley would never have the nerve to accost. Never, unless he were feeling out of sorts, driven, already half-crazed by his weird dream and now baffled by the appearance, here on his train, of its actress.

"Hi you don't know me but my name is Stanley. Um, it doesn't matter. What I... What I wanted was I've been having this thing where... Well I had this dream about this storage crate at work and then I went and found it in the warehouse and it stank like rot and..." He got all of this out fast enough not to be dissuaded by the increasing mistrust in her brown eyes. "The thing is that I had this dream and then it seemed to sort of come true and then just today

soft power

I was... I had another dream and there was this girl and she was sort of... in a bad way. In amber. And the thing was that it was you." He paused here; she was still silent. "In my dream. So I wanted to know if you were ok."

Taking this in for a moment more, she suddenly stood: "Get away from me! Damn! Why does everybody have to be so weird? This is my stop," and pushed her way past him and ran out of the train and out of sight and he stood there, holding the oily, warm handrail, staring after her, silent, and thought about how his words must have sounded and felt horrible about it, trying to hide his face from the curious onlookers. He got off at the next stop though it wasn't his, waiting for another train to take him the rest of the way home.

6. come back to me don't bother me

All the books in the bookstore gave it a smell. You could pick up a book, open it against your face, and breath in its dry, musty, material scent. Tens of thousands of books taken together gave off an odor that, depending on Audrey's mindset, was either a mysterious, pungent possibility or a dank reminder of the waste of so many trees for so many pages of so much passed-over drek.

The End of Books had a small magazine section—God knew why—that tended to remind her of the stifling empty-headedness of people. There was a magazine called SKIN devoted entirely to women's more dermal insecurities, its readership in her store confined to teenage girls without the discretionary income for a subscription, all apparently in the tenuous position of understanding the old issues to be more or less interchangeable with the new ones yet still finding themselves unable to dismiss the whole idiot enterprise. Sometimes Audrey would venture the beginnings of a conversation with the liquid-thin young girls sprawled with careless sensuality across the rough wall-to-wall, and once convinced that she wasn't trying to hassle them for reading without buying they were responsive enough after their saddening, desperately samey fashion. Audrey was young enough to merit some credibility so she'd try to explain that most of them, at their age, were still comparatively flawless with or without SKIN; that, all taunts aside, teenage boys weren't exactly discriminating when it came to teenage girls willing to give time of day; and that they weren't going to get any that was worth having in high school anyway so couldn't they read about something more interesting and start to foment the personality that would precipitate some tangled obsession a few years on? She'd then point them to her picks shelf, and she'd had the satisfaction of seeing a couple of them return periodically to check for new recommendations.

The only other person to pay any attention to Audrey's picks shelf was her father. He'd bumble in six times a year, always selecting from it one book to take home and (she'd deduced by hinting around at their contents) not read. It happened that Audrey was thinking he was about due—one of those moments that makes you question your skepticism—when he walked through the door, in his way, timid and sad and dazed.

"Hey! How are you?" She tried hard to keep worry and pity from her voice but she suspected he could tell, though he never let on.

"I'm really good. I've been, you know, doing my stuff. I just about finished editing together the new thing so I should be able to get a date to you pretty soon for the premiere."

soft power

"This is the one with Howard?"

"Yes that. I think it's pretty good." Having gone down this dead end he paused for a minute, pretending to look at the rare books shelf above Audrey's head. "Did you talk to your mother yet?"

"No! She left me another message last week and was like, 'Oh Audrey I found this unbelievable little seafood place. It's gorgeous. We have to get you out here some time so we can go,' as if I'd spoken to her in the last two years or I was supposed to just forget that I hadn't," she laughed.

"I don't want you being so hard on her on my behalf, Audrey. You should talk to your mother."

"It's not... I know you know what I mean. I can't talk to her anymore really, so why should I bother pretending?"

"But you don't need to be angry for me. Anyway it just ends up as a nasty message on my machine. So I guess I want you to... to not be so hard on her on my behalf." He tried to involve her in his apologetic smile while she unraveled the syntax.

"Yeah yeah so now we get to the real matter," eager at the chance to change the subject.

"What about you? Are you doing anything new?" he looked slowly round the store.

"No, Daniel, I'm not. Nothing new."

"I'm sorry. I know you like this place but I don't think they're really using your talents."

"Thank you, Daniel, but I'm not allowed to talk to recruiters while I'm on the job."

Again, a pause. "Well, anyway, don't mind me. I'm just going to look around a little. You know. Need some new reading." He wandered back into the store, footsteps muffled by the hard sea-green carpet, but even that brushing and his soft swallows suddenly were irritants. He made some show of looking around but didn't seem to spend enough time to notice anything. Audrey rolled her eyes and stared at some words in her book.

Two pages later he returned with the inevitable selection from her shelf. (*Snow Country*, this time, and perhaps it was short enough to fit his schedule.)

"Just this."

"Ok then." She affected the Minnesota accent while ringing him up, something she'd learned from Simone: "You come back real soon now, ok?"

He dazedly smiled to acknowledge the halfhearted humor. "Call your mother, Audrey."

"Ok bye!"

The bell on the door clanged and the door shuddered after him, and she was left alone with the polyrhythm of the wall clock.

How did they do it? Her father had his work to keep him occupied; he juggled projects like a demented jester in a high-ceiled room to make sure of it, but Audrey had to infer that—like the deadening of the taste buds that broadens the palates of adults—his tolerance for loneliness must have increased for him to be able to go days or weeks without a friendly conversation. She had to remind herself that she was technically an adult too, now, but it didn't seem to've happened so far, though dark chocolate had grown on her.

But even for his sake—even for the small, beleaguered figure of him in her mind—she would not call her mother. Always presumption, on every level. Conspiratorially badmouthing Daniel; Audrey couldn't even politely ignore it. Catch could wait another two years, or ten.

soft power

The store stayed empty until Audrey left, walking slowly, thinking. The train was late, sliding into the station beneath its own indiscreet cacophony, dimly annoying in the expected way. And the first thing she saw when she got on was the strangely animated guy—medium-build, stooped, gawky, tapping his heel, manic, on the rubberized floor, elbows forward on his knees—who looked at her as she walked in, looked away, looked back and away again, then stared out the window. Soft, pale, suburban features, a dull bowl of longish kid hair that he obviously didn't notice. He looked like he'd grown all a sudden and now had more length than he knew what to do with. Agitated, but he had the suggestion of kindness about him; certainly he lacked anything you could point to as a sign of danger.

But then as she was reaching into her bag for her book he assaulted her with the long, confused, weird ramble that could have originated anywhere on the meandering road between pick-up and schizoid polemic. And if it weren't for her mood or the heat she might have let him go on just a minute more but she was just scared and she told him off and left, two stops early, walking the rest of the way, angry again, wondering what everything seemed to have against her lately.

7. lost and found

The next day, in his chair at work, trying to put the embarrassment out of his mind, Stanley worried about his immune system. They liked to talk about your immune system fighting off disease. Down in your trenches, those t-cells, your little white soldiers, valiantly battling the tiniest monsters—your cold, your fever. That wasn't quite right, though, because diseases aren't really your immune system's forte; they're its Vietcong. It fights, but quite a lot of the time it loses, at least for a good while. Viruses, especially, have nothing to worry about from your immune system; once you catch that herpes it will be with you, helping you along, for good. No, the palatable metaphor of the soldiers fighting off disease, like a smaller M*A*S*H, was obviously half-truth.

The real virtuosity of your immune system, what they didn't want to say for fear of discouraging the squeamish from noble medicine, was this: your immune system keeps you from rotting. It's got that handled cold. All the little bugs, all of them, everywhere, trying to rot everything, and you go for eighty years unscathed. A piece of ground beef, deprived of the benefits of its cow's immune system and left at room temperature, is rotting vigorously within a day. Hours after you die and your t-cells die with you, the bugs are already realizing that they've finally gotten the run of the place—swarming, enveloping, devouring, bloating, turning all green. But as long as you've got your immune system, which *keeps you from rotting*, you've got nothing to worry about.

Like the viruses, cancer is another thing your immune system is just no damn good against. Cancer, what doesn't infect, poison, or eat, but instead corrupts, perverts. Cancer, willlessly bent on making you into more cancer. What about a giant, autonomous tumor, lying there, alive? Would its genetics occasionally, randomly change into something that knew how to become coherent structure, non-tumor? Of course not, so cancer has the upper hand. Cancer, close cousin to old age, deliberate misdirection instead of slow forgetfulness, but either one eventually turning suppleness, lustre, and uniformity into irregularity, exception, misshape. Even if you're

soft power

lucky or reclusive and Newton's unforgiving mechanics never manage to shear pieces of your matter apart and infection never manages to seduce its way into you, you can't hide from the particles that randomly collide with yours, occasionally flipping your bits around. Sooner or later—no, face it, sooner—cancer or old age is going to monkey with your design to the point that it's no longer tenable. Once that happens, the rot that your immune system so confidently beat down for those few years will win out, again. The winner, and still champion? Rot.

Stanley was by now firmly convinced that something was rotten in #1588; the smell, out in the warehouse, was unmistakable. Nobody else seemed to have noticed, but when Stanley's boss came reeling in, looking hungover in a bad white suit and a t-shirt, Stanley assumed someone had tipped him off to it.

"Stanley! How's everything around here?" Rob's signature quality was insincerity.

Stanley was never disingenuous, even as he now lied: "Good."

"I danced with way too many ugly girls last night, Stanley. You know?"

"Yeah."

"Yeah. Hey I've just got to get a couple of things for the accountant and then I'll be out of your way," walking to the filing cabinet in the corner of the small clerk's room, next to the forlorn ficus tree that almost looked fake—as if somebody had set up a business manufacturing synthetic replicas of weedy, browning, poorly cared-for plants. Stanley waited while Rob rifled, loud and slow, through the files, piling those that he extracted next to him. When he finished he locked the filling cabinet, pulled out his key with his right hand, grabbed the stack of file folders with his left, noisily aligned it against the orange formica of the counter where

Stanley sat, then put folders and keys in a pile on the counter and walked off to the small adjoining bathroom. When the door shut and the aggressive peeing began Stanley grabbed the keychain, found the purple-tinted master key for the storage crates, and began working at the rings with his fingernails. He couldn't pry the two rings apart at first and the sound from the bathroom was already sputtering when he started working the key between them. Trying to mute the jangling he removed the master, replaced the keychain, and was in his seat just as the door opened and Rob walked out.

"Hey, don't party too hard ok? I'll see you later," as Rob grabbed his things and left, letting the aluminum and plexiglass door nastily slap the frame.

Stanley walked slowly through the warehouse toward #1588, his footsteps echoing through the empty space, wondering if he was up to this. Thinking about fingerprints, he put his left hand beneath his shirt and then used the fabric to grab the lock, which resisted the turning of the purple key only briefly. After removing the lock he pulled at the door of the crate in the same way, as it opened falling back from the now unrestrained stench that poured from the dark insides. So dark that he couldn't make out a thing, so he ran back to his desk and grabbed the flashlight that he'd fidgeted on and off so many times in the past.

The crate, the size of a large closet, was empty but for the form at the back left that Stanley squinted at from the doorway. It was a boy, seventeen or eighteen, maybe, dirty blond, pale, thin, with delicate, almost female features. He was sitting with his back to the wall, hands tucked against his chest, and the impression left on Stanley would have been of peace if the box weren't so fetid. Now clumsy with adrenaline, Stanley closed the door and replaced the lock, still remembering not to fingerprint, and ran back out of the warehouse with fear no longer superstitious but righteous and pure.

He was now reluctant to tell anyone about the box, worrying that he might come under suspicion himself (especially with the stolen master on his person, which he resolved to get rid of somewhere), so he settled down to wait out the time until one of the other clerks noticed the smell and told somebody. He tried for a while to speculate about why someone might have deposited a body in River North Public Storage lot #1588 but of course he got nowhere. He then tried to return to his book and couldn't concentrate well enough to read very far but it gave him something else to think about.

The boy had been nineteen at the most and dead. Stanley was 21 and deathly afraid of getting to be more than 25 or so. Not sure that he had to finish what life he'd planned by 25, but he'd better at least have started. Alan Turing was 23 when he published *On Computable Numbers with an Application to the Entscheidungsproblem*, in which he described the universal machine. The *Entscheidungsproblem* that the paper answered was the last of three questions, a tripartite challenge posed by the mathematician David Hilbert in 1928. The first was whether it was possible to either prove or disprove every mathematical statement arising from a set of axioms. The second was whether all the provable mathematical statements were consistent. The third, the question that Alan Turing conceived the universal machine in order to answer, was whether there existed a "definite method" for proving or disproving any given statement—instructions for going about it that anyone could follow. Hilbert posed the questions in hopes that all three could be answered *yes*—raising the possibility of mechanizing the process, putting together a machine that, given the axioms, would methodically crank out each and every consequence, so that if you waited long enough eventually you'd know, given any formal, logical statement, a verdict: true or false—but the answer to all three questions turned out to be *no*, the first two due to Kurt Gödel and the last to Alan Turing.

Gödel dashed the hopes of a generation of industrious mathematicians by constructing a mathematical statement that provably could not be proved true or false. Stanley's book explained that it was a careful formalization of the old *liar's paradox*: "This statement is false." That made the result not nearly so disheartening to Stanley as it must have been to Hilbert since, though it might not be true or false, Gödel's example was so obviously facile. Still, it marked the end of the dream that mathematicians had been working toward—that of a complete, consistent list of all truths deriving from the short list of axioms. If nothing more, you at least had to allow for an endless list of stupid, useless statements that you could say nothing about, one way or the other. It was one more step in the formalization of hopelessness all over the science of the early 20TH century.

Turing, taking up where Gödel left off, showed that any definite method could be described by a paper tape input to his imaginary machine—the machine a prototypical follower of instructions. That meant that if a well-defined problem existed that was impossible for the machine to solve, then the answer to the *Entscheidungsproblem* had to be no, and he found such a problem.

Turing encoded the input to his universal machine—the description of the states and behaviors making up a particular Turing machine—numerically. For instance, he wrote the fickle machine that alternated between "0" and "1" as:

31332531173113353111731113322531111731111335317

This meant that every number corresponded to a hypothetical Turing machine, and that there were two types of numbers. *Satisfactory* numbers described a Turing machine that would operate properly, computing an infinite sequence of digits. Other numbers corresponded to malformed, stillborn machines: machines that were *circular*. Sooner or later, a circular machine would get stuck, unable to print any more digits. Most machines were circular; most machines would get stuck; nearly all.

Turing's insoluble problem, the so-called "halting problem," was to decide, given a number, whether or not it was satisfactory. Suppose, Turing wrote, that a machine existed that could make this decision. Every number corresponded to a machine, and every satisfactory number printed a stream of digits, so a simple modification of said machine would allow it to test all the numbers, starting with one and counting upward. For every satisfactory number, this machine would compute one digit of the output of the machine that that number described. It would find the first satisfactory number, emulate the first machine long enough to produce one digit, and record that digit. It would then count again until it found another satisfactory number and compute two digits of the second satisfactory number's machine. The hypothetical machine would record the second digit of the second noncircular machine alongside the first digit of the first.

Turing had set a trap for the machine that he envisioned. At some point, say with the thousandth satisfactory number, it would reach the number that described itself, and what could it print? The machine wasn't circular, so its number must be satisfactory, and the machine would try to compute the thousandth digit that *it would itself print*. In order to do this, it would compute the first 999 digits and then try to compute the thousandth. In order to this, it would compute the first 999 digits and then try to compute the thousandth. In order to this, it would compute the first 999 digits and then try to compute the thousandth. The machine wasn't circular, and yet it was—a contradiction. It could not exist.

Turing fed the machine to itself—the snake eating its tail, like Gödel's statement. The universal machine was less universal than you might like. So although mathematics lived thousands of years before discovering its own mortality, the computer was conceived in the darkness of its own limitation, never afforded the youthful optimism that we all deserve. That seemed a bad sign.

Stanley's youthful optimism was definitely on the wane. He had a habit of depressing himself by attending the flavor-of-the-month movie about the coming-of-age of some group of young and beautiful friends; he couldn't help making the inevitably distressing comparison between their fruitful lives on the one hand and his, barren, on the other. He didn't want to end up in some storage crate or accident scene or nursing home, nothing ever having happened to him, having no friends, never having produced anything that he liked, the weight of his own isolation, inaction, and virginity eternally on his stilled shoulders. So he was now torn between sorrow for the fellow in the box and the fantasy, ridiculous he knew, that investigating the bizarre circumstance might lead him to something... of note. Temptation getting the better of him, he found himself turning to the amber glare of the universal machine at his desk and querying lot #1588: Richard Holmgren, 4720 W. Sestertia Drive. He dialed the number, more sure after each hollow, mechanical ring that it would be wise to hang up.

"Hello?" It was an elderly woman with a weak voice.

"Hi. Richard Holmgren, please?" Stanley told himself he was making a business call for the sake of courage.

A sigh. "I'll get him." Then the sound of the phone being laboriously, clumsily put down, just the start of a drawn-out litany of creaking, knocking, and a stream of distant voices.

"Richard here," Richard eventually announced.

"Hi I'm calling from Public Storage." No name. "We're having a problem with our database here and we need to check some billing information for some of our customers. Do you happen to remember how you paid for the item that you stored with us on July 15TH?"

"What? Sarah, we don't have anything in storage, do we? No you've got the wrong number."

"Um..."

"When were we out with the kids? Two weeks after... My wife and I were in Wisconsin on July 15TH and we're the only ones at this number. Nobody was house-sitting. You must have made some mistake."

"Right." He tried to draw it out like he were making notes. "Sorry to bother you."

"You sound familiar," and Stanley could feel the slow weight of Richard's words as his mind worked toward some memory. "What did you say your name was?"

The last thing he wanted to answer. "Um..."

"No, don't tell me. I'd swear I recognize your voice. It's..."

Stanley only waited, not knowing what to do.

"Sacks. You sound just like Sacks. Any relation? The lawyer, does wills. What was your name?"

Stanley hoped this last question would be overrun by another but as he paused it didn't seem to be happening. "No, no relation. I'm very sorry to bother you Sir," and hung up, half expecting the phone to ring him back within the minute, but no such thing happened. And settled down to wait, and say nothing to anyone, because he knew there were now fingers pointing his way.

Richard and Sarah hadn't sounded like the type that Stanley envisaged having criminal connections. 4720 W. Sestertia, by the address, would be in the sleepy, grey wasteland of modest single-story homes at the west edge of the city. Retirees like Richard and Sarah would be common enough there, corpse disposal comparatively rare, he would have thought.

It rained while Stanley was at work. Walking home at five he saw puddles accumulated in all the bus stops. In one of these floated a discarded glass bottle, bobbing and spinning playfully in the wind that rippled the water's surface. Then a bus came and the wake from its wheel sent the bottle surfing over the curb where it hovered for a moment before rolling back into the water, bobbing to and fro. Stanley stared fixedly at the bottle as he approached and was nearly flattened by a short but massive young latino man, in shorts and a hockey jersey, barreling along toward his bus. Stanley roused himself to the task of attending to the world.

8. pipe cleaners and popsicle sticks

Audrey woke up energetic on Saturday to an epic of dog barking, the sound reverberating through the alley outside her window. She couldn't say how long the dogs had been at it when the white square of the ceiling, softly greying into the corners, resolved in front of her. Shifting to a fresh spot on the sheet, she felt its heat, more than her own, and became conscious of the late August warmth getting its morning start—the real reason she could be

soft power

roused so early. Everything that she touched was hot or wet or both.

She had time to make some pancakes, clean up the mess, get a start on cleaning the rest of the apartment, shower and dress before time came around she felt good about calling Simone and Oliver as promised, and it was well judged because they sounded still in bed. Still, they said she could come over whenever. With her ablutions she'd also grabbed a rough tongue of hair running up from the center of her forehead and gone at it with a washcloth soaked in bleach from under the sink, ignoring the banshee wails of protest that she imagined from each individual hair. Once she'd rinsed, it looked compellingly repulsive, though it wasn't quite the *Bride of Frankenstein* thing she'd been going for. Still, she hoped someone would say it looked bad so she could tell him off.

Simone buzzed her up when she got there and left the inside door cracked. Predictably, Simone and Oliver had a fantastically capacious apartment that was totally unique in its arrangement, located as it was on the top floor above a Thai restaurant wedged in a corner of one of those overburdened intersections serving three streets instead of two. The building was the remnants of some young, not-yet-jaded architect's gallivant through Algiers fifty years earlier. He'd done the place up like a mosque—white stucco walls, all the windows round and covered by wrought iron patternwork, the stylistic play culminating in the third floor space accessed by a locked door on the second, meaning that the stairway led unobstructed up into the hardwood of their triangular main room, where dim, brown light filtered from two walls and the ceiling through the decorated windows and, in the third wall that bisected the apartment, open doorways on either end led to the kitchen and bedroom, respectively. They'd also got it for a song, again predictably for them, inconceivably for anyone else. The decor accentuated the construction—baffles hung from the ceiling from brown and white-patterned sheets that sagged voluptuously toward the floor from four corners; both doorways veiled by chains of brass ringlets; candles flickering on the low, black end-tables.

"There are cigarettes on the table." Simone's voice from the bedroom.

"I don't smoke," Audrey replied, taking a cigarette and lighting it, with some difficulty, from a candle jar.

"I heard you put on fifty pounds and went on Ricki Lake with your pornographer brother, you skank." She hadn't finished getting dressed, it sounded like.

"I heard you were selling autographed copies of your butt at Seven Eleven next to the weenie heater till your parents got there and your Pa made your Ma take over for you and raised the price to two zlotys."

"I heard your brother shoots naked movies of little kids of Klan members while you watch, you racist."

"I heard your Pa say he brought you up to be 'one fine young money-makin' machine' but you wouldn't stop picking your nose and wiping it on your boobs so the customers kept refusing to pay."

"He told you that? I'll kill him and Ma both," finally emerging through the chains in black jeans and a pale blue wifebeater advertising some faded out band, as dressed down as she got, smiling at Audrey. "Oliver went to the store for milkshake fixin's, and Paul's coming."

"Thank God. This weather is the worst. I was soaking wet five minutes after I left home. He better get something good."

soft power

They'd asked Audrey to help them decorate the wall of the main room between the doorways, because she liked that sort of thing. She gave them her idea and they liked it and today they were all going to get together and with her friend Paul and hopefully do it all. Audrey had a mockup design on notebook paper that she began to transfer to the wall in faint pencil markings. The design was ornamental—wavy concentric rings orbited by ambiguous symbols, curvy and serifed. She sketched roughly, marking the spaces between lines with numbers: ¼", ½", ¾", 1". From the kitchen, Simone hauled in a cardboard box full of identical silver-colored pins—department store surplus—and they started the long task of filling in first the lines and eventually the spaces in between with pins hammered in up to the lengths specified by Audrey's notes, the figures in the design embossed on their surrounding orbits, these differentiated by both height and pin density. Oliver came back with chocolate ice cream and bananas and rum, all immediately triaged into the sputtering freezer, and sat down to help with the travail.

As they worked, all sitting crosslegged at the base of the wall, methodically tapping pins into plaster, Oliver's idea for a business: "There are all these bars and either they play some music or there's a band there, but why does it always have to be that same thing? It's not even that good of a thing to have in a bar. It's too loud and you can't hear except 'What?'. So I want to open this bar and sometimes it will have music but other times something else. It'll be different every night and there will be no way to find out in advance."

"Like what?"

"Like some night you go in there and there's some voice actor reading Nabokov, or the *Iliad*. Or contests for the best crayon drawing or best fingerpainting or best comic strip or whatever with a free Zombie for the best entry from each table and all-you-can-drink for the grand prize winner."

Simone imitated his soft excited voice: "Or best Norman Schwartzkopf quote, or best pussy. A free beer for the best pussy! Any brand you want!"

"Shut up just 'cause you never have ideas. Or they'd be showing some Buñuel movie, or slides from my vacation, or—"

Audrey interrupted, "So it's like camp with liquor and pretension instead of hazing and sports and sexual tension?"

"Yeah pretty much. There could still be sexual tension though. Until Simone got there."

She kicked him in the stomach. "—until your Mom got there. And entered the best pussy contest."

The buzzer rang and Simone let Paul in. About a year ago Audrey had been working when a stooping 6'8" man, about her age, had come in soaking wet out of the rain, his skullcap of semicurl hair dripping, his small, round glasses misted by tiny droplets. He asked, through gentle timbre of New Zealand accent, for books about cheese.

"Cheese?"

"Yes well you know. How to make it, that sort of thing. I'm Paul by the way. Paul Ferrell."

"You want to make cheese?"

"Well it's just that I had a wager with this fellow that it couldn't be all that hard to make, and now I seem to have procrastinated rather badly, and I need to work it out tonight. You follow?" Audrey had showed him how to make ricotta by souring milk with lemon juice, in the process earning for herself $10 N.Z. and a new Food Club devotee.

Paul and Oliver went to the kitchen to work on the milkshakes. They got on well, sharing a tendency to go at everything from first principles to the point of hubris. On the way in, Oliver went to the stereo and turned on some music, just loud enough to thump pleasantly in the throat.

Audrey, pushing in pin after pin, could sense some anxiety from Simone and—wanting to talk but unsure how to begin—began, "How's it coming with you two?"

"I don't know. I'm still feeling pretty much in limbo. A couple weeks ago we went to that party I was trying to drag you to. Good thing 'cause it was pretty bad, all these people who knew each other and then us." Finding herself at the end of this easy tangent, she bit down, "Anyway as soon as we got through the door he found his way to the spot on the couch next to some girl. She was, you know, blond, voluptuous I guess you'd say. And he was sitting there proselytizing about cow antibiotics of all things, her hanging off his every word and all her," not wanting to say it, "flesh hanging off of her, for two hours. And it's not like he's not allowed to talk to other women but there was so obviously nothing going on there above the level of," another pause, "skin. And she was big time butt too, that was the worst part. I feel dirty knowing that that's even appealing to him."

Audrey let the opportunity to respond slip by.

"I think the thing is when we got started it was all this drama, you know? First I was playing 'hard to get' and then he was playing 'hard to get.' We got in the habit. And I know I was just playing, but I don't know that about him. Doesn't seem like it."

"Have you been at each other's throats a lot?"

"Not so much, no. We're almost completely fine, really. I know right now he's happier here than anywhere else he has the option to move to, but it's just... All my fears are gone except the one, now, because I can handle anything with Oliver, but there's no way to know if he needs it the way I do."

The grinding of the blender for a while now had washed around the room, nearly drowning out the music: *Didn't I didn't I didn't I see you crying?* "I don't have much to say hon, except everyone can tell he likes you. I think you'll do ok, if all you want's my guess."

Simone let out the faintest whisper of a laugh, no more satisfied by this than you'd expect. "But enough about me."

"Yeah yeah. I'm still 'too picky'. I did have a guy try to tell me I was going to die or something the other day, though, so that's something. I'll take what I can get."

"What's this now?"

"This freaky weirdo on the el. Comes up to me first thing, says he's psychic or something, his dreams keep coming true, and he had this one where he saw me and I was, I dunno, dead." She made the dead pose here, or the zombie pose, lolling her head back, slack-jawed, tongue out, elbows up, wrists limp. Then, in official zombie or retard voice, "Hep me Thimooone. Um dthead. I cann feel muh legths."

"Ooh," ignoring this last, "you're embroiled in an intrigue. Was he cute? Was he more movie insane or homeless guy insane?"

"I'on'knowhy'on'tyoushutup?"

The blending had stopped now, and there were cold, lumpy pouring sounds from the kitchen. Paul and Oliver shuffled in, each with two big glasses of thick, brown glop that looked appealingly frozen and were, Paul said, "rather stiff."

"Nobody get rocked and start putting pins in backward," Simone warned, "or I'm pissed!"

"You're all talk," Oliver ignored.

soft power

"That's enough lip from you, Tinbergen," Audrey admonished, "and I don't want to hear you backing him up, Ferrell."

It quieted down after that as the four of them sat down to work, eventually moving to chairs and then to stools and finally standing as they marched up the wall. The conversation, when it recurred, was Paul or Oliver with another idea for Oliver's bar.

At six or so they'd finished except for a few hard-to-reach sections at the top that everyone was content to leave to another day, and they all sunk into the couches and chairs at the opposite end of the room to survey the work. It looked good—silvery, flickering, playful with the lights and colors reflected from the rest of the room, the ornate design in relief an absorbing mesh of texture and form. Everyone congratulated Audrey on her idea, and she was happy at the success but eager not to be the subject of conversation, constrained to glowing and humbly smiling.

Finally she broke it off: "Hey I'll see you guys later I gotta go," which took everyone a little by surprise but she suddenly felt like being alone. She went home and cooked some pasta with cheese and garlic and olive oil, then checked herself briefly in the vanity, experiencing the usual resignation, and went out again, selecting from the paper the loudest-sounding show she could find after five minutes' search.

Audrey liked to take part in the rock'n'roll fantasy play—cliché of clichés—that went off thousands of times a night in little clusters, each around a stage somewhere, each pulsing like a magnesium fire on some map, turning the various metropoli of the world into apocalyptic hotzones of light. She'd been enough times to be intimately familiar with the *dramatis personae*, which went like this: we will be the stars, up here on the stage above you, like Gods, each of us with our prototype just like polytheism, whether sneering and elitist, warm and flirtatious, coolly and abusively sexy, timid but adored, or drunken, disorderly, burning out. You will be the faithful, below us, faceless, heads raised to the heavens, adoring, awash in the amplified torrent of sound. Each of you focus your little light on us and you can bask in the reflected brilliance. Push us toward the sky with your screams and we'll strain against gravity to drag you up by the trains of our gowns. And it went off, again and again, because when it worked, it worked. Feedback; power beyond the sum of the parts. And even the low role, the one Audrey took, was to have no demand of identity placed on you, not to have to be witty or pretty or strong, to be able to check yourself at the door and join all this energy as the thick distortion of the guitars and the pounding of the drums carried you away. She couldn't get enough.

Trouble was, then you found yourself wandering away, the ringing in your ears muting out everything else, along one of the octopus of paths that diverged at the door beneath the marquee, fewer and fewer left around you until you were alone again and it was still you and you were no longer angry or sad or elated or anything except alone and tired, and your train was still your train with its raw stench of body odor, and your street was still your street, vacant and still, and your apartment was still your apartment, still empty, still silent but for the noises you made yourself.

9. *lame time*

A little disconnected: suspended between Friday afternoon and night, Stanley waited out the ride home, not quite a part of anything around him. Pulling into the stop three south of his own, he was reminded of a video game he'd seen where you got to build a city from the ground up, indicating where you'd like a stadium, airport, or Godzilla, and one appearing instantaneously, prefabricated, already fully functional. Because there—just below the station, in the space occupied by a vacant lot the last time he'd noticed—was a big, shiny supermarket surrounded by acres of pure blacktop, looking for all the world like someone had plopped it down a moment earlier with cars already in the lot, customers already in the aisles, and two colorful flags already attached to the lampposts, all set to flap heraldically in the wind.

But if that left him disconcerted—he got off the train, realizing at the sight of it that he needed groceries—then what he saw next made disconcertion seem easy. On the sidewalk, below the station, beside the prefab supermarket, a small crowd had gathered, and Stanley, arriving in the midst of it, paused to see what it was about. In the clearing at the center of the crowd was a mime apparently preparing for his routine. He laid out a big bowler on the ground in front of him, pulling from his pocket a crisp dollar bill and placing it deliberately in the hat. He produced a piece of chalk, which he used to mark an excruciatingly regular box across the sidewalk, separating himself from the crowd. He returned the chalk to his pocket, arched his back, stretched his arms along various chords, then stopped to take a deep breath. A mother's baby cried out in hunger or pain or boredom, and the mime stridently shushed at it, index finger to his lips. Silence restored, he inhaled again and coughed, then set his eyes forward as if to begin, and here is what he did: he slowly, ceremoniously reached forward, both arms sweeping out, meeting a few inches before him, fingers curved as if to hold a baseball bat, and then entered a furious, prolonged, two-fisted, full-bodied caricature of a certain repetitive motion only too familiar at least to the males in the crowd, who stood, still silent, agape, until somebody mustered the pluck for the requisite "What the fuck?!" and the mime, aware of how these things progress, bolted through the crowd, down the street, and out of sight around the first corner, leaving the bowler forlorn on the pavement in the center of the crowd of astonished onlookers, still with its single dollar bill.

Stanley—feeling like a foreigner who'd accidentally gotten off at the el stop not for Argyle or Granville but for Horror—made his way through the harsh expanse of parking lot to the supermarket. The cars prowling their lanes seemed to threaten him with their momentum. He presented himself to the door and nothing happened; he had to wave his hand before it gave lazy, unimpressed acknowledgment by sliding open. Green peppers, pound of mushrooms, cream. Pasta: rotini-63 or fusilli-34? He tried not to think about the pasta numbers conspiracy or what it might mean. Furtive glances at the other shoppers. Trash bags, deodorant, six pack of mexican beer, oh, one lime. Checkout, pay, door, cross the parking lot, cross the street.

September and still warm out, warm but yellowgrey, and sweat dripped down his leg as he carried the two plastic bags toward home, about a mile from the store. Jaywalking across the big roads, and the cars all seemed to speed up, offended by the encroachment on their turf. Nobody stopped to give him a lift.

Inside his apartment he attended to the list of immediacies: put down groceries in middle of floor to lighten the load, strip off pants and open the windows for the heat, urinate, put away the groceries. He cut up the vegetables, put on water for the pasta, began to assemble a cream sauce, then remembered about the beer and attended to that. Covered the cooking mushrooms in the saucepan with the oversize lid from the pasta pot, then remembered that the pasta water should be covered as well, set on it the tiny saucepan lid, and was surprised out of his inattention when it vanished into the water in the brisk manner that gravity demands. Irritated at this stupidity, he grabbed the lid and pulled it out of the water, near boiling hot as you'd expect. "Fuck!" As the lid slashed across the tile floor with an awful, raucous clatter, Stanley plunged his rapidly reddening hand into a stream of cold water from the sink. "Fuck fuck fuck!"

Despite these setbacks, by seven o'clock everything was progressing well: the pasta cooked, the sauce waiting in the saucepan. Stanley served himself a bowlful and went to the main room to eat it. With the bowl in his arms, he couldn't see his feet and by accident kicked a shoe—more obnoxious noise. Finally he collapsed onto the ratty brown sofa and began to appease his tired hunger with big spoonfuls of mediocre pasta, trying to favor his unburned hand, staring intently at a blank wall, not caring.

Afforded thought for the first time in hours, Stanley thought about the visits from the police over the past two weeks. He'd hardly seen them himself, meekly sitting in his chair as occasionally an officer went from outside to warehouse, warehouse to outside. Somebody had finally smelled the smell, as he'd expected. It took longer than he would have thought. Toward the end he began to wonder if it were a test—Rob measuring how blatant and repugnant an odor Stanley would pretend to ignore. Rob was brave enough to open the crate himself when he first learned of the smell. He remade Stanley's discovery and without touching anything more called the police who came and took their notes and photographs. Stanley had heard a few things from Rob, who had a certain oily charm that he was able to put to use getting gossip from the police. They hadn't found much, apparently: the employees were interviewed, and none had seen anything unusual, and there were no prints found anywhere in or around the box except those of the employees who'd picked it up. Those and the ones on the victim's hands, of course. The only item of new information was the identity of the victim: his name was Nikola Tesla—a coincidence or circumstance that no one besides Stanley noticed or cared about.

He finished eating, washed the dishes, and it was eight o'clock—dusk descending on his softly buzzing neighborhood, subduing the uneven chatter of dogs, cars, shouting, horns, faraway music, a woman's laugh. Each of these like a harmonic of a single voice that whispered expectations of the Friday night to come as people hurried to parties, dancing, drinking, a lover, a brawl. Stanley went out and walked through the pleasant cool of the new dark, hoping to percolate the ambient sense of action, keeping to himself, thinking.

The sprawling bible of a paper that Alan Turing published at the age of 23 didn't earn him legendary status until years later; at the time it went almost unnoticed, leaving him in quiet, postcoital repose to continue with various mathematics as he saw fit. This until World War II threw Great Britain—the faded naval superpower—into a state of confusion from which it never fully recovered. Under blockade, the British convoys fled a faceless enemy in the form of the German U-boats. The once-mighty Admiralty wasn't even able to keep track of the whereabouts of its own ships, let alone the invisible U-boats that, at the start of the war, could inflict terror with impunity from their hiding places a few feet beneath the surface of the ocean.

Young Alan, a few years older now than Stanley, took a job with the Government Code and Cipher Service, doing his bit by challenging the German *Enigma*—the machine they used to send coded orders to the U-boats. It was a system of three rotors in sequence, each with twenty-six inputs and twenty-six outputs, randomly connected, so that depending on the turning of the rotors an input letter could be permuted to a coded letter in any of 17,576 ways. There were six canonical rotors in each U-Boat. Any three could be put in the machine forwards or backwards, giving a total of 16,872,960 encipherments. That wasn't all—puzzle piled upon puzzle, a nightmare vision of German engineering—because each time a letter was enciphered the rotors clicked over like clockwork to a new position, a new encipherment. The U-boats had a book detailing the initial state of the rotors for every day of the calendar, so that even if the British managed to capture an *Enigma* machine and decipher one coded transmission, their enlightenment would last only until the end of the day; the next morning they'd again be faced with sixteen million wrong answers.

But cryptography is mathematics, and Alan Turing had a knack. He'd got word of work in Poland, where they'd discovered how to defeat an earlier version of the *Enigma* by exploiting the rare circumstance in which the machine happened to encode a letter to itself. Such a letter, for a particular configuration of the rotors, was called a "female"; what would you expect them to call the elusive puzzle piece that, if you could only find one, could solve all your problems? With his crew at the GC and CS, Turing devised a new machine—this one a hodgepodge of intelligence workers making educated guesses, mechanical calculators that clacked through possible configurations of the Enigma, an army of clerical recruits, and his particular contribution: a trick with a pile of punched cards that let you simultaneously discard thousands of wrong answers in favor of the right one. He put this system together and made it function, and soon British convoys were skirting mystified U-boats, where it was assumed until the end of the war that the Enigma code was still impregnable and the failures of intelligence must be due to the dapper machinations of Her Majesty's Secret Service.

They called Turing "the prof" in deference to his untidy brilliance, at once both respecting and patronizing him—the typical mechanism for handling the one who's a little too much himself for comfort. The wartime machine that he'd built learned to work on its own and little by little he became irrelevant—too flighty for day-to-day operations. He got a medal—the one civilians get. He put it away in a drawer somewhere and left it. He was paid decently. He bought two silver ingots and stashed them for safekeeping, buried under a bridge until after the war. He forgot where he'd buried them. They were never recovered. The war ended and he went back to mathematics, and back to his plans for the universal machine. Having experience with electronics now, he thought he could build it. His position the enviable one of having his own personal Grail burning brightly a few feet before him, well within reach, consuming him, distracting him from the mess of his personal life.

The further Stanley walked, the more the excitement in the air seemed to fall away from him like smoke as people, one by one, left the streets in favor of wherever they'd been excited to get, until there remained only Stanley, slouching toward home, and a couple of aimless drunks who had long since given over to their reflexive mutterings.

soft power

10. fractal compression

The cold snap hit Oliver stiff and sudden as a wall, raising goose bumps on his arms—now underdressed—in an instant the world coming to seem ferocious, malignant, and capable of anything. He was spending his Sunday alone, out looking for a gift in the sun that now did little to warm him. He rubbed his hands against the skin of his forearms and picked up the pace, window-shopping twice as fast.

Gifts were just so difficult—the damning combination of ambiguity and indelible permanence; trying to set a feeling to a thing. This one, for Simone's birthday, was typically over-constrained, having to be significant enough as a token of affection, but not so much as to seem weird or inappropriate, intimate yet universal, sexual yet intellectual.

He kept at it, getting colder, passing store after store selling all manner of things intended to suggest, "the purchaser of *this* mass-produced item is an individual of wit, charisma, and character." Oliver felt the paradox of this—more and more people caught up in the process of designing, assembling, marketing, distributing, and selling things that tried in vain through voice made hoarse to scream, on behalf of the purchaser, "I am not a part of this machine." More and more people for whom *buying* was a hobby, a talent, an outlet, an escape, a need. Oliver walked through these crowds on the street, thinking, *This can't be right. It didn't use to be like this*. But doubting it, all the same, as he passed personal fountains, movie posters, acidwash furniture, colorful ceramic kitchenware, mass-produced handmade silver jewelry, and then passed it all again in the next block. None of it remotely right.

The chill got the better of him finally, and he ducked into an empty little restaurant hoping for something warm to drink. And come to the right place because there, up on the menu, as if written in holy fire, was "Best Hot Chocolate."

Oliver immediately announced, "I would like the best hot chocolate," to the girl behind the counter. She had Louise Brooks' look, flapper haircut sleekly contrasty against pale skin, her smile self-possessed.

"Sure."

Oliver sat down, looking around the place—a nice enough space, high-ceilinged and well lit, but somehow sterile, plastic. He felt momentary paranoia as if some other customers were thinking, *Stick to waitresses of your own kind. Don't be bothering our girls*, but decided to assume he was imagining things. She set down his cup and saucer with a reassuring rattle, and he tried it and indeed it was the best—like drinking straight liquid chocolate; rich and creamy and immediately warming him throughout. Figuring Simone would never forgive him for letting this secret go by (and he didn't even want to think about what acts of violence Audrey might be capable of), he flagged the waitress again.

"Is it the best?" Smiling again as she asked it.

"I think maybe yes. How do you make it?"

"It's pretty simple; just dissolve some chocolate shavings in milk and a little bit of cream warmed on the stove."

"Ah-hah. Healthy."

"You look like you could stand to put on some weight," looking him over sort of boldly. "Enjoy," and walked away with one of those girls only tricks—looking him in the eye while turning around to walk off then, at the last second, lazily twisting her slender neck to look away.

Oliver found her a little funny but was hardly paying attention, still caught up in the problem of the gift. He searched absently back through their history—going on three years now—for the seed of an idea. There had to be some tidbit there he could use.

Back in his days as an ornery philosophy major he'd been the sort to be called "cool" without anyone actually knowing him. Even then he'd had his cultivated mystique keeping people away, and most of his conversations sooner or later turned to venomous expressions of distaste for the philosophy program that frowned upon the students thinking for themselves, and—worse—the complacency with which the students assimilated this prohibition and made it their own. The thing that got to him was when he'd explain some idea or other of his to another student and could see, in his eyes, or hers, that dropping away into the distance, the implicit shock—who did Oliver think he was, talking about philosophy and his laundry in the same breath? Couldn't he just go along with the established dialogue, and what was his source on that, anyway? Popular opinion said he was prepping for a career as a crazy—haunting diners and smoking too many begged cigarettes. Oliver, for his part, took up a programme of advanced research in avoiding people. Some of his methods were tried and true, like the obligatory seat at the back of the class on the left or right extreme of some welded-together row of wooden-backed theatre seats, all of them wrenching back and forth in unison with each sneeze or change of posture by one of the students. But some of the unorthodox choices for venues of study he believed to be entirely original, from dorm bathroom stalls to dank old sports bars to the token pea-green-upholstered chair that waited out its time in the vending-machine lounge of the school of engineering. To flee the chatter of his roommate he'd head out the window to the fire escape and look down at people walking along the sidewalk, to whom it never occurred to look back up.

Simone had been the exception to this; he saw her for the first time tearing ass around the corner, her sandals slapping painfully against the road, frantically looking this way and that and, yes, up at the fire escape and right at him with pleading panic in her eyes. He skipped down two flights and lowered the ground stairs with his weight, helping her up and through the window into his room, where they'd hunched, peeking out the window, she panting and muttering thanks.

"What was that about?"

"I signed up for that poster-selling gig, driving around the country to different schools selling John Belushi in the 'College' sweatshirt out of the back of a van, you know?"

He did, but that didn't seem to explain much. "And...?"

"Well, the guys I got assigned to sell with were jerks, you know? Kept eating all the food we'd buy together and they hoarded all the stuff that sold well for themselves and left me trying to sell the ad for some disastrous year-old kids' movie nobody ever heard of. Anyway I got so sick of it that when we got here and they went to sleep I opened up the van and put up a sign advertising, 'Free Posters.' Cleaned them out pretty good." She flashed a wide, unselfconscious grin.

Just then an ominously rusted-over van came squealing around the corner and stopped, two collegiate-looking heavies getting out, looking the area up and down, eventually giving up, and Simone—safe for now but still AWOL from her poster sales summer job—stood up from behind the window and looked around at the hideout she'd happened upon.

The cute waitress, back again on a break, asked if she could smoke in his extra chair. She razed ¾ of her cigarette before speaking with sudden energy: "You live around here?"

soft power

"A couple miles south."

When he didn't go on, she exhaled, tilting her head and studying him with the indiscreet gaze again. "I have to say I find men who appreciate good hot chocolate absolutely irresistible," she deadpanned. "I get off work in an hour. Maybe I'll see you?"

He laughed, feeling awkward now. "Sorry... I'm just out looking for a birthday present for my girlfriend."

She, pouting a little, "Oh. What's she got that I don't?" And fixing him with the thousand-watt stare.

"You know." Apologetically. "When someone just makes you comfortable. Some people are like that. Comfortable. Able to make the best of it. Other people go the other way—you look like one—toward restlessness. Always that feeling that there's somewhere else you should be leaving for that's so much more... No offense. Me too. I would hook up with someone like you and it would be nice, you know, intense, but all the nervous energy just drives you crazy after a couple months. Simone's comfort caught on with me and I never feel bored anymore, or like I'm missing out, except when she's not around. Only worry is that my restlessness is infecting her, in the symmetrical way, you know, and she'll lose interest. Sometimes she doesn't seem to care where I go even, or who with. It isn't that I want her to be jealous, but something you know? I get the feeling recently I'll come home one of these days and she'll just be gone, but not like I'm not going to stick around to see." He looked up from his hands, finally, thinking for the first time that she was unlikely to be interested in all of this, but she was still watching, the coquettish stare now replaced with a look of some small sympathy.

"You'll be alright I think. Like I kinda said, I'm here if she's not, and knowing my luck that's a good sign for you. Get her something nice for me ok?" and she stood and went back to work, leaving Oliver to his puzzle.

Simone had lain low for a while in his room, the two of them playing cards and getting to talking. She behaved toward him then as she'd continued to: not believing every thing he said, in fact calling him on it viciously when one of his flights of fancy went a little far, but at the same time it was obvious her acknowledgment of his capacity for working things out, granting him as much right as anyone to have an opinion—the very thing he so often missed. They'd gone together to a little Mexican place whose authenticity was called into question by, among other things, the black-lit fishtanks built into all the walls, its clientele limited to grad students and retirees. The sort of place that would normally drive Oliver mad with its sleepy irrelevance (it was her idea), but they'd ordered two boatlike and suspiciously colorful margaritas and their evening still felt like time that couldn't have been better spent. And it went on like that—whether eating waffles in a breakfast joint with her parents or just loafing around exhausted in the heat of their barren white first apartment— always blessed and for the first time in his life with the feeling that he was making the best of it.

And there it was, staring him in the face, and he paid and left with the excitement of planning eating him up and thanked the flapper for her help on his way out.

11. schoolboys sucking down your cloud

Most people just bought books. Hundreds a day, probably, would come in, maybe say, "Hi," but otherwise quiet, browse around, maybe pick out five or six things, bring them up, pay and leave. Audrey never minded that. A few would come in needing help, and she enjoyed that, telling somebody where something was or what she'd recommend for his daughter. Every so often, though, came guys like these, and it was always guys, and almost always pretty much like these. You'd get people coming in decked out in leather and chrome, a ripped sweatshirt, a full-body tattoo, or a prostitute dress, and inevitably these people were deferential, polite. What you had to worry about were these two—eighteen or nineteen in khakis, belts, Adidas, tufts of short blonde hair sticking out the hole in the regimental baseball cap. A lot of people look like that, of course, and most of them are fine too, but Audrey had learned to recognize the warning sign posture—the walk, torso motionless, the weird sort of chest-out, lazy, butt-wiggling, high school athlete lurch, trouble nearly every time.

There were two of them, today, and she saw them first ambling pointlessly along on the other side of the street; no surprise when the loitered their way back and into her store. Then the usual pastime of walking around pointing derisively at things and sharing gruff giggles. No doubt *The Joy of Sex* and *Everything you Ever Wanted to Know...* provided a few rich laughs. She did her best to ignore it all but one of them, the blonder of the two, prevented it by coming up to her and asking:

"Do you have the Kama Sutra?" The other one, the sidekick, hidden clumsily behind an aisle, enjoyed a spastic laugh at this. The one that asked just stood there fixing her with his "I get chicks" stare.

"Upstairs."

"Do you like that book?"

"Never read it."

"Oh, really? Why not?" What really got to her was the ease with which he stood there jerking her around—like his total insincerity didn't bother him in the slightest. Robot.

"Not my kind of thing."

"Oh yeah? Hm," and robot stood there, still staring at her for a few seconds, exercising some imagined power, until he went away finally, the sidekick chortling merrily along.

She read for a while—it nearly time for her to leave—then, realizing they were still around somewhere by the giggles, called out, "closing time."

They walked guiltily up from the back of the store—who knew what they'd been doing—still with their air of entitlement, in no particular hurry. As the sidekick passed in front of her desk and toward the door the other one stopped and turned to her again:

"Can I have your number?" looking her straight in the eye, not even blinking, standing there like he had every right.

She knew better than to say anything—just glared silently for a moment, and not even very long because he couldn't quite muster the restraint that the timing of his joke demanded.

" 'Cause you look just like my dyke sister's type." His friend, in back, laughed uproariously at this but had the conscience at least that he couldn't look her in the eye. Not so for the other, who still just stood there in front of her, still with the stare.

"Oh, you mean you don't want my number? That's too bad 'cause oily little high-school baller worms out cruising in daddy's minivan are such a turn-on for me. Have you ever even seen a lesbian? Not counting the ones on pay-per-view in Skinner's basement now. I'm sure you'll be the date rape superstar for a couple years yet but look me up when you're out bulking up your gut with

soft power

your buddies who all hate you and whistling at strippers 'cause you can't get a date. And get out or I'll call the police."

They left—still fronting but wary of any real confrontation—and Audrey's anger faded fast into despair. Rational or not, you had to hate everyone when confronted by two like that.

Her first thought was this wasn't her day when she stepped onto the train and saw, looking the other way, the weirdo from before. Still, weirdo or not, she couldn't picture him pulling a performance like the bookstore boys; not with that goofy, cowering posture. Maybe cutting off her head and archiving it, sure, but anyone who wasn't capable of standing there flashing a billboard smile and fucking with you at the same time had to be better than anyone who was.

Weirdo wasn't smiling right now, but just looking listlessly out the window. Not vacant, though; she could see his eyes tracking back and forth at things outside—could see him thinking. He looked so genuinely sad, but resigned at the same time. Then he smiled, with his mouth at least, weakly, and she looked out the same window, to the far end of his line of sight, and saw a crowd gathering around a mime. And despite a clunky build, the hunch of his shoulders just made him look so small. Fragile. And so she thought she'd give him just the slightest chance.

She walked over and sat down on the outside of his row. "I'm Audrey. We, um, spoke a few weeks ago. I've been calling you Weirdo since then. Thought you should know. Is there something you'd rather be called?"

It took him a while to notice somebody was talking to him. When she finished he stammeringly whispered, "Stanley," and that seemed to be all he was capable of for the moment. She held the curious pause for a few seconds, giving him the chance to continue, and eventually he came out with, "I'm... um... sorry about that whole thing it was..."

"Oh say no more I'm over it." She stared out the window for a minute, reaching for the only bit of smalltalk she knew, having learned it from Simone: "So, you know any good conspiracy theories?"

"Um..." And then the change, because suddenly he was talking, quickly now, though still almost inaudibly soft. "Actually yes. Did you know that if you plot the variations in skirt lengths... according to what's fashionable at different times... the graph looks like the stock market? They go up and down together."

She didn't quite know where to go with that, all its fearsome implications aside. "Ok but that's not exactly a theory right?"

"Um... I guess not. Ok here's another one. Guess what the average ratio is between the length of a river if you travel down it and the crow-flies distance from the source to the outlet."

It was so strange the way he'd suddenly animated. "I don't know that one either."

"It's about three. Three point one. Four. It's hard to measure. There's not that much precision but it's 3.14. And you know what a group of primates is called?"

And this was a surprise, because she did: "A shrewdness!" Then she realized how nerdy this sounded and hung her head a little, glancing around to see who had heard, and noticed where they were out the window. "Hey this is my stop. Why don't you come have dinner with me and tell me who's trying to kill me."

"Um..."

"No pressure. Friendly thing. C'mon," grabbing his forearm and pulling him with, having some idea how these things were done.

soft power

They got off and she set out, striding along, conscious of him—a little tentative and behind. "What's the story then? I'm curious."

"I'm sure it's nothing. I was underslept. Imagining things."

"Yeah yeah I'm sure too. Now tell me," and waited for him to be ready to talk as she led him down the street, the golden hour heightening the intensity of everything—pleasant weather but cool enough to make your nose run. Storefront neon flickered in here and there. A block or so and he finally spoke:

"I had two dreams. I mean, I have all kinds of dreams but two that stood out scary. The first one was. Well, I work at Public Storage, you know what that is?"

She did.

"Yeah I was asleep at work and I had this dream about one of the boxes in storage. Something about it was," and she winced hearing him considering the label she'd just given him, "weird. But I saw what number it was before I woke up and I found the real one and started to notice that it smelled. I stole my boss's key and opened it. This was after I told you now. I opened it and looked inside and there was a guy in there."

"A guy? What was he doing?"

"Um... He wasn't. He was dead."

This was more than she'd expected so she put off responding. "Hey what do you think about Korean?" A shrug, little enough resistance so she led him on into a place that in English at least had no name beyond *#1 Barbecue*, past the glossy bar and its overhanging serpent—wavy like a road or a river, backlighting on the wall—and through plots of deserted white tablecloths to a four-person booth in blue vinyl, taking the two inside seats with views out the window where the sun set down the street, fading across dirt, brick, and telescoping iron security gates alike. "How did he die?"

Stanley shrugged. "I don't think he probably wandered in to somebody's storage crate and couldn't find his way out. The police came. Nothing's turned up."

"Can't you check who stored the thing?"

"I did, it was this old couple. Richard and Sarah. 4720 west."

"So it's a suburban crime syndicate?" Audrey was starting to enjoy herself now, hunched forward at the high table, elbows out, playing detective games in the seclusion of the dark restaurant.

"They were out of town. They say they didn't call or anything."

"So somebody gave a false name when they dropped it off?"

"No, it was a pickup from that address."

"So somebody ordered the crate to their driveway, put a corpse in it, and had it picked up?"

He shrugged again, still leaning back from the table, his eyes cycling between menu and window, she unable to catch them in between. The waiter came and took their orders—chicken and pork—and she kept watching Stanley looking as if he wanted to say something but never able to come out with it.

"What does all this have to do with me again?"

He stared fixedly at the tabletop while reciting this part. "Before I found the body I had another dream. It was just the image of this girl and I don't think I really could have seen what she looked like but that night I got on the train. I hadn't really slept, I was sort of nervous. Um..." He was reluctant. "I try not to drink coffee 'cause it makes me real shaky. Not that I'd had any coffee that night but I felt like it I was—"

She prodded, "In the dream, what was she doing?"

"She wasn't." A small silence. "She was just sort of lying there curled up. And everything was orange, like she was... preserved... in amber."

Again, Audrey didn't know where to go with this so she waited, staring out at car lights with their halos of red and white, suddenly wishing she had some coffee herself, feeling limp and deflated. Silence for a few minutes until the waiter arrived with a portable gas stove rig, lit it, then away again and back with a ripple of plates down his arm like seashell, and a ceramic chime as he set each in turn down on the tabletop marble, lettuce glistening wet, thin slices of raw meat smeared with reeking brown sauce, and he transferred these again to the stove where they popped and sizzled. Audrey felt her appetite stir.

She raised her eyes from the food to Stanley to find him staring, and looking very awkward as suddenly he blurted rapid, "It's 1930, right, and the bottom has just fallen out of the stock market. Suddenly everyone's wearing these long skirts. And at the same time in physics and mathematics comes this incredible, crushing, backward windfall where for the first time people are proving—literally proving—the limits of human possibility. You cannot know both the position and the momentum of an electron. Werner Heisenberg, 1927. No formal system can be complete. Kurt Gödel, 1930. Some problems are not computable. Alan Turing, 1934. And he was 23. I'll be 23 soon." The food cooked on and as Stanley chattered about universal machines and Enigmas and World Wars she snared a slice of chicken between her chopsticks and yanked it away from the sticky heating surface, wrapping it together with a clove of garlic in a lettuce frond and working the whole bundle into her mouth. Stanley watched this and imitated her competently enough until eventually the food was gone, talking all the while:

"Don't know why I'm so interested exactly. Ironic because if I'd been around back then you can bet I wouldn't have gotten conscripted to Turing's department. I would have been storming a beach somewhere, getting immediately shot in the face." And here he pantomimed himself at Normandy: "What's going on. I'm scared. Oh. I guess I'm dead."

She allowed herself a little laugh at the pathos of this.

"Anyway, it's funny because I don't think Turing would have called them 'females'. He was sort of an embarrassment to the folks at Cambridge and later the GC and CS because he was gay and not so discreet. That made him a security risk in those days and they didn't want him working on cryptography after the war. He tried to get involved in one of the first computer projects but they didn't quite know what to do with him and it wasn't well managed so nothing ever came of it. He just got frustrated; he could have built the first modern computer but he couldn't. It didn't work out. Somebody else beat him to his own idea. He did some game theory stuff. There was this idea called a minimax where everyone in a game tries to steer it for the least bad of the possible outcomes. Five years later he started working on the chemistry of embryology, figuring out how the cells know to differentiate in an embryo so that your arm turns into your arm instead of your pancreas. And how the leopard got its spots. In the meantime there was this incident where he picked up some jailbait, took him home, and then was robbed a few days later. Then he made the real mistake which was reporting it to the police, so he got put on trial for indecency, convicted, and sentenced to hormone therapy."

soft power

Audrey was, by this point, fairly absorbed.

"'The Cure,' that was called. Which didn't stop you being gay but at least you got to grow breasts. He did his year at that getting depressed I guess because not too long after they found him lying in his bed with a little foam around the lips, and with the core of an apple on the bedside table that he'd laced with cyanide. I've heard cyanide smells like almonds; maybe that was the least bad of all possible outcomes in his game. He was 38. Twice nineteen. When he'd been at school and he'd had an infatuation with a boy who turned him on to science in the first place. Christopher was his name, who liked telescopes and experiments with rainfall. Christopher died at nineteen from cow tuberculosis, and maybe that was Turing's midlife crisis. It was a waste."

That was the end of the storytelling, and she sat in silence feeling a little down about all this, and also not knowing what to say. "I gotta go, but I want to hear the rest of the big mystery when it comes out," as she scribbled her number on a corner of the beer list and handed it to him, then was in a hurry to pay her part of the bill and get out into the dark. She walked home, stinking of garlic and reflecting on Stanley who now seemed no less strange for getting to know him a little—his quietly authoritative way of speaking and his curious story of the wasted half-life of a mathematician dead fifty years.

12. death games

Stanley, for his part, left sitting on his palms in the dim closing noises of *#1 Barbecue*, felt that minutes ago he'd somehow become an enantiomorph—the same atoms arranged in a mirror pattern—with the property that someone now saw him instead of seeing through him. He thought about the story he'd heard about thalidomide, a sedative sold in the late fifties, "for morning sickness." The R(+) entantiomer of thalidomide had a sedative effect. The S(-) entantiomer, looking glass thalidomide, was teratogenic. *Teras*, from the Greek: monster. Women who took the drug while pregnant gave birth to children with flipper-like wands where their arms should have been. Who knew what looking glass Stanley was capable of? Flipperkids?

Witness the appearance of this girl who not only paid him attention but seemed actively interested in the things on his mind he never had the nerve to talk about with anyone else. As if to confirm the theory of supernatural intervention, he noticed on the restaurant's cashier counter a bowl of fruit with a banana, and the banana sticker said not "Chiquita" nor "Del Monte" nor any other ex-foreign corporate moniker but instead "MAGIC" inside the spiky explosion-bubble shape, bright red. (He took the banana home with him and was vaguely dispirited to notice it rotting like any other banana a week later.)

This euphoria lasted all night—nervous energy forcing him awake as he lay in bed, staring at the ceiling, shunting endlessly back and forth over his recollections of the evening, trying both to edit it together into the most promising montage possible and by rerunning the footage to preserve the ghostly, fading grains of memory's image.

But by morning tacit forebodings and bad little hints had found their way into his edit of things, and he began to suspect that maybe she'd just thought he was strange and this wasn't such a good thing after all. No longer intoxicated, she seemed awfully attractive, intelligent, and above all seemed the sort of person capable of getting whatever she wanted. The idea of her interest in Stanley, who wasn't all that smart or anything else really, began to seem suspect. So caught up was he in this enduring doubt that he walked unawares into far more immediate distress.

Distress the cloud that trailed Baker, waiting for Stanley when he got to work, reclining in the spare vinyl waiting chair in the Public Storage office, showing off the sort of weariness that cannot be slept away. Baker was the head detective who'd come to investigate #1588, interviewing all the employees, giving each a dose of his considerable inertia, remaining at rest as he sat questioning him, occasionally troubling to mark something on the legal pad that seemed to be his accessory. He wasn't aggressive, wasn't mean, and it wasn't that he didn't listen. It was that he did, sitting there, stern and severe, immediately betraying the inestimable experience of his years, soaking up everything you said, and you felt him, sad and reluctant perhaps, but intentionally or not still a force that could never be mitigated once set in motion—once you'd lied or done something wrong.

Chris, coming out of the shift before Stanley's, outside the building sucking in the last drag of a cigarette just as Stanley arrived, gave warning with his eyes that Stanley wasn't sure what to make of, then the hot cigarette butt bouncing flicked to the hot asphalt and Chris said goodbye, warning in his voice but still Stanley was unprepared when he walked into his little room and found it occupied by Detective Baker's persona, expanding to take up space like a foam or a weird gas that whatever it was certainly wasn't oxygen.

"Hello," said Stanley, and got back the eyes that expected the world to disappoint them, tired of it.

"We need to talk again, Mr. Rollick. I don't want to upset your schedule so I came here during your work hours. If this isn't a good time, I could come back."

"No, this is fine." Stanley, eager to please, trying to guess one step ahead at what was about to happen—failing. Failing spectacularly: Tacoma Narrows Bridge.

"Oh, good, I'm glad to hear it. I know I warned everyone last week that we might need to follow up with some of you, so I hope it's not too much trouble that I'm following up with you, Mr. Rollick."

Stanley still couldn't figure where this might be going.

"We're all working very hard to figure out what might have happened to Mr. Tesla. That was his name. Tesla. My name is Ian, by the way. And there are some things that don't make sense to me yet, Mr. Rollick, so we need to come back to you and get what facts we can. Phone records, for instance. Do you ever need to make phone calls when you're working?"

"Not really, no."

"Whatever calls you might make while you're here, while you're working, those would be personal calls?"

Stanley thought about this, and it seemed safe enough. "Yeah."

Ian Baker stopped to write on his legal pad, writing with the sort of force that would leave his thoughts embossed on the second page. "I don't really know how businesses like this operate, Mr. Rollick, and I guess you're as good a person as any to ask. What kind of hours do you work?"

"Most weekdays, 9 to 5. Sometimes not. Sometimes Saturday or Sunday. Other guys work nights."

"I see. What kinds of things do people store, besides corpses?"

soft power

"I don't really know. All I see are the boxes."

"How do you mean? Don't you have to pack things for people?"

"No." Thinking that surely Baker must know all of this, but he just waited for Stanley to continue: "They order storage and the guys in pick up and delivery bring them an empty crate. They pack it themselves, they keep the key. We pick up the crate and store it, then deliver it to their home when they want it back. Either that, or they just rent a space, unlock it, and leave stuff in it. So like I said all I see are the boxes."

"Oh, I see. They keep the key, and you never need access, so you don't have one?"

"I don't, no."

"But someone must. In case they never ask for their stuff back."

"Yeah. My boss has a master that opens any of our locks, but the only time I've ever seen him use it was when he opened the—"

"Yes I see. That master, that must be the one that Mr. Lecht told us he recently lost. Strangest thing, he said, because it was gone right from his keychain. Of course we don't know if that has anything to do with Mr. Tesla," again writing on his pad, appearing to grow wearier by the moment, as if the whole thing were a rerun he was forced to watch.

Stanley, by now, was beginning to worry.

"There's just one more thing then, Mr. Rollick. About that key. I was wondering if you could return it to us."

"What?"

"Well, it's just that when we heard that Mr. Lecht's master was missing, we did the standard thing and had his keychain checked by forensics. And the strange thing is your fingerprints happened to be on some of the keys along with Mr. Lecht's prints, and he claims he didn't lend anybody the keychain. So I'm assuming that he left his keys sitting around one day and you took the master, leaving those prints on some of the other keys. Am I wrong?"

"Um..."

"I see. Those guys in forensics, they can do amazing things these days. Fingerprints are what people think about, you know. Movies and such. But fragments of hair and skin, stuff you can't really help leaving wherever you go, that's most of the action these days. For example, we found a strand of hair on #1588 that matches you but doesn't match any other employees, even though you aren't in the records as having processed that lot. Are those records incorrect?"

"Um..."

"All of it makes me wonder, Mr. Rollick, whether maybe you know more than you're letting on. Because it seems like you're here, every day, and you could pretty easily have stolen Mr. Lecht's key and used it to open one of the crates and leave something in it."

"But why would I—"

"Why does anyone do anything? How would I know? I used to try to speculate on that sort of thing but I've given that up. It's too hard. More to the point is that unlike most people, you could have, which makes me think maybe you did, Mr. Rollick."

Stanley, by now, was relying on the pure intuition that his innocence would protect him. "But that doesn't make any sense. Why would anyone pay to store an empty box?"

"Well, maybe you took out whatever was in the box."

"But they didn't even order the storage, so—"

"Now how would you know that, Mr. Rollick?"

And he just sat there, wide-eyed.

soft power

"Could that be because you called Richard Holmgren on August 28 and asked him about the storage order?"

And he said nothing.

"Because that's what the telephone records show, is somebody making that call during your shift, and Richard told us somebody called him, and somebody, from his description, sounded an awful lot like you, Mr. Rollick. Sort of an awkward guy, he said. No offense, of course."

And still he said nothing, all panic and despair.

But to his surprise, Ian Baker also said nothing, for a while, having played his hand he sighed, sat back, and stared—jowls and eyebrows still tired and sad, his hair neatly and expensively trimmed, very short, greyblack, in the style of a divorcee, it seemed to Stanley. And slowly, a bit more with each breath, the expression softened. "Awkward. Good word for you. You're not enjoying this I'm sure, but don't worry. We know you had nothing to do with it."

At this point, that made Stanley nothing but suspicious. "You do?"

Baker sighed again. "Yes, Stanley, we do. Because like you say, we know that Richard and Sarah didn't place any order and we took the guys from delivery over there and verified that they picked up the order from that address. And we examined the body, and we know it's been in that crate since roughly the date of the pickup, and you stole Mr. Lecht's key only two weeks ago. We don't work miracles but we figure a few things out, which is a good thing for you, Stanley."

So that was it, a scolding.

"I understand that people make mistakes, Stanley. And you made a mistake. You probably smelled that awful stink before anyone else, and wanted to check it out yourself, so you took the key and you peeked, and then you didn't want to arouse suspicion so you kept it to yourself, right?"

Stanley just nodded, tiny as a mouse.

"I understand that people make mistakes. So I'm not going to have you prosecuted, even though I could, and I didn't tell your boss about your fingerprints on his keychain. Someone's looking out for you, Stanley. Call it a reprieve."

Hanging his head, looking guilty, Stanley waited.

"But you need to understand that this is important, Stanley. Mr. Tesla was murdered, and that's important. You can't be playing detective games. You're going to get yourself into trouble. If you know anything, if you hear anything, I want you to go to the police. Do you understand?"

Stanley nodded.

Baker shook his head. "That's not good enough, Stanley. I need you to take me seriously. Now tell me you understand."

And it was all he could do to say, slowly, "I understand."

"Good. Have a nice day, Stanley," and he left.

The adrenaline buzzing through Stanley turned stale and left him aching, all day, of anxiety and relief at the same time. Every shrill ring of the phone made him start; he kept expecting Ian Baker to call.

Audrey, too, was on his mind, the impression of her pretty face still with him but not the face itself even just a day later. The sensation of the food they shared—a panoply of spices each burning, stinging, gently torturing in its own way—had stayed with him better. The whole S&M thing had never appealed to him—he just didn't get it—but maybe it was just like spicy food, your appetite

soft power

and the taste of it compelling you to eat more and eat faster as the pain accumulated on your lips, drawing the pleasure into sharper focus. Till your eyes were teary and your nose was running but the burning made it feel worth it—like you were earning it, and like it meant something. Distracted you from any considerations other than the sensual: the pain and the pleasure, the conflation of the extremes.

In the middle of this the phone rang again, jolting him from his thoughts. He scrabbled at the receiver to make it stop.

"Hello, Public Storage."

"Hi, I want to schedule a delivery."

"Ok Sir," tapping forward through the computer, "what's your lot number?"

"1588."

And all at once, another sort of conflation: animal fear for life that doesn't understand about telephones, human love persuaded Audrey wanted these answers, and schoolboy mischief flirting with Baker's rules. "Sorry, that's 1588?"

"1588."

"Ok, when did you want that delivered?" Only his familiarity with this script kept him afloat.

"Any time this week is fine."

Searching the calendar, "How about this Friday, at two pm?"

"That's fine. Oh, and we've moved, so I'll need that delivered to 5020 West Florin."

"Ok sir. That's Friday, September 21, at two pm, at 5020 West Florin. Anything else?"

"No, that's it. Thanks," and he hung up, Stanley straining to catch any detail of the unremarkable voice. He immediately dialed, for the first time in his life, 911, asked to speak to Detective Ian Baker, and told him what had happened. He could imagine Baker's face, fallen at the edges, on the other end of the line.

"Thank you Stanley, you did well. If he calls again, go along with whatever he says and call me," and gave his number, and that was all.

13. *indirect light*

Everything's aspect a little yellow in the room: the walls, the portraits of children or grandchildren on glass shelves, his shirt, the skin of his hand. His feet sunk into the blotchy short-long patterns of the plush carpet—maple syrup brown, synthetic looking. The venetians, tilted just so, passed slight lines onto the carpet, his pants, his hands. The one-time-only feeling—a home's first impression on an outsider. A chemical odor.

He picked up one of the portraits, the bronzish frame sucking heat from his palm: two kids lying on the grass, somewhere on the east coast, beneath a sculpture—a rough figure from rust-orange car salvage; its right hand, lobster-asymmetrical, a claw metalworked from a big diesel muffler; its head grotesquely shrunken, the familiar leaping jaguar hood ornament. Quicksilver icon of agility, muscles frozen at the lightning instant of contraction.

He imagined the thick, gloppy weld at the base of the head; anything less and it would disappear after a few days; there are worms about, on the east coast as anywhere. Baker was wary of the danger of his attitude, of the risk he took by unconsciously segregating people into people and worms—wary of becoming one of those lead-fisted TV cops, becoming Cop Violence. He did it anyway; he

soft power

couldn't help it; the world did it to him; the worms did it to him. He saw something every day: worm lying in the bakery for the sake of two dollars, becoming indignant—sincerely indignant—but lying and knowing it. It wasn't the real criminals that got to him; they had their own economy of desperation and violence and tit-for-tat. It was the crashed-again taxis, the tainters of food, the businessmen cheaters, the drowsy cops, the stealing congressmen: all those who take no responsibility. Parasites. Worthless. He wary of the power of that word, the weight of the assertion that someone had no worth, but he used it anyway. That was the legacy of twenty years.

Time had gone all vague on him somewhere in there. When people stopped asking his age—thinking better of it—somewhere in the hinterland of forty or fifty. Or before that, when people stopped commenting, one way or the other, about his appearance. Just like the guerilla force of grey hairs, these things came little by little until before you knew it you were permanently attached to your job and its worms, detached from your ex-wife, your ex-daughter. Baker was recovering workaholic; not because he'd gotten better, but because his condition had finished off all its would-be victims. Jill forgave him, he knew, but still wanted nothing to do with him.

Every few seconds, between paces, he verified that 5020 West Florin, just across the street, a flat brick affair like this one, remained still. He checked the baroque wall clock: 1:50.

Polly—by what could only be called contrast—wouldn't go so far as to forgive him. Would never go that far, he was sure. Jill sent photos of her every so often: Polly at twenty, her head suddenly shaved. Polly at 21, her hair grown longer, with friends at a bar somewhere—a single among couples.

The troublemaker Stanley, Baker had noted, was probably about Polly's age now. One of the things that made Ian like him, probably. That and however odd Stanley might be, however clumsily he might befuddle an investigation, he was not a worm. Baker had a nose for that, and dangerous though he knew trusting it to be, it had proved itself accurate over and over again.

When he and Polly had been on speaking terms, when she had been merely resentful of him, when she was a late teenager, Stanley, younger then as well, would not have been the sort to interest her. Her tastes were calibrated, consciously or not, for ill effect on her father. An obnoxious rich kid that she let hang around their home at all hours to make him irritable. A chew-spitting precriminal bruiser that she disappeared with until late in the night to make him worry. A smarmy, mustachioed predator of no appeal whatsoever into whose car she traipsed, from whose car she staggered too many hours later, willfully into the lecture—she'd have known dad would wait up, sit her down, she choosing to sit so that he couldn't help but notice, the way her dress rested, the absence of color when she drunkenly recrossed her legs. All to make him... something. It had to go wrong, sooner or later.

1:54. No cars drove by, nobody in the house, nobody around it. The owners, he learned from their neighbors, were on vacation. He'd checked the travel agents, the airlines, everything. No leads, no connections. Except that PS lot #1588 was picked up from the home of one vacationing suburban couple and was now to be delivered to the home of another. The stillness of the cloudy street and flat houses belied the hidden state of alarm—police everywhere, preparing to spring the trap when somebody received the delivery.

Baker got flashes of the hotel room from time to time—less often as time went by but no less vivid. The ice cubes sparkling up from beside the upturned silver champagne reservoir, the television lit and softly whistling but showing pure black. He wasn't, of course, allowed on the scene, but the unwritten code for that sort of thing allowed him in, if he wanted.

1:58. Beneath the ugly clock was an upright piano, sagging a little toward the center, which had plinked dissonant when he tested it earlier. The one item in the room that you wouldn't have expected was the vase of flowers on the coffee table—a spare, line-drawn pyramid from razor-sharp crystal, faintly smoky, exhaling a billow of violent red-budding vines. Outside a car crept slowly by—the crunch of tires stretching over pavement almost unbearably loud—but went two houses past 5020, the garage opening automatically, consuming it.

Twin stains—one a cluster of droplets toward the center of the bed, the other a wide pool spilling over one of the pillows—had turned the dingy white sheets redblack. The champagne bottle, empty and inert, lay on its side on the nightstand, hushed about its role as accessory to two acts of violence. What struck Baker most about the man was how old he looked: almost bald, almost obese. She'd done well, because it really would have bothered Baker meeting him, he imagined.

2:03. The truck pulled up in front of the driveway. Two big officers in Public Storage uniforms slid down from the seats, walked to the front door, and rang the bell as if there would be someone inside to answer it and not just an empty house. If anything were to happen, it would happen now.

When the need arose, she had fought. If he had felt like taking credit for anything, he might have taken it for that, though it could just as easily have come from Jill. She had fought and failed for what must have been minutes until the bottle, just discarded, had found its way, still slippery, into her hand. Champagne bottles are strong—much thicker than beer or wine bottles, reinforced to resist the high internal pressure. So when subjected to external pressure the bottle hadn't shattered as Polly expected but had continued forward intact, stressing and collapsing the indentation—matted with hair, blackened and encrusted, a ruby diadem—that Baker had stared into for a moment, his eyes unfocusing, before he'd turned and walked out of the room. He'd returned to his daughter, crying in the arms of her mother, he knowing enough to stay out of the way, on his tongue the foretaste of final exile.

Nobody answered the door, nobody approached the delivery men. They walked around the house, shouting was anyone home but no one was, of course. Eventually they gave up and left.

Baker, sitting alone in the yellow room with the photographs and the flowers, listening to the clock, waited a while before leaving himself, thanking the worried woman in the kitchen for the use of her home. Back in his office he was still thinking of Polly's face at 21, and feeling charitable he called Stanley and thanked him again for his help but unfortunately nothing came of it. Just another vacationing couple, and not a peep from whoever had called. But please let me know if he calls back again. Thank you. He lingered on the line for a little while, holding onto the link, however tenuous. Estranged was a word you felt unnatural using in the context of your own life, but that was what she was: his estranged daughter. The line was closed at the other side, and when the phone began to yelp angrily he did as it wished and hung it up.

soft power

14. how to get a date

The phone call was a gift to Stanley—pennies from heaven. Sitting on his swivel chair, swiveling, shivering from the processed air, looking out the window at what he knew to be low-grade even heat suffused with dust—a couple minutes in it and a wash of convected air would lift some particle painfully into your eye, the hot insistence of the wind annoying but better than this cold—he was wanting for an excuse to talk to Audrey again, despairing of finding one when the phone rang and there it was, nascent but perfectly formed.

Just off the line with Baker he picked it up again to call her, got halfway through her number before pressing the hangup and asking, was he up to this? He dialed again, this time reaching the penultimate digit, then stopped—taking advantage of the chance to go forward or to abort—waited a few seconds and hung it up again. Why should it be so difficult? He wanted to talk to her, he had something to say, she'd want to hear it, but he couldn't quite— the image of her furious countenance giving him pause, paralysis cold and sure and real as any affliction.

The dull roar of the air conditioning muted a jet cleaving the smoggy sky outside the window, the knife-edge vapor trail pointing from the plane to the apparent source of the sound behind it. Cars drove, pedestrians walked, everything moving forward but Stanley who was stuck. Finally he forced himself to use the only trick he knew for getting past this: dialed, fast as he could, the entire number without hanging up, and imagining the ringing at the other end he was finally prohibited from hanging up. It rang three times, on the verge of providing him with excuse to give up when it clicked.

"Hello?" It was definitely her, which was the first thing. And there was nothing miraculous about it, just the sound of anyone answering the phone.

He didn't want to talk, but again politeness badgered him into it. "Hi. It's Stanley. Um, Rollick. The, uh..."

"Yeah yeah the detective I remember. How are you?"

"I'm good. I—I heard something; you said I should call if I heard anything and—"

She waited.

"Well, they called about the box. Somebody called and wanted it delivered; they gave an address and a time you know. The usual thing."

"What are you gonna do?" He could hear the fascination, and found himself hoping the little mystery would keep up.

"Well, I called the police and told them about it, and they set up to hide and watch the delivery and see who picked up the box, because the people living there were out of town. That was today at two, but the detective called me back and said nobody showed up. So they don't know anything." It had taken longer to explain this in his head. "I guess there wasn't much to tell."

"What was the address?"

"Why?"

"Come on, what was it?"

"5020 W. Florin."

"Do you work on Friday?"

"No."

"Come over here on Friday morning." She gave him her address.

"Ok." Shocked by this apparent good fortune, he just waited.

She noticed his awkwardness, he guessed, and gave a little laugh. "Ok Stanley. See you there."

And the word, "bye," and the little click, and the subtle change in the tone of the background noise, could take on such different character depending on the circumstance, but it was always the noise itself and never the listener that was slow or sad or lonely or anxious or, as now, elated and terrified both.

15. *art history*

Oliver and a Bus: Greyhound Terminal, ten am. *Oliver looks very small here under his big backpack and the tire that's almost his height. The chrome bolts are bigger than his eyes. There's a puff of steam from his breath. We both look a little nervous, but I'm behind the camera so nobody knows.*

Blurring into the frame at the far right who should happen along but Audrey's friend Les, who turns out not to remember us. We watch him walk by and then he is accosted by a homeless guy selling a benefit newsletter for a dollar. "Buy Streetwise, help the homeless," and then a surprise 'cause Les says, "Um, I dunno man, it isn't very long, I'll give you 75 cents," and of course the guy is taken aback but they end up settling on 85 I think. Jerk.

Nervous 'cause I can't see this working, really. I'll take the trip, sure, happy to get it, but a bird died and its wing, just the wing and nothing else, is down there pasted onto the sidewalk beside the bus behind Oliver, and I can't help thinking that this is what the bird's last few swoops through the air must feel like, 'cause there has to be a way to tell, some suspicion a hundred meters before the big chrome grate slaps you out of the sky. 'Cause that danger is what it's always been about, I think, Oliver for me everything I could want and so attractive the idea that I'm getting just a little of his time before he moves on to grander things. However famous he might get or whatever his wife looks like there's always going to be this picture, getting yellower, not quite focused, not quite composed, but of him about to take a trip out west with me. 'Cause photos last a long time, relatively.

16. in a convent

Down the tunnel of sidewalk he went toward her address, stepping along the bent and cracked slants of concrete. The street felt very old, the old trees and the old houses closing on either side of him, the old cars sitting astride their old oil stains. Out of a window somewhere the abrasive noise of someone too old to learn violin, trying anyway.

Toward him a man with some kind of defect of musculature or bone structure, so that he didn't walk so much as hurtle headlong, stumbling jerking perpetually forward. Like you'd have to reach out and catch him at any moment but he never quite needed it. Always falling, in a very low earth orbit. Stanley looked away.

He found the building, a 3-flat, brick, nice woodwork. Thought about the concentration of lives on these streets, and what it would look like if you knew the people in each of the hundreds of apartments up and down the block. Imagined himself floating up through the walls, along the second-story cross-section of homes. Not to peep or voy, but just to sample the possibilities—just to compare decors. Woman living alone, staring at her cat framed by a parallelogram of sun reflecting off the floorboards from the window. The barren intensity of an apartment of students, the torn posters taped messily to smudgy walls and invested with such significance by their scarcity, by the ashtrays and dishes left lying around because there's no time for that. The secreted criminal lair that had to be here somewhere, where the bored gangster's molls wait for the gangsters and talk about their siblings. And somewhere here were the lovers just now roused from their late night's slumber by the outside sounds, the boy going to the kitchen, wiping the sleep from his eyes, bringing back a plate of apple slices, no, mango slices, feeding the girl, her eyes still closed in a smile, he rubbing her belly, never quite satiated of her nakedness.

And the apartment Stanley wanted, where Audrey lived, what would that be like? But at the inner door he found himself without the apartment number, the nameplates by the doorbells having worn illegible. A column of identical ivory buttons, each secure in its brass collar, stared him up blank and silent—a question posed in a nightmare, behind every wrong door a hulking sweatball jonesing to chase him, beat his ass.

He just stood there, transfixed by it, struck dumb. His hand groped forward as if it had an idea; he stopped when he found there was nothing. Of course it had to go wrong. Stupid to hope otherwise. He slowly stepped back, too disheartened to really move much, stumbled backward into and through the outer door, clumsy and shellshocked. She would think he hadn't wanted to come. Outside again he stared up at the building but it revealed nothing. He noticed for the first time the glare of the sun lighting up his left profile, making him squint and feel he didn't belong. Imagined people in the windows watching him stand there. Somewhere he heard shouting. *Hey!* What was it about? *Hey stupid! Up here! And get a haircut!* Oh. Up on the third story, beneath the guillotine of a window, Audrey was leaning over, laughing at him discreetly. Her hair was pea-green now, refusing to complement her baby blue t-shirt, which read "Muffins!" with a picture and everything.

"Hi! Come up," as she slid back from the window and went away. Then the door was buzzing and he was rushing forward to catch it. It was heavy. The stairwell smelled like food and pet. He went up it to where a door was opening and Audrey appeared again.

"I didn't know which door. I like your shirt."

"Yeah me too. I like it 'cause it has no reason to exist. I prolly shoulda given you the number, sorry. Hey come in." Head slightly down, she gave him just a moment of eyes towards her eyebrows and a faint smile before going through the door, and Stanley followed her through feeling like he was about to knock something over.

Times like this were the justification for his disembodied-eye spy fantasies, because her room had that feeling of the new and foreign or like a room in a movie. Such a contrast from his own nasty small space. It looked so comfortable—all kind of bold colors from the midnight blue linen dustcover on the big fat lumpy couch to the red velour drapes with the improvised theatre-style up-and-down mechanism, the fabric pleating into lazy half-moons. And a tree in the corner! The branches of the tree were hung with those inimitable little point-drawn portraits clipped from the *Wall Street Journal*—a yearbook of faces balding, faces stodgy and white, faces weirdly pointillized in someone's idea of an aesthetic. It was cool and breezy and the light was just right; Stanley sat at the big old desk or table, staring into the aged burls of the wood, feeling the desire to stay and spend time, grow older with the wood. He looked up at the bookshelves that hid most of the walls, his eyes hopping between stepping stones of familiarity in the titles, which were few, as she came back in with a glass of something, cold tea; it was good.

As much as he was enjoying the setting Stanley didn't know what he was supposed to do next. She kept him from having to do, though, saying "Essreese." He didn't know what to make of that.

soft power

"What?"

"That's who lives at that house. S. Reese, 5020 W. Florin," and the phone number.

"How did you—?"

"Went by the house, the mailbox said Reese. I looked for it in the phone book." She held up the phone book to illustrate. "How's your tea?"

"Good." He looked around the room for a change of subject.

She was half a head shorter than him, looking up at him with excited eyes, having none of it. "Well, I want to know what happened. Let's call them."

"Um, I think the police like that sort of thing to themselves."

"Yeah nobody's gonna know and talking to people's not illegal," and reached for the bright red nuke-launching telephone on the desk.

"That's what I thought before but—" suddenly thinking better of admitting this story.

"What?"

"Um..."

"C'mon, what?" Her arms were on her hips, her head angled forward at him, staring at him, staring right at him.

"Well, the detective, he found out that I'd called the other house and... told me I'd better not. I got in trouble. I don't think it's a good idea. Let's just make sandwiches or something."

"Quit your whining. I'll call them and you don't have to do anything but sit here," as she reached for the handset again, dialing the number.

He could tell what was going on but didn't care just then, snatching the handset from her and waiting as it rang.

"Reese," it answered.

And prodded into this as he was Stanley found his mind empty of things to say. His reflexes said "Hi," and then waited, like a child that wants a response and is prepared to say it again if need be. And more words, they just came out, but slowly: "I... um... I was wondering." He could hear his watch. Audrey was staring at him. Her pupils were enormous in her pretty brown eyes. Her skin looked soft. Reese wasn't saying anything. "I was wondering if you—"

"Spit it out, Sacks," and Stanley froze, because his name still was not Sacks. He felt his heartbeat throb out like a tree's root system through his body, wondered if Audrey could hear it but she just stared probably thinking *Why isn't he talking?* And that all he could take and he'd learned something already anyway so he slapped the hangup on the telephone and then put up the handset. She wanted an explanation.

"He called me Sacks."

"So? I'll call you worse than that, Sacks." So tempting in all her fierceness, but the rules say never let it show.

"No see when I called the other two the people whose house it was picked up at the guy told me I sounded like Sacks. Some guy named Sacks, who was their lawyer maybe? I forget. Anyway I sound like him. And this guy called me Sacks. Thought I was Sacks."

"Are you Sacks?"

"No!"

She stared at him like she wasn't convinced for a couple seconds then launched into it: "Ok so both these peoples were out of town and somebody must've known about it to be able to use their driveways, and it sounds like they both know somebody named

Sacks who sounds like you. And you sound kinda weird, so I'm thinking this Sacks guy is some weirdo and he uses people's houses when he hears they're gonna be away."

"Uses them to get crates with bodies in them delivered and picked up." He smiled.

She was having none of it. "Right well I dunno. Like I said you sound weird. Want some more tea? I've had five cups!"

She disappeared into the kitchen, and Stanley took the chance to run for the bathroom, which made the magic living room seem drab. First thing through the door the assault of color and texture and shininess—the feeling like a cathedral or a mosque. She'd torn out the tiling, he guessed, and filled it in with this incredible mosaic. From the section near him the tiles seemed to be haphazard bits of things: a triangle of embossed seafoam tile, a sliver of chrome, curvy blue glass from a bottle, a scallop shell. It stretched from waist high to eye-level, wrapped all the way around the little bathroom, into the bathtub and out again at the other end. There was a river through the middle of it, behind the river a green canopy of trees and underbrush. In the river there was a crocodile with its teeth around an elephant's trunk; the elephant strained away on the shore, stretching the trunk grotesquely. Also on the shore was a pink fleshy crab without its shell hiding beneath a rock. Other animals were scattered round the room, eyes gleaming out of dark hollows, tails protruding from things. There was a big old guy's head peeking out from behind some clouds that he was spreading with his wrinkly hands. There were a few people in some kind of Indian-looking clothes.

"Everything ok in there?"

Stanley snapped out of it. "Just looking at the animals." That was a dumb thing to say.

She laughed. When he came out there she was with another big glass of tea, gleaming at him all wired. "You like it? I made it myself."

He did, but not wanting to gush, he said, "It's very exotic."

"You should warn me next time you go in there and I'll get you some khakis. I don't wanna get sued by your next of kin when the lions eat you."

"I don't think they saw me."

"You can't be too careful."

"He was helping with their will, that's what it was."

"What?"

"That guy said Sacks was helping with their will. Maybe they went somewhere on safari for their vacation and were preparing to get eaten by lions. In case I mean."

"Let's find him. I'll get the phone book." And she did, and Stanley just stood there and then just sat there not having a place, feeling impressed by all this diligence, while she ran numbers in the phonebook asking for Mr. Sacks. Needed something to say for when she finished, but could think of nothing but that need. Which didn't make for good conversation. Waiting for the phone to ring, she saved him: "My mom taught me to make this tea. Reminds me of her."

"What's her name?"

"Catch," as she raised an eyebrow and adopted a highfalutin manner, "Catch Livingston," then let it go again. "We don't get on so good." She talked a little on the phone; Sacks didn't work there.

"Why's that?"

"She and Dad split up just after I left. She split up with him. I feel bad for him. I think he's lonely. Every time I talk to him I get angry at her. Every time I talk to her I get angry at her too. How bout you?"

"She died when I was little. Hit by a car. It runs in the family. Dad's ok. We don't talk much; he's a little..." He made a face that he knew could mean anything from "complacent" to "insane."

"When you gonna switch to detective work full time?" He could never quite tell because of the smile how much she was insulting him.

"I was in school. I sorta ran out of money. Or ambition."

"Studying...?"

"I hadn't really gotten that far. Whatever looked interesting."

She didn't answer here like he expected, just waited, which was worse. Stared at him, right at him, right in the eye, like she could have done it all day, and he had to put his eyes to the floor. More phone business, more staring, like she was trying to suss him out. Why wasn't she talking? Stanley was scared. "Oh, he does? Yes. Yeah. Mr. and Mrs. Stanley Livingston. Yeah. Ok, thanks." She put up the phone and turned to Stanley with this amazing wide-eyed excitement: "Four thirty today," it was two, "and it's a free consultation, and your name's Livingston. Like me!"

"That's weird. I didn't even feel anything."

"That's how good I am."

He couldn't argue with that—couldn't seem to argue with anything when she was around, went all docile, didn't know what to do, didn't know what to say. So he followed in the same sheepish sort of way when she led him out of her apartment and all its content, its many textures, unsteady piles of things, rich old smells, memories and possibilities. The big door painted white over black resounded after it closed, shutting him off from all of it, from the books he hadn't read and the meals he hadn't eaten. Shut him out, said *You're just a visitor, time's up. Sir, move along. Sir.*

"C'mon," she said, with that enthusiasm that never seemed to let up, seemed to bubble up like lava from the center of the earth, cooling immediately against Stanley as if he were the underwater—lava orange and toothpastey oozing out and then freezing, but there was always more where that came from.

---

17. *children grow up to be adults*

"Hi, we're going to die."

Blink, swallow. Blink.

"...so we need a will, right?"

Blink. Blink. Sacks was small and looked to be made from balsa wood. His chest seemed to bend beneath the weight of his big idol's head, all out of proportion. His teeth were yellow, his hair frayed. He peered out at them like an owl, and said nothing, just blinked, and each time it was a big event.

"That's what you do, right? Wills for people who are gonna die?"

Blink. Swallow. "Well, yes um, I'm sorry I didn't... I didn't get your name." And it felt weird because he really did sort of sound like Stanley, even to Stanley.

"Yeah, I didn't tell it to you. I'm Audrey. This is Stanley. We're going to die."

"So you said. Hmm. Can I ask why this is on your mind? Most of my clients are a little," his eyes looked huge behind his glasses, "older."

"I'm not sure. I've just been feeling like fate is against us lately. You know?"

Blink.

She kept on with it: "Well, it's not like you have to be old to die. Not anymore. You never know when you're going to end up, you know, spread across the front of a bus, or laid up in quarantine with some new disease, or tossed in a gutter, full of knife holes, by some guy who thought you were cute."

Blink.

"Or, you know, discarded in a storage crate somewhere. Could be anything."

Swallow. "Well, Audrey, what you say is true, but writing a will isn't about fixating on your mortality. I don't think most of my clients feel like they're at a higher risk of death than they ever were. The purpose of a will is to ensure that your assets are dealt with in a way that's consistent with the way that you lived, and that begins to be important to people who've spent years accumulating those assets. So when I ask why this is on your mind, I'm really wondering what sorts of assets you've acquired recently or what new reason you have for trying to protect them." He made a nervous face, trying to figure them out. "Children, for example."

"Nope, nothing like that. We are po'."

Sacks laughed, finally, at this. "Ok. Well, certainly you could hire me to do your will. I work for you, and it's your decision. But, to be honest I think it would be a waste of your money and time to do that at this point in your lives."

She thanked him for his time. They went out. Passing, as they did, a girl of nine or so. Probably his daughter. They walked out of the featureless waiting room that they'd waited in, before, where

Stanley had looked up periodically, always to see the secretary's stare change in panic to a makeshift smile. Audrey waved to the him on the way out, natural as anything, and then stopped out on the stoop, nestled herself in the crook of the banister, and lit a cigarette. Made the stooping, hunching, sheltering pose, carefully guarding her eager new flame. Stanley liked watching the cigarette rite, especially the little moment of silence that she observed now after inhaling for the first time.

After the drag she spoke: "Well, I wouldn't call that conclusive, but I didn't get anything from that guy."

He waited, squinting out at things.

"Just seemed normal. Were you watching when I asked about the crate?"

He nodded.

"He do anything?"

"No."

"Yeah, I didn't see any—"

The door opened, and she hushed, and the little girl came out again, but he wasn't with her, and she stood there on the steps with Stanley, doing a nervous little step-step thing, waiting for her father, probably.

"Hi!" said Audrey, all smiles.

The girl looked distrustfully at the cigarette, which Audrey quietly smashed out on the concrete beside her hip and then turned herself, dangling her feet non-threateningly toward the girl, who finally—sounding a little disappointed—said, "Hello."

"I'm Audrey. What's your name?"

The girl shifted her wait around. "Lydia."

"Hi Lydia! This is Stanley. Don't worry, he's harmless. Doesn't he need a haircut though?" Here she grabbed at Stanley's head and gently tousled his hair, and he wondered if she had any idea what that meant to him. She did it like it was nothing; maybe it was.

Lydia laughed. "Yeah."

Audrey sat there, bouncing her feet off the step and smiling, so very warm.

She looked up at Audrey. "I like your hair. It looks like soup."

Stanley had never really figured out how to be gracious, but Audrey could do it. "Oh, thank you! That's what I wanted. I was thinking 'I want my head to look like soup.'"

The girl blushed and looked down at her shoes, whitewall denim. Nobody said anything for a while. A car drove by, slowly. She looked impatient, like dad was taking longer than she expected. "He cries at night sometimes."

Audrey asked, "What?"

"Sometimes I wake up in the middle of the night and I hear it. I used to think it was an animal on the roof, but it's him. I've gone in his room. The lights are off, but he's crying. It's slow, and it repeats. If you wake him up, he doesn't remember. He asks if I've been having a bad dream. I say yeah. Do you guys do that? Why are you here?"

"Well, he's probably just having a bad dream himself, and when you wake him up he forgets it. You forget your dreams sometimes too, right?"

Lydia sighed and rolled her eyes. She was wearing a backpack, which gave her a little extra momentum as she swiveled back and forth like a mechanism in an old clock. Then she took off the bag, sat down, and pulled out a pad of paper—stationary—tore off the top sheet, flipped it over, started drawing on it against the pad, the pad on her knees. She seemed to be drawing sort of absently, like it gave her a reason to stab this way and that with her pen. "I like to draw while he's reading me stories at night, after we eat. That way I have ideas. Right now I don't have any."

Stanley was jarred by memory to speak: "Yeah! I used to do that when my mom would read to me. I could never really draw, though. Couldn't draw actual things. But it was something to do with your hands at least."

Audrey had the thing, though, the talking to kids thing. "What kind of stuff can you draw?"

"I can draw places."

Audrey waited.

"I can't draw people. They look scary."

"I dunno, people look kind of scary," Stanley joked.

Audrey ignored him. "What about animals?"

"Nope. They look dead."

"What about plants?"

"Yeah, plants are easy."

Stanley butted in again: "What about plant people?" but was again ignored.

Then Sacks finally came out, said "Oh, hello," in a gentle sort of way, and "Sorry Liddy. You ready to go?" She packed her things into her backpack and went off, he taking her hand, and because he was so small and she was pretty normal they made not so asymmetrical a pair, except for the bobbling of his giant-sized head, as they walked off down the street. Stanley noticed, after they'd gone, that she'd managed somehow to leave her drawing behind and Audrey picked it up.

There were lines going this way and that, messy; it didn't look like anything; it was random. The only real feature was a blackened rectangle as if she'd written something and then crossed it out:

compulsively scratching across the same little area, covering black with black with black. Audrey flipped the page, as if whatever had been written and then covered would, being closer to the opposite side than the rest of it, show through there. It didn't, but weird because the crossed out section had embossed a rectangle, outlining one particular area of the letterhead on the back of the drawing with eerie precision. Below Sacks' name, the name of the law firm, and the address, where it said simply, for no obvious reason, "Westin-Rodant" and to the left of it a generic little black-and-white insignia with fourfold radial symmetry.

She lit a new cigarette and smoked this one all the way through. Stanley thought about Lydia. Then he looked at Audrey, still dangling from the guardwall, sort of tiredly splayed there. And suddenly he was worried that she'd be getting bored of him. 'Cause what had he really said today? He worried a lot about overstaying his welcome. It was better to leave people wanting more. You couldn't go wrong erring on that side.

"Hey, I have to go."

"Um, ok." She sounded sort of surprised.

He wondered if it was a mistake, not really wanting to leave, but too late now. Tried to think of something to say by way of acknowledgment that didn't sound too desperate. Couldn't. Tried to smile, but didn't feel quite right about it, couldn't quite manage it.

She noticed anyway. "Yeah yeah, we both had fun. You fuckin' oddball. I'll call you. I wanna look some things up." And then, as if trying to teach a small child what was expected of him, "Bye, Stanley."

He waved and then left, not knowing how fast to walk, feeling like when you start consciously regulating your breathing and then you can't remember how to stop, and you want it to feel natural again but it won't.

☥

18. *art history (continued)*

Out of Dodge: *On the bus at North Avenue, eleven am. Oliver is looking out the window and notices in one of the store windows, one of the fancy furniture and kitchenware sort of stores, there is a bed on display in the window and there is a man who looks like he is probably a bum sleeping in the bed, like he got in there somehow and they haven't noticed yet.*

It didn't turn out that good, but you can sort of see the window and the outline of the bed frame. You can't see the guy in the bed at all 'cause the sun against it is too bright and the whole thing is a blown out wash of white, but you can see Oliver's hair at the bottom left where he is in the way, but it's blurry and looks like a fungus or black foam that's taking over the picture.

We both laugh at that for a while and then feel weird and quiet while the diesel engine chugs and the bus heaves forward. Then he makes the joke again—the one he keeps making every ten minutes or so, the joke by now just being how annoying it is—where he gets real sober-looking and then says, "Listen, happy birthday, ok?" Like he's presenting me with it over and over, and will keep doing it the entire trip. And then when you ignore him he acts all stern and keeps repeating, "Ok?" more earnest each time until you answer. Knows I hate it 'cause what can you say you're expected to answer but no answer appropriate, the joke has no punchline, nothing you can say adds anything but just sounds prescribed, one way or the other. So finally I say "You asshole!" and finally he stops and doesn't do it again.

And, Hottie: *A couple minutes later. There's a guy on the bus who stares at me. Wish he'd stop 'cause it just makes me feel self-conscious but*

soft power

every time I look up, there he is looking at me again, and each time he takes his time about looking away, no matter how bad I glare, like he thinks I'll like it or he's saying something like "Hey, I'm looking at you." Cut it out nasty, olddirty. So one time when I catch him at it I raise the camera quick and take his picture and that makes him stop; he stares straight at the back of the next seat the rest of the ride.

So there's a picture of this sort of affronted-looking guy which, as soon as we got the film from the photomat, I circled his head and wrote "Hottie" below it, and Oliver kind of got mad like "What, you really think that guy's hot? What the fuck? That guy?"

There's things to look at in the city, shops, buildings, people, taxis. Through the city, west, it gets more and more run-down and then switches over to the rows of small houses perched above the face of the running poured-concrete cliff, which keeps the cars down. Less to look at there, although we do pass a van—a dark red van with old-style bubble-windows—full of naked people. The other cars probably can't see, closer to the ground, but up here from our bus we can see: the driver is a naked guy; next to him on the passenger side is a naked woman with her foot out the window, against the mirror; and in the back are three or four more who you can't really see but they're all naked too. The woman in the front has big, proud, womanly breasts, the kind that seem to stretch the skin taut around all their bulk, and as we're watching I feel jealous and wish I hadn't pointed out the van. Then the driver looks over and sees the bus pulling by and notices we can see and just sort of grins at me and shrugs, maybe embarrassed, I can't tell.

Before long we're out in the middle of a soybean field, where there's really nothing to see, nothing at all, and for half an hour or so we play threats. I start:

"I'll beset you with vermin."

"I'll sell you into slavery in Egypt."

"I'll purge your family's name from the earth, one crying child at a time."

"I'll do unto you as my grandfather did unto your grandmother, and his unto hers, and likewise for time immemorial."

"I'll give you such exquisite torture as the minstrels will sing of it for generations, evoking with my name the very spectre of earthly horror."

"I'll rain down upon you with blows, so many blows."

"I'll hit you back."

"I'll poke you in the arm a couple times."

"I'll call you names. Bad ones."

"I'll be angry at you."

"I'll feel some reservations about inviting you to a party."

"I'll leave you off my list of the most influential voices of the twentieth century."

"You wouldn't! I'm warning you, I'll disbelieve you."

"I'll nullify you."

"I'll prove you don't exist."

"I'll incite the hairshirted faithful to wailing and self-flagellation so as to ward off your dark spirit."

"I'll drench you with humiliating corn and lead all the kids in laughing at you."

And so on. After that trails off we quiet down, and I nestle my head in the cavity between his chest and his arm, and it is comfortable but trying to figure if he wants it there, if it is working.

✝

soft power

19. stick that fork back in your eye

Stanley worried about the timing. She'd said they were coming at eight. Not to have enough time would be the worst thing, but he didn't want to finish too early and have to sit around and wait.

The clock inched forward and the scary noises from outside the window came more frequently. It was dark and so cold out, having snowed for the first time two days ago. The snow hadn't lasted, but the cold was enduring. Maybe they wouldn't come. That would certainly disrupt the timing.

Able to stand it no more, he set to work. He'd thought about using a plastic fork, but that would be slapdash. A plastic fork was for children, for amateurs, for suckers. He had a hacksaw that he'd stolen from his dad for something and he had a mind to use it. The metal fork would be impressive—would set him apart. It wasn't too much, was it? He set the fork on a chair, braced it with his foot the best he could, lacking a vice, and started sawing through its prongs about midway along their length. Couldn't quite hold it there—it slipped around—so took some time to get the cut started, but working at it for a while, longer than he would have thought but not too long, he managed to shear it pretty well. He went to the mirror and lumped putty onto his eye, closing it and then covering the area with a thin layer. He stuck the sawed-off fork into the putty, but it wouldn't stay; it drooped then fell off.

He broke a toothpick in half, braced it against his eye socket, and then glued it to the fork to act as a buttress. Now the fork pivoted out of the putty as soon as he let it go. Ok, not having time to mess around, pulled away the putty and glued the fork to his eyelid, then replaced the putty around the juncture, replaced the toothpick and covered it with putty. It seemed pretty secure after that. He covered the whole thing with the liquid gore that he'd bought, then checked it all in the mirror, and it was good—he was every bit the victim of an unspeakable accident. He imagined people at the dinner party and to underscore a point somebody—a few drinks under, maybe—waving his fork around and suddenly it's not in his hand anymore and then the soft wet sound and everyone looks over and Stanley's just sort of swaying in his seat, mouth agape, with the unruly fork from his face, and then he'd try to look at it with the good eye but it would just swivel out of the way, of course, and at that someone would vomit. Now he had a half hour wait, sweating beneath all the putty and with the fork tugging at him, and he tried to keep his hands from worrying it so it wouldn't all fall apart. Of course, they might not come.

It didn't seem to make sense that they'd come—didn't fit the pattern he'd established. People dressed up, went out, went to parties, he knew, but it was other people. Those things had always been denied him. They wouldn't come. Running late, they'd omit him; he was expendable. They were late.

"Have a good costume. If you don't you can't come, ok?" she'd said on the phone, and he'd had to dutifully repeat, "Ok," before she'd let him go. What if he had a good costume and still couldn't come? The smudges on the walls stood still. An hour earlier there were footsteps from upstairs, but they'd gone out, tromping down the stairs—hustle and bustle everywhere but here. The things that always made noises made noises. He tried to read for a while but couldn't concentrate.

"What are you doing on Friday?" she'd asked, completely straight.

"Um..."

"Wanna come to a party?" she'd asked, completely straight.

"Um..."

soft power

"Have a good costume. If you don't, you can't come, ok? If I show up and you're just standing there or you've got some weenie little mask, I'm slamming the door in your face, ok?"

So, the fork, which had come to him the day before and he'd woken up early, unable to sleep, and bought the putty and the gore. An excuse to try to impress—nobody would have any reason to suspect. The last party he'd been to was with ROTC friends. He was thrilled to be asked along but it was uncomfortable—a packed small loud little box. The floor had bounced up and down, inches it seemed like, from everybody's weight—all the big imposing men and bland blonde women who wanted him out of their ways. Every few seconds he was asked to move this way or that, shoved or jostled. His friends dispersed to talk with their friends. He finished his beer and snuck out. Maybe it wouldn't be so bad if she didn't show up.

The phone call was just the latest in a series since he'd last seen her. They were short because she'd had other things to do, but each time she'd had a bulletin for him, some new tidbit in the continuing saga:

"I found there's gonna be a funeral for Nikola Tesla November tenth. You wanna go?"

"Go to a funeral?"

"It'll be fun. We can wear sunglasses and stand off to the side acting mysterious."

"I don't think I have the clothes for it."

"Oh come on, you're just stalling now. You know what else?"

"It's catered?"

"No, I mean about Nikola Tesla: he's named after a famous scientist."

"Yeah I knew that."

"Are you holding out on me Stanley? You don't want to trifle with me!"

"No no I just knew that. He's from a hundred years ago or so. 'Tesla coils,' that was him. He was this crazy eastern-European mad scientist guy. Had some insane plan about generators broadcasting electricity through the air so nothing would need batteries or gas. Except there's some drawback to it where if you actually tried it people would burst into flames or something like that. I forget how it worked exactly. Anyway I knew that."

And then there'd been the call about the party, saying she'd come by, that it was only about five blocks from there. It was 8:23. She must be tired of him.

Then the buzzer toned and Stanley went to the door and opened it and there was Audrey, at least he had to assume.

"Jesus," she said, studying his gash, and he felt perfect for a second or two as she inspected, approving. She was a sight herself—normally dressed but her face entirely obscured by a layer of glittery-red paint and framed by a matching old glittery-red motorcycle helmet.

He stared at her, trying to figure it out. "Um..."

She rolled her eyes and gave an exasperated sigh, then dutifully turned away from him and tilted her head back to reveal an isosceles triangle in three big, solid-black circles. "I'm a bowling ball, stupid!" Of course. "Let's go. I wanna show off your gruesome injury."

As he was shuffling out the door she peered inside at the apartment for just a second, then thought better of it and eagerly led him off down the stairs to the street where a small crowd milled.

"Ok everyone this is Stanley, and he had a little accident while he was eating dinner so we all have to be extra nice. Stanley, this is Paul..."

Paul was extraordinarily tall and stooped and had a paper bag over his head—a big plain brown bag and nothing else—but there were no eyeholes, no holes at all, so how could he tell where he was going? From inside the bag a voice, quieter than you'd think and sounding Australian and sort of apologetic, said, "I'm groceries."

"...and Oliver..."

Oliver looked like Stanley might if you took off twenty pounds of fat and put back twenty of muscle. Same height at least. He had a platinum blonde plastic pompadour wig and was caked with pink-flesh-colored makeup and lipstick. At a slow, steady deadpan, he said, "I'm white, Bro."

"...and Simone." And here Audrey's voice went shrill and staccato: "Nyeuh I'm Simone my costume has to make me look byoo´-tee-ful´." Like three notes.

Simone was tall, taller than him, wrapped in a pointy tin-foil bra and matching skirt, her smooth brown long stomach and legs all exposed, and these incredible chrome shoes up on scary tall, scary thin rods for heels, and the heels were orbited by green wire coils. "I'm from space. And *shocked* at how rude you guys all are. Hi Stanley it's very nice to meet you. And don't worry, on TV I saw Freddie Prinze Jr. arriving at a movie premiere with a fork *just like that* and Joan Rivers' daughter assured me it was darling and that look was going to be huge this year, even if his date was looking a little droopy. Let's go I'm cold."

And she must have been, the air searing Stanley's nostrils and making the sidewalk beneath his feet seem especially brittle.

Simone's footsteps against the frozen concrete echoed across the street as they walked past darkening sunroom windows. There weren't many people out on the streets by now. Each streetlamp blasted them with bluish light, igniting the rolls of their breathing. Nobody said much. Maybe they'd talked before getting to him, or maybe they were too cold. He felt a part of them—felt a little thrill as they passed a man in the opposite direction at not being the one against the group, at the strength of his numbers, and at the army march toward dawn.

20. the devil in miss livingston

Twenty minutes inside the door and this crew of co-dressed guys comes in, on each a pair of black sunglasses and a big, curly, black wig. They're laughing to each other; they're big and ruddy. There's a little group of girls that sneaks in behind, and they're all the same amount shorter and they're all thin, and they huddle together in glazed smiling silence.

"Haha! A little afro action! Welcome, gentlemen," Les says, high fivin'. They're embracing each other, solid and meaty, as if to test: "I'm still here. Are you?"

The instant should have been there, in her memory, when he switched over, *zert*, and became such an ass, but it wasn't. Hadn't she noticed? It didn't seem right that she could have missed it or forgotten it—didn't seem reassuring. Maybe it was a slippery slope. Maybe she was next.

But it didn't matter; it didn't bear thinking about. Here they were at this lovely party, and the clientele were nice enough mostly,

soft power

and the drinks were big and strong. She shook her head to clear out the revulsion and went off to find company.

There was fried chicken in her hand, a drumstick, and Oliver asked, "Where'd you get that?" It was almost gone already—warm and crisp and slimy and just right, soaking up the ache in her stomach.

She pointed across the room, but he didn't see. "You can't see from here. On the table. See the Pubic Hair and the Cataclysm? Behind them. It might be gone. There should be some bread still." He went.

Audrey chewed at the chicken, Simone sipped her drink. They were sort of alone on one side of the big dining-room-cum-hallway, which was shadowy and colorful with light from cellophaned-over lamps. Simone stopped with the sipping, then, taking a big gulp for the nerves, said, "What do you think I should do?"

"You don't want to go?"

"I don't know. Maybe. Could be a bad idea." There was a stereo playing, the pounding bass metronome resonating everything, resonating her.

"I mean, it must be a good sign that he wants to go, right?"

"Well, yeah, unless he's just sort of going through the motions. I guess it means he's being honest with me, just maybe not himself. But it's crazy, right? I feel like every conversation we have nowadays is just back-and-forth dropping hints and accusations, you know? This annoying little tennis game of trying to get the other person to say something more definite than you will yourself."

"So don't go."

"But on the other hand we haven't done this. Haven't gotten to ourselves and tried to talk through it. It might work, you know?"

"So go."

"But I'm worried about getting stuck in Utah by myself."

"Ok, well, go, and if that happens you can call me and I'll beat my way out west and come get you. I ain't scared'a no bikers or hitchhiking murderers! Let me at 'em!"

"Yeah shut up."

Up came Paul, still inside the bag, which nobody had figured out yet. "These are a bit much," he said, holding up his drink. "I'm almost too drunk to notice I'm lonely, and with this music I can't concentrate on being bored. This is great!"

Audrey looked at a bookshelf—a typical Les sort of bookshelf, a few too many big names, or maybe it was that you sensed that those thirty books there, those were the thirty he'd read. Like if you struck up a conversation, now, in front of the shelf, he'd allude to one of them within a couple minutes.

"Did you see the fellow dressed as Don King?"

Her theory was Les fell in with the wrong crowd. What it was about them, exactly, was a little hard to pinpoint. Self-satisfied, prancing around, joyous all the time, being young and beautiful and blessed by the sun, presuming themselves the pinnacle, presuming everything, but every conversation some bland pseudo-philosophy about the path to an ideal life, something meaningless, "Really being open to things, you know?" "Everyone doing their thing." Or worse, in Les's case, a kind of dull amoral hedonism, but not in so many words.

Paul hung for a second in the quiet, having failed twice at conversation. "Oh, pardon, were you talking about boys? I'll leave you to it, then," and he did, clumping off, heavy and drunk, across the old wooden floor to the kitchen linoleum, which was more solid— the better to hold him up, she imagined. Then Stanley went through in the opposite direction, in his usual forward, single-minded lurch.

Simone indicated him after he'd passed. "He doesn't say much. Sort of cute though in a weird way. What happened with the murderin' lawyer, anyway?"

"Oh, I'm not so sure he's murderin'."

"He didn't seem like the type?"

"No, I guess not. Listen to this, though: they had this stationary which said 'Westin-Rodant,' in tiny letters. You know what that means?"

"Um... No."

"I thought it might be the printing company, like Avery, but I looked through a list and it's not. Then I looked in a phone book, and it wasn't there either. Then I looked for somebody famous named 'Westin Rodant' or 'Westin' or 'Rodant,' and didn't find anything. I had about given up, but the other day I was dying my hair and I had the newspaper spread out on the floor to catch the mess and the business section happened to be under me and there it was, 'WSRT Westin-Rodant Corp' in the stock listings. It was up an eighth."

"All right! See you in Maui."

"Listen to this, though, this is where it starts to get kind of odd: I looked up their SEC registration and it says they conduct no business of any kind, and they have no plans to at this time. That doesn't seem to have stopped people buying the stock, though."

"So are you to going to catch whoever did it?"

"Totally."

"You better hurry, 'cause you're next right?"

"Totally." She paused for a minute, drinking her drink. "Yeah, Stanley's great though. He sort of seems to know about everything.

How it works, that kind of thing. He's got all these little stories. He was talking the other day about people who discover some huge new thing. Like Isaac Newton, who went for all these years being the only person around who knew about calculus, figuring all this stuff out on his own. All those years when he had a huge book in his head of ideas that nobody else knew about yet. Except that hack kraut Leibnitz. Stanley was saying what was that like, and how it must have been weird to be Newton, walking his dog, smirking at everyone because he knew calculus. And then he says how Isaac Newton was a virgin when he died."

"Whoah."

"So he claimed, anyway. Can't imagine why he would have lied about it."

"That is pretty strange. I'm not sure I can imagine being enough into calculus for that not to bother me."

"It's fun though, you know? Stanley will just sort of come up with this stuff spontaneously. And it's sort of refreshing 'cause there's not a lot of artifice to him. Not like some other people I could mention," and she shot Simone a big-eyed glare of accusation.

"Hey, I got the best artifices of anyone. You know you love it."

"Yeah ok. But you know what I mean, right? Like when he just walked by and his pointless haircut was bouncing around? I love it. It's the dumbest."

"It is very dumb."

"What?" said Stanley, who had just come back.

"Oh, we were just talking about my retarded dog again."

"Oh."

"Yeah. Sparkey."

"Cool." Stanley had an extra drink, which he handed to Audrey, who wasn't sure what to do with it.

soft power

"What is it?"

"I made it. It's called a Green and White. Try it, it's good." It was pretty good. "I was reading the paper today and there's this article about an Indian reservation in Nevada where people keep dying from some weird type of cancer that's supposed to be really rare, and not contagious of course. The incidence among the people on the reservation was something like 500 times the national average, and nobody can figure out why."

"It seems like I read about something like that about every other week. I remember I saw one just a month ago about a series of murders on a reservation. There's all these old bums around—alcoholics sleeping under bridges—and somebody was going around drowning them, pulling them into the water while they were passed out. This had happened five times maybe. I can see why it might be hard to get medical or legal attention."

Simone put in, "But they've got such great casinos. That must count for something."

"Yeah, the gambling industry gets no respect. Not only a breeding ground for crime and corruption, it's got a beautiful tradition as a scrap for the disenfranchised to kill each other over. Makes me proud. Right up until the government takes the reins and then you have The Lottery, which offers poor people the opportunity to prove themselves equal to the rich, if in nothing else then at least in paying taxes. 'Cause everyone deserves a chance."

Excising this anger she began to worry, as Les appeared at the end of the hallway, coming to see what it was about, and stood watching her, dubiously. He had dubiousness down pat. (Dubiosity? Dubor? Dubiety.)

"You're angry," he said, mockingly laughing, at her, or at himself. Laughing at the idea of anger. But his derision carried such sway, with her as with anyone. Intelligent. Charismatic. Yet you couldn't quite respond to it, because the attitude was under the surface, leaving nothing to attack, soft belly concealed by irony's tough shell.

"What?"

"Oh, nothing." Because he'd never, ever take a stand that wasn't amusedly detached at the same time, undercover chuckling at the very idea of disagreeing with him or with anything.

Fuck that! She knew—they all knew, and he knew that she knew—what he meant. "Does that make it easier, to write me off as a lunatic so you can ignore all the ways that your comfortable little life is stoked by unlivable conditions in all kinds of places too far away from your Halloween party to think about? 'Cause you tip your waitress and you smile at the dishwasher no matter what language he speaks and what else can be expected of you? 'Cause you had the same chance as everybody else, and if they weren't able to make the most of their parents' paying for their absurdly expensive college educations well then it's not your fault? Why wouldn't I be angry? What do you mean?"

"Yeah. It's all my fault, not directly of course, but just 'somehow.' 'You know.' And you caught me. Me red-handed and you with that big Green and White. You're 'making a difference.' You might be acting locally, but you're *thinking* globally."

"But it is. It is your fault, just as much as it's mine, because neither of us has really objected. It's as much your fault as anyone else's, or more, because you don't even seem to mind." You never seem to mind, unless seeming to mind would be funny.

He just sort of shrugged, smiling indulgently, patronizingly. "Maybe you should have a rock and roll benefit show. You could call it 'No Reservations.'"

"Yeah, maybe. Fucker."

Blank, conciliatory smile, absolute dismissal. "Hey, that's not party behavior. Let's keep it down, ok?"

So she just walked away, 'cause what else was there to do? Out behind the kitchen was a deck where smokers were huddling in the shelter of the building with their bright little embers. She bummed a cigarette and smoked it furiously. The few stars stood out against the night—not moving, anchoring everything.

One of the afro guys came up the outside stairs from who knew where, smelling of bong. "Hey, have you seen Les?" His eyes flitted off, just above her head, not bothering to conceal rank indifference, as if she were a refrigerator or washing machine in his way, but one that might happen to know where Les was.

"He's sucking the devil's cock in hell."

"Whoah, alright. Sorry."

She turned to the alley, which was still and crystalline beneath the sodium vapor lights. The building across the way had a little access tunnel running into the back with an incandescent flood angled down it; somebody at the far side was standing there, casting a severe shadow down the tunnel and across the driveway, a shadow hulking and top-heavy like a superhero, like a communist-poster worker. She wondered what they were doing over there. The shadow didn't move much, standing watch, sturdy but calm.

Apart from that one offending shelf there were no books to speak of inside. He had a television in every room, but no books. It is more useful to think of television people and book people than to think of dog people and cat people. Television and books hiss and fight when left together.

TV shows advance the Murdoch school of literary criticism, which holds that the way to understand a book is to construct a sentence that supplants it. "Though Samsa transforms to a giant insect, he is still the same person on the inside." This is called "the Point."

TV news doesn't even acknowledge the existence of print, unless it's in conjunction with money. If a book sells many copies, that is news. If a book is auctioned for a large sum, that is news. Other books are not news.

Television and money are friends. You cannot learn much from television, but you can learn to invest. Audrey had a notebook where she wrote down things that she'd read or heard and had considered telling. On the list was a topic, coming up soon, from TV News: "How can I profit from mapping DNA?"

There was some chatter from inside, clamoring and moving. The Gay Pirate came out the screen door and addressed one of the other smokers: "You gotta come see this. He's starting." They started to file into the kitchen, and Audrey followed, eavesdropping.

"What's this?" he asked the Pirate.

"It's this guy Denny. Everyone says he's amazing. The best."

Back in the dining room the guy in the cataclysm costume was sitting at the center of a little crowd with a newspaper. Somebody shouted, "Italy," and he grabbed a sheet of newsprint and started clutching at it, frenziedly, his head bent over, his hands wadded up in his lap and you couldn't see what he was doing. Despite all the obvious effort it was sort of strange and quiet. Everyone standing around to see the show but it wasn't really a performer, just somebody's idiot kid brother who can put his thumb through his ear or something. With no flair to entertain awkward impatience set in, everyone watching Denny's facial spasms and twisting palms. A couple seconds later, not long at all really, he slapped the floor with a pretty decent silhouette of Italy torn from paper, followed just a second later by Sicily, even, and to scale.

Some people clapped. "Isn't it amazing? He's the best," Audrey heard a voice say.

So she shouted, "Uzbekistan," and went off to find a dictionary. He'd finished by the time she found the map, and sure enough there it was, not half bad.

"Lithuania." The voice Simone's. "Let's play pin the tail on the former Soviet Republic."

He did a couple more and then staggered away, sweating, and she could still hear the murmurs of "the best" here and there. She stood there for a while, nursing her drink, not really wanting any more. It was late. Two thirty, maybe. The walls were dirty. Her head was spinning. Oliver was with her.

"I heard you're going cross country," she said.

"Yeah, well, we'll see. I keep remembering Emerson's thing about travel, you know? People talk about it as an 'escape,' you know, like 'If I can just get away from my boss, everything will be so much better.' And of course his point is they're really just trying to get away from themselves, so it never works. Not if your expectation is that you're going to go somewhere and everything will suddenly be, you know," and made a sparkly, magical little hand gesture here. "So I wonder if we're going to go out, you know, drive for a few days, and then there we'll be, at our heels, clinging to us, and we won't be able to tear ourselves away." He shrugged.

"Yeah." 'Cause he hadn't really left anything for her to say. Stanley, she'd just noticed, was standing across the room, against a wall, alone, staring at the floor. His shoulders were hunched up and his hands were in his pockets, making him look small. He was just sort of staring, and he looked so sad. Wondered what it was. Then she watched him out of the corner of her eye as he stood up straight, surveyed the room, and walked up the hall to the door and quietly went out. "Hey, I gotta do something I'll see you later," she hastily explained.

Oliver looked surprised. "Ok."

She could hear Stanley below her, footsteps on the carpeted steps in the stairwell that smelled like turmeric. Sort of plodding—neither fast nor slow, just heavy. She hurried a little so he wouldn't get away.

Out on the street the cold felt good to inhale, cleaning out all the hot and smoke and sweat. Stanley was down the street to the right a little, walking down the sidewalk, hands still wedged in his pockets, head between his shoulders against the cold. He'd mentioned something about being hit by a car once, and it sort of made sense now, looking at him—standing alone in the wide valley of brownstones, the smallest thing around, looking totally fragile and totally at everything's mercy. A pinball in play. Puffs of white came up over his head now and then.

She trotted after him, down the street, mid-speed. A muffler backfire somewhere, far away, and she winced. A few feet behind him he heard her and turned around. She waited for a minute for him to say something but he didn't.

"Hey, where you going?"

"Um, I was sort of tired."

"Yeah well," and then this strange silence descended, falling around the two of them in the darkness and the cold, and she could feel the stares of the angels in the parapets, and the light from a window where somebody could be standing, staring through blinds—like it was suddenly a set, these cars just props, and the audience was hanging off her line. And it wouldn't come. She always had something to say, but his eyes were grey and he was staring, expecting, looking at her from a questioning sort of distance, giving up

soft power

nothing, leaving her nothing to say in the middle of the night, next to a van. Headlights spanned them and then a car passed, achingly slow and measured, marking the time, and he was still standing there, and so was she. "You're supposed to say goodbye before you leave, you know."

"Yeah, sorry. I was feeling quiet."

Still she felt stuck, glued in place. Wasn't sure what she wanted, but it wasn't this. "Alright. Well, I'll see you later, ok? Bye." 'Cause that cured the paralysis at least, jogging back through the cold, back to the party, and she felt relief to have gotten away but it wasn't what she wanted, and she looked back a couple times at Stanley who was making his same progress away toward home, his head still down. For just a moment, five seconds maybe, she felt rushing over her every rock'n'roll oath of fealty ever sung, wanting to run back and take retreating Stanley's hand and she wouldn't even have to speak because both of them would have and hold the same certainty.

✢

21. ...

And Stanley looked back, too, but they never caught each other at it.

✢

22. *art history (continued)*

Time and Distance are the Same: On the bus in Kansas City, midnight. *This is my first one. I'll try to follow Simone's pattern. It isn't very good. I took a picture of the map that I was looking at, the United*

States map. I know that because I took it but I'm not sure you could tell. It's blurry and dark and there is no contrast. It shows film grain and little else.

At first I was trying to plan our route. It becomes uncertain here. After I got tired of that I started reading the names of all the cities. They fade like colors across the map. The colonial Norfolk, Charlotte, and Amsterdam wash up against the Spanish Pasadena, Sacramento, and Santa Ana. And through the middle a bright streak of Wichita, Milwaukee, Chicago, Delaware. The record of the history plays out across the surface—comings and goings, killings and new beginnings. Each clan and each generation has its own ideas about what a place should be called. I thought what if you could see it all—look at the map and see in your head everything that had happened, like a chart but millions of tiny lines hither and thither, migrations, trends, disasters.

After a while, finding towns, comparing longitudes, I started feeling down. All the time and distance that separates me from the places I could pinpoint, the places where I've been. The old, dirty, wise East with its Boston hospitals, frozen aluminum railings that held me up waiting for my grandma to die. The big, pretty, lonely West, Cheyenne outhouses, homes smell like cowboy, trails lit by stars and hurrying past the possibility of scorpions. Did I have any idea back then that I'd be here, so soon but so late, with nothing to show for it but this tiny, useless impression on my memory? All those years and miles wasted because what had I done since then with my locales and my highway snapshots? Would I be gone just as soon never having returned to the places I swore to bring Someone? There, mapped out on the page in two dimensions, one of them curved, at 1 to 10 million scale, the limits of my speed and duration and the area of the places I'd never make it.

Because you can't conceive of time or distance, really, and if you try you better hope that there's someone there to rescue you, on the rattling silent dark bus, when you feel air-conditioned cold saturating your clothes and freezing you, cutting off blood to your extremities, slowing your breath, and you can do nothing but reach feebly for the warm embrace of those arms and cling, cling, tight and desperate as you can, cling for dear life because what choice do you have in the midwest at midnight, at the middle of a bus full of people like you, who don't have a choice.

And, By the Night or Hour: in a Room in Kansas City, two am. *Centered above the headboard of the bed is a dangerously ugly, decaying oil painting of a woman lying on a bed. Simone, on the bed, is attempting to imitate the pose for the camera. The two of them make a nice pair.*

We are both very, very tired. We just figured out that if you wait until midnight to stop, all of the hotels have become full. Because full hotels will not rent you a room, and because of our narrow price range, we spent about two hours dragging our bags up and down every street in the city looking for some place to stay. We passed a guy curled up in a doorframe who looked up at Simone and said, "Girl, you're so beautiful, your daddy musta dumped your momma for you." He told it straight. Just down the block from him was a little hotel where the manager had to open a gate to let us in.

The sounds of us walking—the sheer fabric rubbing of the bags and the off-balance footsteps—seemed very loud in the cold quiet street as we approached. Through the gate we could see him sitting there, long hair and thirty or so sitting at a folding card table watching TV, looking over maybe with disbelief when we rang the bell. He got up, slowly and deliberately, turned away from us, walked back to the desk to buzz the gate open and then came up to the door to talk to us. There was another man, older, shorter, browner and bald, who looked up with annoyance when the bell rang. He went back to watching the television immediately. The first man came to us and stood there, apparently feeling he'd done his part, and we wondered if it were really a hotel. Were there any vacancies? There were not, even when we said please. Did he know of anywhere where there might still be vacancies? He stared when I asked him this, stared totally blank like he was still waiting for me to talk, for five seconds or so. Yeah, he knew a guy. He would call and check. There was a vacancy.

We thanked him and walked back down the street and as we passed the guy said, "Girl, you're so beautiful, your daddy musta dumped your momma for you." We laughed. After two blocks, we looked at the numbers and realized we were going the wrong way, so we went past the same old guy one more time. This time he must have noticed, 'cause he said, "Girl, you're so ugly, your daddy musta dumped your momma to go back to the circus with the other monkeys."

This place had a gate too, and a plexiglass cage around the manager just inside the door, and a sign with weekly rates. We talked him into letting us stay just one night. Simone went ahead of me up the hall to the room because I was carrying the heavy stuff, and when she opened the door she just laughed. It's filthy here, an old filth that has long held the corners and edges. It is spreading, feebly pushed back but irrevocably forward, onto everything, into everything, through the air and paint and wood. The new grime is washed away from time to time but each time what's left is stained, dirt-dyed, a little stronger and more permanent. But I guess it hasn't taken long to get used to because we are both sprawling in the dirt like little kids, eating it practically.

And so back to the photo: I come back from the bathroom to find her lying there, pointing to the painting. She asks how she is doing. The ragged circles under her eyes make her look like a ravaged noir bombshell—looking you hard in the eye, with long weariness that doesn't mind if you come along but doesn't mind if you don't. Her head rests, her cheek against the arm that extends straight off the bed toward me, limp and cradling an illicit cigarette in bed. The way her body arches and twists—from her hips down on the sheets to her upward shoulders—makes her ribcage show faintly, its form just hinted at by the crenellations of skin in soft shadow. The meat of her breast spreads and pushes the skin outward; it is shallow and circular, gently rippling in the wake of each hard exhalation. All along her the flesh buzzes with tightness, stretching skin smooth. She looks at me still with no expression, watching me watch her.

She keeps asking me questions: "Why do you look? Do you have anything, having looked? What is it about my jumble of parts? Why is it never enough? Doesn't that bother you?"

I have nothing to say.

"Do you want to hold me? Do you want to fuck me? What's the difference?"

The window is open. Outside the window is smoke-blackened brick.

"Which is better? Which makes you more happy? Does it make you feel good, or feel better? Does it make a difference, tomorrow?"

And when I go to her and brush her I only want to touch her more and to be closer. We move together until we can get no closer but still we try, tearing at this flesh that would keep us apart, to hold so tight that our skins dissolve and meld and as one we don't fret time or distance because you cannot grow apart from yourself.

23. *mafia stylee*

The dead are a powerful lobby in Chicago, the joke goes. But it's true, just look at a map: Oakwood Cemetery, Rosehill Cemetery, Graceland Cemetery. It seems like half of the land is brown and featureless on the map, devoted to all the dead, who've been piling up in the old city for years. Chicago had its fire to burn people up and its mob to knock them off; they don't weight you down when they throw you in the lake, they just stab you full of holes so the air can get away and you'll sink, but there's still a headstone for your somewhere. "When there's no more room left in hell, the dead will come back," but what about when there's no more room at the cemetery?

So far Audrey felt safe. Looking down into the cemetery from the el, there were great rolling green hills still unused. And should a problem arise, those high, thick walls would keep in the walking dead. But does barbed wire work against zombies? Maybe it's just to keep out the graverobbers. Do they still have graverobbers? Where would you go if you wanted to apprentice?

Stanley was standing at the entrance. It was grey. It was raining enough to get you wet, eventually, but not so much that you didn't feel foolish with an umbrella. He was looking at his feet. She was about to call out but thought better of it and held her tongue. He had a suit, but no haircut. He looked good though, like the orphan at his mother's funeral in Dickens or Roald Dahl: the boy done wrong. How long would he have been waiting? She couldn't sneak up on him though, because her heels knocked the pavement. He looked up when she was a few feet away and smiled, with surprised recognition.

In retrospect, the black hair might have been a little much. Black hair, black heels, and she'd borrowed this old hooded black silk gown from Simone that Grace Kelly could have worn. It didn't really fit her, but close enough.

"Wow," he said, "you go all out." That was probably as close to a compliment as she was going to get, considering, and close enough: she beamed, despite the setting.

"I told you before—" The asphalt path into the cemetery was new and pure grey. "—I don't fuck around."

"You know we could still leave. We could go to a debutante ball or something."

soft power

"Don't be a coward. Come on."

She yanked at his arm, which was heavy but without conviction beneath the black linen of the suit, still dry under the patina of tiny water droplets, each defiantly maintaining its perfect spherity. They walked down the path, and she was more nervous than she let on. The padding of his smooth mirror-shiny black shoes against the asphalt was a comfort, calming the sharp uneven cadence of her wooden clock-tick steps. They passed the undertaker's building—its lead-pane windows gone wobbly with age, dark inside, reticent. She'd gotten a big cup of coffee to make herself feel better and it hadn't worked, and now she was shaking. Once she'd got Stanley moving she let go of his arm so as not to let on. The sunglasses were supposed to help—were supposed to deindividuate—but that wasn't working either.

There was no litter in cemeteries; it was jarring. There were no tags and no stickers peeling away from the eye-level surfaces. Mayor Daley did not silently say, "I hate it here," and Tattoo from *Fantasy Island* did not admonish, "Grow." The little path wound around and over the small gentle hills like a car commercial before leading them to the dour assembled—a much smaller number than she would have expected.

The minister was speaking. He was young and bird-faced—nose too big, chin too small, pale and quiet. He seemed to expect someone to interrupt him at any minute and chide him, "You're not doing it right."

"...be little comfort at a moment like this to be told one more time that all things happen for a reason, or that this too shall pass, or that any of the..."

To his right was evidently the mother. She looked as if she might fall to pieces at any minute—not cry but literally fall to pieces, like her face and her body might give up coherency and collapse into a heap of various ashen, doughy lumps, a foot tall or so, covered except at the top by the now-rumpled black lacy gown. Because it seemed to be only an act of will that was binding her together at all, holding the round red nose that might otherwise tumble right off. She looked alcoholic, weighed on and softened by years of slow poison. She looked fifty but probably wasn't.

Next to her was another woman, an older version of the same. Then a stern, well-dressed, severe couple, and their obvious daughter who was twenty or so. She had a dress to compete with Audrey's own, flattering a shape not thin but still good, still alive. Her hair was dark and straight, framing her small cleft-chin face in a box of razor-sharp bangs. Between her clavicles was the knife-point of a single, slender black line of tattoo that quickly vanished beneath the high-cut dress, and could have been anything.

"...not to allow yourself to be made a victim of this. You must feel that in a world where your loved ones can end up as Nikola did everything has gone beyond your control, but you still have the choice to live through this, and to deny those that would take him from you the satisfaction of taking you as well. And even that must..."

Then the girl was staring right at Audrey with no sunglasses, and the pupils were small in her pale green irises. She had the kind of eyes that smoldered with a deep and abiding conviction that she, at least, was in the right. And not only that, but you believed it too. She stared with something that could have been anger or curiosity, and she wouldn't stop, not for a minute or more. Audrey hadn't seen Nikola—only heard Stanley's description—but she saw this girl now, identified by her position in the crowd and by something in her countenance as a close friend. On the great vista of human

soft power

possibility at the turn of the century, this girl was about two degrees from Audrey, it was obvious. She had to fight the urge, out of nowhere, to giggle, as if she were twelve and had made a joke with a friend and every time the phrase repeated in her head she couldn't stifle the laugh. Finally the stare moved on toward Stanley, and Audrey felt some blend of relief, sympathy, and schadenfreude.

There were some others: a middle-aged, perhaps teacherly woman, a balding man struggling to wear a suit, two young boys trying to hold still, and a big man probably better for his pall-bearing ability than for his knowledge of the deceased. The gathering was quite small. Also there was a stout, tired, finely wrinkled but hardened rather than softened man with grey-tinged short-buzzed hair, wearing a long overcoat.

The speech wound down and stopped, and then the mother wearily and sorely thanked everyone for coming and then it was ending and people were breaking from their spots, milling apart.

Stanley leaned over quietly, "Why did you want to come here?"

"I forget."

"I'm cold."

"Yeah. We should probably go."

And they turned around and walked but not too quickly away, but then a voice behind them, and Audrey didn't have to turn around to know whose, stopped them dead.

"I'm Ada."

Stanley, of course, said nothing, so after a pause: "This is Stanley. I'm Audrey. Nice to meet you."

Ada gave her some more of the inquisitor's eye. "How did you know Nikola?"

That was a tough one to answer. Audrey inhaled, thinking, and hoped it looked sort of natural. "We, uh," and then pulled out a pack of cigarettes and offered one to Ada, who—thankfully—took it, buying time. "We didn't, we just heard about it. Stanley—"

"Oh, ok, you're that Stanley. I remember now. Don't worry I'm not going to get offended or anything. You look nervous. Don't worry about it. Want to get a drink?"

It was Sunday afternoon; an empty bar sounded like just the thing. Ada walked off to say goodbye to her parents.

Stanley, who she'd just noticed looked constipated, said, "I really need to leave," indicating something behind his left shoulder.

"What is it?"

"In the overcoat."

"What about him?"

"Remember what I said about the detective?"

"Got it. You can go. I'll call you. Look, I'm sorry I made you come." And she was. She took his hand then, on impulse, took it between hers that were much smaller and pressed against it, looking up at him. Then she remembered about her sunglasses and wasn't sure what to do next and let him go, and he waved and walked briskly away. But she noticed that the overcoat man was moving to follow. She stopped him. "Do you have a some change? I need to make a phone call and I'm all out."

He rummaged, coming up with some, while Stanley, out of the corner of her eye, double-timed it away, and after overcoat had gone a few feet Audrey came again, "Actually—that was stupid—I need to make two phone calls. Sorry to bother you. You're not in any hurry are you? That's a really nice overcoat; where'd you get it?"

She held him up so that, she estimated, Stanley could make a getaway, and then Ada was back and they wandered around looking for a bar. They found one soon enough, an anonymous place marked only by a sign advertising Schlitz, and it was as dark and wooden as Audrey had hoped.

The bartender, the only person there, was big and slow-moving. He looked at them. "Where are you two coming from, a funeral? Ha!"

Ada glared at him: "Yes," and kept staring, stone-faced, and so they got their Guinness—which felt least inappropriate on a grey Sunday after a funeral—on the house. They sat in a booth, the only customers. It was pleasant there, the air warm and the stone-topped tables cool. The beer was chilled but not cold, black and strong and sustaining.

"I've never had to go to a funeral for someone really close. I can't imagine..."

"No." Ada glared and let this hang, horribly, just like with the bartender, and then smiled and it was just a joke. "Like I said, don't worry about it. I'm fine. After all the waiting and not knowing, and then the waiting and knowing, this is pretty anticlimactic."

Audrey listened, looked, and sipped.

"Here, I know," and Ada reached into her wallet and pulled out a picture of Nikola, a tiny frail black-and-white matte rectangle that showed him looking up, as if in surprise, from a plate of food. He was light and boyishly beautiful, a year or two younger than Ada, who was in turn a couple years younger than Audrey.

Ada got up to buy cigarettes. On her back, at the base of the neck, was the identical beginning of another tattoo. Audrey stared at the photo and tried to connect it to her own life, because what would it be like to hold a photo of dead Simone or dead Stanley for that matter? What did it feel like at the point where the photo becomes not something to tide you over but just something to postpone you forgetting?

✝

24. tesla coil

"I like your boobs." That was the first thing he said to her. It was funny, at the time. At the time, Ada had a roommate, an art-school girl named Anya who was nice enough but strange and strangely naive, seeming not quite capable of dealing with the world.

The quintessential Anya story took place one night while Ada was sleeping. She woke to a meek knock at the door, a wedge of awful light and Anya saying "Ada?" like a sick child. She didn't know what was going on at first; the red digital said 2:11.

"Yeah Anya?"

"If you wanted to make a tent to hang over your bed, how would you do it?"

"Um, you mean like a mosquito net? You can buy those."

"No, a black tent over your bed."

She was very tired. "What? I don't know. I guess I'd probably go get a screw hook and put it in the ceiling and make a harness from some dowels and rope and drape some fabric over it. Why do you want to do that?"

"Um, no reason. Thanks."

She flopped back onto the pillow and her heavy eyelids fell shut. Anya was weird.

Knock knock. "Ada?"

"Yes Anya?"

"Do you think it would be expensive?"

"Um, no, I don't know. It would probably cost you thirty dollars at a hardware store."

Pause. "Do you think you could help me do it?"

"Yeah, I really want to sleep right now, Anya. Can we talk about it tomorrow?"

"Oh, um, ok. Good night."

"Good night Anya."

And that was the last Ada ever heard of it. Anya never built a black tent to hang over her bed; she never even mentioned it. Figure that one out.

Anya left at year's end, left her things in the place that they shared and went to stay with her Aunt Katerina in Pennsylvania, and she called Ada halfway through the summer asking could Ada, at great expense, ship a certain large and cumbersome art project? She wouldn't say why, and Ada couldn't talk her out of it so she agreed.

It was a plaster-and-gauze cast in a three foot rectangular frame made from two-by-fours. An impression Anya had made of herself, her torso in flaky, white relief, shoulder to shoulder, neck to hip bones. It was much heavier than you'd think. Ada carried it all right out of the building, avoiding all the corners, and down to the end of the first block, but then her hands were tired and wouldn't hold and she had to set it down and rest. It was terrifically hot.

By fits and starts, her arms aching, resting every couple-hundred yards, she lugged the thing two blocks up and three over to the local shipping outlet, heaved it up on the counter and started nursing her splinters. The bemused woman said she didn't have the right supplies to wrap it well enough to send safely—couldn't insure it—and was Ada sure she wanted to ship it? *Don't blame me.* She should take it home and get a box and pad it like such-and-such and bring it back. *All right, but can I just set it here for a while before I carry it back home?*

That was when he came in, seeming to taunt her Sisyphean struggle with his trivial errand, merely picking up a roll of packing tape. A slim, buoyant roll of packing tape. He was small and adorable; he had a happy, open look, smiling at her while he picked out the tape and purchased it, casting inquisitive glances at Anya's art object. He was slightly younger, but not too much. He was blonde, had carelessly sculpted little-boy or rockstar sort of hair. The attraction of sad people is the challenge of making them happy; the attraction of happy people is that they might do it for you. And if neither ever happened, still that was the idea.

"I was wondering," she asked, finally, because she really was, "you keep smiling at me. Is that on purpose?"

He seemed to enjoy this chance to say the line: "Yeah. I like your boobs."

She just looked at him for a few seconds and he didn't look guilty or defensive or away, just open and true, bright and straight back at her. "Not mine actually." It made her smile to say that. "I guess you could have figured that," because Anya was slimmer.

He didn't say anything for a while. Finally, "What's that for?"

"My muddle-headed roommate wants me to send it to her in Pennsylvania."

"Why?"

"I have no idea. Because she's stupid."

He stared at it some more, now with a look of suspicion. "Maybe she wants to make the robot look like her." Ada smiled at this, and then laughed.

"Yeah, maybe. You know, I think that's probably it. Anyway, she says I need to pack it myself, so now I have to carry it home." She shrugged: what are you gonna do.

"I can help if you want. All I have is this," indicating his roll of tape.

She thought this over but did not answer.

"I'm not a murderer or anything. I don't even exercise." That seemed to be true, and he was so non-threatening and she so loath to carry the thing home that she said ok and off they went, the two of them, walking down the late July sidewalk with the chest hanging between them. The trip back was easy; it seemed like seconds before they were outside the building and he was saying, "Well, good luck."

"No, please. Help me get it up the stairs. I'll make you some lemonade. Only fair," and so up they went, and it was easier for him to take the thing himself, which was surprising because he looked so small but men have such grotesquely strong arms, even the little ones.

Inside she started squeezing lemons, looking now and then out of the kitchen where he was wandering around looking at things.

"Can you play this?"

"What?"

"The guitar."

"Oh, kind of."

"I can't."

"Oh." Was it enough sugar? One of those things: you add a little, and compared to how bad it was at first it tastes great, but you know it's still too sour. Didn't want to add too much though.

She brought it out. He was sitting on the couch. His hands were folded in his lap. He thanked her.

matt segur

"Play something."
"I'm not really very good."
"Shut up. Play."
"Um, ok." Strum strum. Tune. Strum. "This is called *Tom Lightning*. I wrote it myself." It went like this:

> First from the gate was *Scotland's Pride*.
> Flanks like satin! A thundering ride!
> Other jockeys knew they hadn't a chance:
> it was written on Tom Lightning's jockeying pants,
> written on the rear as he hurtled ahead.
>
> The crowd saw it coming a moment away,
> that fat man's beer flung careless astray.
> The tripping rang awful, the crushing of bone,
> as horse fell and sent rider flying, alone.
> A grave disappointment, the horse owner said.
>
> No one could squarely inherit the blame.
> Fingers were pointed—the usual game.
> For a chain of events that they couldn't explain
> had sent rider with horse on the rendering train:
> they had made Tom Lightning soap from the dead.
>
> [and the chorus, which went:]
> Tom Lighting Glue, it works like a champion.
> In the glue crop, this glue is the cream.
> There's no glue like his glue when you're in a hurry,
> 'cause he was so fast and so lean.

Nikola seemed to like it. He chanted, "One more!"

"Sorry, that's the only one I know right now." She futzed a little and then put the guitar up. "What do you do?"

"Um, I fix bicycles. How long have you been playing guitar?"

"Three or four years, on and off. I suck. How'd you get started at that?"

"I don't know. They asked me if I wanted a job. How many songs do you know?"

"You're not really answering me."

He stopped for a minute, looked into the lemonade, and for the first time couldn't meet her eyes. "Sorry. Evasiveness is a habit."

"Yeah."

"I'll stop, I promise. Here: ask me three questions. I'll tell the truth. How often do you get an offer like that?"

There was something very alluring about that—that willing relinquishment of power. "I guess you like old movies?"

"Um, yeah. This is good," indicating the lemonade. Then he noticed what he was doing. "Sorry. I didn't used to. My mom would to take me on Sunday morning sometimes. Her name's Junette. There was a tiny little theatre just down the street from us. They only had a ten-foot screen or so but they'd show all kinds of old stuff. She just needed somewhere to put me on Sunday I think. I hated it for a long time. I thought it was just as bad as when Dad dragged me to church. I complained like crazy.

"There was this one time, though, when I was nine or so, and she and Dad had been fighting the night before and I got up on Sunday. Dad was gone, and neither of us said anything all morning. I knew if I complained she'd start screaming, or crying which was worse. It was a cold grey Sunday morning, and she made these incredible greasy scrambled eggs, probably 'cause she was hungover, but anyway they were incredible. And she got up to go and I just followed without a word. They were showing *Kiss Me Deadly* and I don't know what it was about that movie, really, why the change, but I just loved it. We came out and still neither of us said anything; there was this mist falling that was nice to walk in and we went a couple of blocks to the park and walked around for two hours, just walking around in the mist looking at the condensation on the leaves and the bums. Then we went out and got spaghetti for dinner, and she bought a pack of cards at the convenience store across the street and we sat there in the restaurant and played Rummy until way past my bedtime.

"I never said anything about it because I couldn't think of anything to say that didn't sound—I don't know—dorky, but I think that day was the best time I ever had with my Mom. After that I always looked forward to going, and I tried not to let on but I think she could tell. So I've seen old movies. Horror stuff was usually our favorite.

"By the time I was twelve or fifteen Mom had stopped wanting to go I could tell, and she wouldn't have gone if I hadn't kept prodding her into it. You know, mostly to get her out of the house. I try to make it out like it's still her making me go." His eyes were unfocused on her knee. "Anyway, that's one."

Warming up to this game, she asked, "What do you think of me?"

"Um, gee, that's a little unfair isn't it?"

"You promised."

"Yeah, ok. Um..." He stared furiously out the window now, into the opposite window, as if there were something going on there. "I, uh, in school I was pretty bad at all of the... stuff. I had a couple of friends but not really. People thought I was weird 'cause my Mom came to a parent-teacher night one time and picked a fight with Mrs. Curtner. So yeah, none of the girls ever really talked to me. Um. What I mean is, I don't have a lot to compare to, but, um—"

"Ok, that's two." And she saw her chance and took it, turning the tables. "Ok, here's the third one. Say you could tell me to do anything and I'd do it. What would you want me to do?"

And he stared, looking intimidated and cute. "Now you're really getting unfair. Ok, um, a deal's a deal. What I want is... Don't move."

And he leaned over, all tentative, and kissed her, his lips soft like a girl's, and she kissed him back. He smelled like linen.

"Hey, I said not to move."

"Sorry." She really liked him. Janine said it was better not to the first time, but fuck her. His cheeks were high and bony and pale, like an elf's. His hair was really soft.

Ada had a tattoo; she called it her reminder. She'd hung around a tattoo parlor for a while when she was seventeen because she knew a girl who worked there. There was a guy who worked there too, older, and she had a crush on him. He had a vicious sense of humor that she loved. He would talk about the customers after they left—just tear them apart. You wondered what he said about you after you left, but somehow it was still attractive; you tried to tell yourself he didn't. And there were the paintings on him, of course—the orange and green lizard-scales up both his arms.

She thought maybe he might like her, too. She wasn't sure what to do about it though; he was intimidating. So she came in one day when her friend wasn't there. *She's not here. I want a tattoo. Oh, of what?*

It was this idea that she'd had for a while. She really did want it. She thought. It wasn't totally about him doing it, anyway. She explained it: *A line. A line? Yes, just a line.* She pointed to the top of her back. *It starts here, and it goes down and around and ends here*, pointing to the front of her neck.

Ada was fine with how she looked these days, pretty much. A little on the heavy side, but in a good way. But back in the day, in retrospect, she'd been a star—body suspended perilously on the cusp of youth, for just that instant sleek, firm and fragrant. If she'd only known. No surprise then that he agreed to do it. Did a nice job, even. She still liked the idea of the tattoo, but she hated finding it again in the mirror every morning.

Nikola, though, he fixed it. He asked about it when he saw the edge, and she told him the story, sort of, and they talked about it a little. They went to the full-length on the bathroom door and together they looked at the reminder. He liked it. He made her like it. Made her happy.

25. younger than that now

He never shifted his weight. Just stood there, hands clasped against his waist, like a stone. A dead stone. Stanley kept trying to use Audrey to hide, inching forward and back to slide behind her silhouette. He couldn't tell if it was helping. If nothing else, it kept him from seeing Baker. Given the choice, he didn't want to see the knife spin through the air—he preferred to pretend. Bullets were fine, or a bomb, but how quickly did they really finish with you? It was impossible to believe you didn't notice being burned alive, even if it did happen in a millisecond. Could those forces really tear you apart before you noticed? Didn't seem like it. It seemed like there had to be a moment as the guillotine cut when you thought, "Ach, me neck!"

The people at the funeral were mourning. They were not like him. They had lost something; he had only found it. Standing in the grey he looked at the coffin and the smell was stifling, all around him. He looked at Audrey, standing there like Jackie O., every bit as much a force as Baker, shook himself and felt better. These people couldn't all know each other; his was just another overcast face. He and Audrey would stand there with their heads down and try to pretend they belonged, and soon enough it would end and they'd leave. Baker wouldn't see him, and wouldn't have anything to say if he did. What could he say? "I could have you arrested for coming here?" It made no sense.

The minister talked in singsong, shrilly failing to help. His shoes were too big. He was taking too long. To pass the time, Stanley tried to think back, think of something he'd giggled at in church, but no. He could remember what it had felt like, but the things themselves were gone though they'd seemed so funny at the time—so timelessly and indelibly true. Finally it was ending and he could feel Audrey just as anxious to leave. He kept to the silhouette still, and Baker was not moving. Then the voice and the hard-eyed girl was behind them, looking for all the world like she expected the frame to zoom in and dolly out around her like she was Wednesday Addams. Stanley was petrified; good thing about Audrey, handling it like an ace.

He took his chance and fled across the grass, stepping around the deep, old stones so as not to trip. He was getting away. Then he glanced over his shoulder and Baker was no longer there. Where? There, moving, and their eyes met for just a second before Audrey's block intercepted him perfectly, and Stanley couldn't help but laugh at the sight of Baker's Agent Badass form confounded by Audrey's smallness. His foot cleared the grass. The exit would be just up the path. He pictured the street outside the cemetery wall; was there anywhere to go? He turned around and saw the crest of a hill hiding him from the sight of the others. How long could she stall Baker? What if he were going off the path, around in front of Stanley to catch him? Then he ran, trying not to make a sound, the jolt of the pavement making his feet ache in thin shoes. Then he was outside.

The cemetery wall was long. Beyond the gate, the street stretched two directions—a blind alley. He tried to imagine the confrontation.

"What are you doing here, Stanley?"

He would have to play like he had every right. "What do you mean?"

And Baker would sigh heavily, "You should know better, Stanley. I warned you. You told me you understood."

He would be defensive: "I haven't done anything. The service was open to the public."

"I know you're not this stupid, Stanley."

Or maybe Baker wouldn't care about the funeral. Maybe it was worse—maybe he'd found out they talked to Sacks. "Are you sure you haven't done anything, Stanley? Nothing at all?"

The el track came out of the fog, spanning the street in the distance, filthy black, still far away. There weren't many cars on the street. The few that drove by drove fast and quiet. There ought to be a time when you were old enough not to have to worry about standing guiltily before someone, thinking what to say, what they knew, how to defend yourself. Not yet. If he could get around the next corner, maybe he could hide in a store. The el platform was no good—no telling how long it would be before a train came.

A car approached behind him, taking a long time. Why hadn't it passed yet? It was slowing down. It was pulling up beside him. Baker must have gone out the other exit to the lot.

"Want a ride somewhere?" But that was not Baker; that was a woman. Leaning to the passenger window, it was the woman from the funeral, the mother.

But there just wasn't time to make the decision. When the moment arrived and you turned your mind and said, "think!" it became an imbecile—left you stranded without it. Ok, couldn't be any worse. He opened the door and got in, and behind him, as they accelerated, he saw Baker coming out of gate.

"Stanley," he expected to say, but she didn't ask. Didn't say anything—just stared straight ahead and drove. The car was stale with cigarette smoke. Smoke could smell different, depending. Audrey made it smell fresh and spicy and at the same time rich and aged like a library. Here it was just dirty and sickly-sweet, tired and wasted, evoking four am casino gamblers sweaty, pasty, and well onto the bad side of drunk.

"Well?" Finally she spoke.

"Um, I'm Stanley, I, uh—"

"Let's start with where you're going."

"Oh, right. North as far as you feel like taking me."

She rolled her eyes at him. "I don't exactly have a tight schedule alright?"

He wasn't sure what to say.

"I never saw you with Nikola. Not that that means anything. I don't see a lot of things. Ha!"

Each sentence that she finished had a small pause, but just before he started to answer she'd say something else. This time she seemed done. "Why Nikola Tesla?"

"You know, I keep asking the same thing."

Oops. "No, I meant—"

"I know. He was my favorite. Einstein's evil, slavic twin." Stanley understood that. "Marriage got me half the name, I might as well have finished it. I'm Junette: my role is 'the great burden,' or it was."

She had one hand at the base of the wheel, a few fingers draped across it, the minimum. The other hand out on its own, skipping across the dashboard controls, fussing with things. The radio was too quiet to hear but the hand stabbed at the channel scan every couple seconds, in between toggling the air conditioning, angling the vents, and slapping the gearshift, arrythmically, like an alien trying to understand music but he just gets it wrong.

"Don't you talk? You're making me nervous."

"Yeah, that's my role."

"Ha! Good show." Then she picked up strain of the inaudible radio somehow, maybe straight out of the air, because she turned it up just in time for the chorus and sang along, "Oh but I was so much older then I'm younger than that now." Her voice was husky and ruined but assured, like she knew how, breathy, the straining of her diaphragm making the sound urgent, right there. She stopped after the chorus.

The car was a big old Detroit boat, and Junette pushed forward and back and between lanes, jumping on first the gas then the brake, hardly paying attention except to now and then mutter at another driver under her breath.

soft power

"Now is when I'm supposed to tell you some funny anecdote about him, right? Sharing fond remembrances and all that shit? I remember watching him when he was tiny, I had to turn around every five seconds to pull him off whatever he was trying to climb up or knock over, because he was always walking into some disaster. I was shocked he made it out alive with only me to watch him. There was one day I was buying some ice cream for him because it was hot, and while I was in line he walked over to this guy, the scariest guy in the world, this six-and-a-half foot, 300 lb. guy with muttonchops and a septum-ring who'd just gotten off his motorcycle to get some ice cream I imagine, back in the line. I don't know what the story was or whether he knew, but this guy actually had blood drying on his face. Not dry, but drying. Nikola, who was about as tall as the guy's knee, walks over to it and starts poking, poking the guy there, in the knee. I had just seen this out of the corner of my eye and I went back to stop him and I see the huge guy turn and look down, slow and massive like, like an elephant on a nature show that's about to stomp on a monkey or something, and then Nikola, who didn't care if it was a blood-drenched ogre, says, 'How fast does can your motorcycle go?' And I'm picking him up thinking that maybe I can get away before we both get killed because how fast can a guy that big run, and he laughs and says 'Fast as you want.'

"By the time he was eleven we'd already switched. Once, he figured out how to drive the car standing up, standing on the pedals and hanging back from the steering wheel to see over it, to take me to the hospital after I passed out. I could have just slept it off, but I woke up in the hospital and Nikola's sitting there asleep in the chair at the side of the bed, and I'm expecting the doctor to come in and give me a lecture about how expensive ambulances are, so I pulled off all the stuff and changed and woke up Nikola and started sneaking out, and then he says 'Don't forget the car.' Piece of shit. I need a goddamn drink. I hate Sunday."

The backlit plastic signs all along the strip looked cheap. They were all organized by type, because there was some insane librarian re-cataloguing the city. Right now they were under "bail bondsmen."

"Earlier you were starting to mention how you knew Nikola."

He couldn't tell the truth. "Um... yeah... met him through, uh, Ada."

"Did he ever talk about his drunk bitch mom?"

"Uh, nothing like that. Same as anybody else I think. You know. Parents are parents."

"Oh, great. Now I got people lying so they won't hurt my feelings. Save the effort, ok?"

Ok.

"Oh, never mind."

"Do you have any idea who might have..."

"Yeah, the CIA. Didn't you know Nikola was a gay Pinko and he was having an affair with Castro? How the fuck should I know?"

"I just thought maybe—"

"Yeah, I got a pretty good idea what you thought. You thought there might be point in speculating about what flavor of insane bastard might have stuffed Nikola in that box, as if it mattered. It's weird, so it's not private, it's news. Just like I told the detective, I have no idea. He fixed bikes. He took care of his soused mom. In his spare time, I assume he went around trying to have a normal life, but for all I know he might have been selling crack on playgrounds."

"Ok sorry. Right here is fine."

She didn't say goodbye or anything, just stamped the break and sat there waiting while he got out.

"I'm sorry about—"

"So am I, Stanley."

---

26. art history (continued)

Blur of Road: Still on the bus, afternoon. I took this one out the window, showing a smear of grassland beneath a featureless sky. There's a telephone pole in the center of the frame—a vertical wipe. There's a dark, scary blur at the bottom left, the shadowy passing of a monster, but it is only a cow. Maybe I shouldn't say that; maybe it's better not knowing, letting it be a fleeting glimpse of a Loch Ness on a lake.

We've been too long on the bus already. Oliver is at me again to start looking for a new job. I know it's not what you want to be doing. I don't want you to settle for something. *He's never really tried, though. He graduated and then went back in the fall after working in Kinko's for a summer. The way he sees it, it's so easy, you get fed up with Kinko's after three months so you leave; you go do what you want. He did it, why can't I? You don't understand the looking for months and finding nobody that wants you and nothing that excites you. The boring businesses want you to know their trade because you're too stupid to learn, and the ones that should be interesting are always small and incompetent and beaten down and powerless, and the people in charge are defeated and sad. And not everybody wants to go back to reading Heidegger and writing stale papers that fewer people read than read Heidegger even, and the white girl flirts in your recitations aren't as appealing if you're not trying to get with them. Maybe you should try to get with them then, and then you can be just like me.*

So he is sitting, still is sitting across the aisle now, and we're each looking out our window, and I have a feeling his side is better but I'm not going to look over and check. Instead I pretend I'm interested in the cow and I want its picture. Which is better than I expected: it's nice and foreboding. Like the camera is a radon sniffer or a Geiger counter or a canary or an x-ray, and you take a picture of a normal-looking cow only to find when you develop it that a demon has taken that one and is using it to do things the cow never would—the cow that died days ago—and if you shrieked "Stop!" to the bus driver, sat bolt upright and screamed and he stopped and you got out while the other passengers shook their heads, if you held down the barbed wire and ran across the field to the cow you'd see, when it turned its head, that the other side was eaten away by flies. So it's up to me.

27. darkdrinkers

A handful of others came and went while Audrey sat with Ada. Plodding, determined drinkers, comfort drinkers, in denims and plaids, comfort clothes. Two white-haired guys came in, with matching caps that said *Olds*, and Audrey thought, *yes*.

The ceramic-top table by the window had a view of the street and the cloudy sky—grey and turbulent and charged in a way to make you glad you were inside, holding your pint between your two palms. Most of the people who came and went would pause to examine the curious pair of them in their Hollywood black formalwear.

One came over and sat astride the extra chair—a bald, sprouty, avuncular fellow in glasses and button-down short sleeves, probably a high school chemistry teacher.

soft power

"I hope I'm not bothering you, but I... I have to tell you this story: When I was sixteen I was with my parents on vacation in Los Angeles, and one night after we ate I was walking around to get away from them and I went into the hotel bar. At one of the tables, back in a dark corner, there were two young ladies, or ladies to me at the time, just like you two, dressed to the nines all in black. I ordered a Coke and sat watching them, trying to figure out what the story might have been, until they left. For years after that I used to make up stories about them. What they were doing there, or why they were dressed like that, or where they went afterwards. Sometimes it started with one of them seeing me watching them and coming to talk to me. Anyway, here you are again."

Ada smiled. "I'd explain, but I don't want to spoil your opportunity for speculation."

"No no, I won't hear of it."

"You're the boss."

Nobody spoke for a minute, which started to feel awkward. Audrey queried Ada with her eyes. "After all, I need something to keep me busy." He gave a forced little laugh, and then more silence. "I'm sure you two can imagine how it is." And then she caught him giving her a look, she was sure, this avuncular man.

Suddenly she pictured a strip club and the weird atmosphere of regulars with, doubtless, daughters the same age as the strippers. But what if one of the strippers *was* one of the daughters? And what if neither of them ever said anything about it, at home with Mom? She found herself laughing hysterically and saw Ada, looking on with distanced curiosity at first, and then laughing with her. Couldn't stop, having drunk too much—cackling horribly she was sure. The man got up and walked tentatively away, which made it all the funnier, and she saw him return to his table out of the corner of her eye. She explained the fantasy to Ada, who laughed anew, and they traded elaborations:

"Do you think he'd order a lap dance?"

"Then say 'Who's your daddy?' 'Um, you are, daddy.'"

"That's great! As if she doesn't get it."

"Or maybe he gets his lap dance from one of the other girls because he's angry at her."

"Right, because she got a C in algebra."

"'I'm very disappointed in you, honey. Now Vera here is coming with me, and while we're gone I want you to think about what you're going to do differently next semester.'"

And as they continued to laugh the chemistry teacher got up from the other table and actually left, but she could hardly see it through the tears streaming down her face.

Ada, by now recovering, said "I think you need another one."

"Yeah, I think so too."

"I think I need some pancakes." Audrey stared Ada in the eyes, which were down on her hands as she spoke. "Nikola was a genius of pancakes. He was obsessed by them when he was little. He said he went days sometimes refusing to eat anything but pancakes. He said he'd scream about it with his mom. She couldn't break him of it, so she gave up and started making other kinds of food in, you know, pancake form to get him to eat. Eventually she got sick of it, wouldn't do it anymore, so he started doing it himself. He'd take whatever she was making and figure out how to make pancakes from it. And he never really outgrew it. Pretty much everything we ever ate that he'd cooked was pancakes, one way or another."

"Didn't that get tiresome?"

soft power

"No, they were great. He did so many different kinds. Potato pancakes, pumpkin pancakes, noodle pancakes, banana pancakes, apple pancakes, chocolate cake pancakes, shrimp and tomato pancakes, onion pancakes, squash pancakes, cheese pancakes. What I want right now, though, is a big fat steak and eggs pancake."

"He should have written a cookbook."

"Oops. Too late."

The bottles behind the bar made a neat array of sparkles that followed your eye. There was a video poker game, but nobody played.

"I should stop that. It's a bad habit, dropping lines like that. You know, to show how detached and unconcerned I am. How healed I am. And at the same time, I get the chance to elicit sympathy. And I get to make the person I'm talking to feel uncomfortable and not know what to say. Obnoxious. What a child."

"I don't think anyone would blame you."

"I would."

Outside the window, storefront lights brightened with the dusk. The window was faintly dappled by streaks of dirt. Audrey tried to think what it would be like, could not. When it came to it, she didn't trust her mind for "appropriate affect." At the instant, in that lifeless fluorescent office, that she'd signed her first lease, finally committing to stay and abandoning the return half of the drowsy, empty night flight from Albany, she hadn't felt relief or excitement or terror or anything really except mild relaxation at being done with it. And it was easier to cry at a movie than at anything that had ever happened to her. People never made her cry or even angry, just resigned and dead inside. What would she do at the message, she could hear it: "Audrey, this is dad, please call me as soon as you get this. Your mother... just call right away." God, there was something wrong with thinking that way.

"A few months ago my boss called me into his office and said they had to make some cuts and newer employees had to go first. He'd give me a recommendation and make some calls to try to find me something, etcetera. So I was out looking for a job for a couple weeks, not finding anything. Finding something marginally interesting but low-paying, or decent pay but absolutely stupid. I found two of each one day, alternating, flip-flop, flip-flop, and dragged myself home wanting to kill myself. 'Hi, I'm the curator's assistant. I get to do clerical work with words like "art" and "Chinese" and "wood-cut," which are much more interesting to type and alphabetize than most other words. If I had two of this job I'd make a scrappy but liveable wage. Nice to meet you, too.'

"Nikola saw me come in, in our paint-peeling little place but it had nice floors at least, and he didn't ask how my day was, or how it had gone, or what was wrong. He just came over to the couch where I'd landed, and he had a plate in his palm so it looked like a tray, and on the tray were two glasses, and in the glasses were two shots of the bourbon he'd got as a birthday present for his dad. He held my head up like it was cough syrup, and we did one each and then another; good stuff. He never made me talk, and he didn't tell some dumb story about how darkness always turns into the dawn. Just sat with me and sipped the bourbon and eventually we went to the window and sat with our bare legs out in the summer evening like a wading pool and watched people on the street, and the glasses grazed the scratchy concrete of the window sill and made a nice sound. I have a picture from that night actually here."

She pulled out a wallet-size photo of Nikola from the shoulders up. It was black-and-white, apparently taken by Nikola himself

soft power

from arm's length as he lay on a sheet. His eyes were closed and he had no shirt and his skin was pale. His hair looked soft.

"I forget where the autopsy pic idea came from. I whitened him up with some powder. We did one each," and she produced a photo of herself, likewise. Audrey set them side-by-side in front of her. Nikola and Ada were the dead.

"The sun was on the other side of the street while we sat, and it still heated the buildings and the air above them. The air smelled like sun. Nikola said it was strange how many ways we remember things. We have this word 'memory' like it was all the same but there are so many kinds. There is memory of facts, memory of names and figures and dates, school memory, forced memory. There's muscle memory, how to ride a bicycle, how to fret a guitar, how to hold a tennis racket, how to fuck. There's narrative memory, each of us penning our personal story and the old pages getting mutilated and lost as we go, but there are always a few good excerpts that have a climax and denouement and whatnot. There's sensual memory, images, sounds, smells, tastes, faces. There's nostalgia memory, the memory of your past state, how you felt and how the world struck you back then. Nikola said for him that one always went with smells. The smell of the air on the window sill reminded him of the feeling of high school, walking home in the afternoon wondering when it would end, or when something non-school would happen to him, something like me I guess. But it's a stupid lie to try to call all of it 'memory' as if that were the whole story.

"'I can't remember anything before school,' he said. He thought it was scary. He said even with school everything up to third grade was pretty much a wash. You know, just the memory of remembering a few things a couple years later. It was a good smell, the window-sill smell. He said we should remember each other by it in our nostalgia memory. I said we weren't dying or anything."

Somewhere in there Ada ordered coffee, and somewhere she lit a cigarette, and now the steam from the coffee and the smoke from the cigarette rose in twin coils. Audrey was surprised to see they looked very different: the cigarette smoke had a bluish cast, the steam was bright with refraction, tan. Cold and hot.

"He said to remember the smell, just in case. I made fun of him and said don't be so morbid. 'What are you, goth or something?' That was when we did the autopsy photos, because I·was making fun of him, calling him goth. That's the last photo I got. He left for work one day, made it there, left there for home, didn't make it home." She shrugged. "It's a big mystery now. Ooh."

Ada and Nikola were still laid out there, each in a little coffin of a frame, side-by-side, the Tesla-Tucker memorial. They were pretty together—mismatched kind of but not—the scrawny little blonde choirboy and the voluptuous bangsy brunette vamp, good and evil. Audrey shuffled them together gingerly and handed them back to Ada.

"Ok. I've already had too much. Time to go."

"Ok."

That was anticlimactic, Ada thought. They exchanged phone numbers, and as they walked out Ada asked "What's with you and the corpse-guy?"

"What, Stanley? I don't know. He's shy and I'm cautious, so nothing I guess."

"Come on, you'll never be wracked with loss that way." She pretended to be fraught and trembling as she said that, *wracked with loss.* "I still like the window-sill smell you know. Sometimes you have to cry havoc. See you."

28. art history (continued)

The Driftwood Wall: *On the beach, afternoon. Fast forward half a roll through too long on the bus feeling cooped up, through splitting the halves of my headphones so my left ear was sore and her right, but at least it was something to do, through long straight roads cutting like alien infinity across Kansas, across Nebraska, across Colorado and Utah and Nevada, through colored neon steakhouses and diner omelettes, through the mad swerving quickie up and down of mountains in California. The gear-perforations frame the negatives like train tracks. Maybe we'll take a train home. Crank forward the track of perforations—there's no sync sound— skip the rest of the buildup, watch us jerk forward willy-nilly like a strobe light, invent some jaunty, mechanical music to make us look silly while we skitter across the country, but wait, slow down, stop, we're* On the beach. *Fifty feet above our heads, out of sight behind the face of the cliff, cars fly up and down Highway 1.*

It's cool. The sun is out but doesn't warm the skin. Its reflection on the ocean is a cold band of white hot brilliance, backlighting the planks of driftwood in stark silhouette. Simone, to the left of the leftmost plank, is distinct only because she's slightly rounder, smoother, and more symmetrical than the other planks.

This is not our fault. We found it this way. We are curious: who might have staved in the membrane of wet sand with these five planks all in a neat row, pointing proudly skyward? Who wanted this small, unconnected fence? Whose fork is it, left stabbed in the ground? We passed the driftwood twice on our walk up and down the beach, walking as far as we could north and then south until we reached impasse.

We are staying with Simone's friend Pancho Villa, whose real name is Dwayne. Pancho Villa is a short order chef and amateur insurgent. He perpetrates acts of spuriously random sabotage against local political and commercial figures of whom he disapproves. I asked him what this terrorism was supposed to accomplish when he never claims responsibility for any of it or leaves any sign that his motive isn't simple mischief. His only credited works are the words "Qué viva Pancho Villa" which he writes here and there in tiny, timid script, as if he weren't sure. Either he's quite prolific or he's amassed a following of imitators, because the phrase is everywhere here—in bathroom stalls and alleys and along the edges of tables. He said that the new way is not to threaten those in power explicitly or to say, "change or you will be hurt," but is instead to instill in them a deep foreboding that they had little chance against the rank violence of the world. How long could you go, as each day brought a new slashed tire or broken window, someone else that shoved you in the street and called you "Bruce," or some new foreign object lurking in your meal—flower petals and candy hidden beneath the surface of your ostensibly plain cream cheese—without beginning to doubt? The new way, he said, was to make them feel small and at risk, so that in the end it would take only the hint of revolution and they'd stand stricken or even lean forward, weak and resigned, into the knife.

When he's not talking about the terrorism of the subconscious, Pancho Villa is pleasant and easy-going. His apartment, next to a park, is small and cramped and full of wall-to-wall content, books and records and clothes and electronics and other things that he simply found and took a shine to: a two-stroke lawnmower engine for something. The bathroom, the only clean room in the apartment, smells like bleach and cold air through the trees outside the window. The window that the air comes in by is in the shower, and it's wedged open six inches or so at waist height. It looks out on the park and *some other apartments and I thought this was strange, a shower with an exposed midriff, but Pancho Villa said not to worry, they can't see your face and your ding-dong at the same time so what's the harm? The morning sun filtering through the distorted, diaphanous glass casts a bubbly pattern on Simone's wet skin; the open window allows a horizontal strip of direct light like a noir-film on her glistening pubis. She is beautiful. We are beautiful. We are lazy and slow-moving and decadent and relaxed, walking and eating and talking, caressing in the shower after Pancho Villa has gone to work. We have taken walks all around the city, looking at people and things in the chill, and each night gone up the street to the wholesome, all-natural granola little city market to buy things for dinner—mushrooms and shallots and pasta and wine. Pancho Villa is glad to have someone feeding him.*

Last night we went out for ice cream and played Hearts there until they closed, and today we're On the beach. We are two happy brown streaks on an impressionist canvas aglitter with light. We are leisurely. We are the platonic ideal of leisure. We are not at all at risk. There is no danger. The fork of driftwood that was thrown here was not aimed at us, except perhaps aimed to amuse us with its weird beauty during our carefree getaway. Carefree getaway. Whee!

29. art history (continued)

Suspicion: Dwayne's car, before noon. *It feels guilty to be suspicious here. The air smells of good intentions. Maybe it's the lines of the old Spanish missions, or maybe it's just the idyllic weather, the blue ocean, the golden hills. It eats at you, to be suspicious in paradise. I've always found the hippies tiresome, but around here you can understand the beginnings of it, at least when it was simply: I'm moving up that hill, to that little house, to raise my child in the shadow of the mountain, where he can run around the carpet of pine needles*, and we'll eat fruit and bread and cheese. The possibility and the hope in the air like poison gas, traces of it are still here, slowly diffusing. Homeopathic hope. You can still smell the pure form, and it's a shame about how it went, but still.

I overheard this: "You going to hempfest?" "No, man... I forgot about it." "Yeah... I forgot too."

I wanted a little time to myself this morning, so while Oliver and Dwayne were eating I said I wanted to call my Mom and I went for a walk. You can walk through the meat of this town in just a few minutes, hitting the grocer and the drugstore and the hardware store and the bank, all the essentials pleasantly distilled right here in a couple blocks. Off the main street the sidestreets slope steeply up and immediately into tall, colorful, sunny little houses. All of the houses seem to contain little clans of one sort or another— five firefighters sharing a place, or two friends and a child, or a man and a woman, an architect and a doctor, just friends. Families beyond family. It makes sense to me.

I didn't really want to call my mother, who is all disapproval and stern hope, annoyingly close to stereotype. "Be a doctor." Doaktor. I've tried asking about it even, hinting at it, this or that character in a book that's just like my mother. There are so many it's simple, and I know she's too smart not to notice, but I've never gotten anything out of her. Those of us who've been misplaced in our families, we feel cheated. I don't understand the idea of a special, privileged category of person that shares my last name, that I care more about. People like me, our monkey brains scream "Have a family!" Some of them run out here to a family town and get a house, just like a family, with a family garden to work in, to be with people that think like they do, that they can sit with in comfort, who'll take them to the emergency room. I do the same thing with my city-folk, at dinners and parties in warmed up little apartments full of family cheer. Not the same, but it's something.

soft power

So there I was, walking past sunflowers, and a stringy, leathery old guy came up around the corner, with faded denim jeans that fit him like skin and a big beard that I couldn't see his shirt. His walk was shuffling. His eyes roved. He was probably homeless—mentally ill. He could have been an authentic hippie. Soon nobody will be able to say that, but this guy could. But he didn't. What he said, walking the opposite way, was, "Hey, smile!"

"What?"

"Why—are you—so grim?" He said it slow, in parts like that, like it was scat. I could have ignored him, been cynical, assumed he was a dirty old man. Maybe a vet with an Asian fetish. I always wondered how you could develop a fetish without getting any more specific than that, because intuitively it should be specialization, specificity.

But here in paradise, cynicism makes you feel guilty.

"Let me guess." He spoke in staccato now, all of the words evenly spaced. "You found out that the communists have learned to control lightning with satellites, and they are using lightning to start forest fires. For political gain." I guess he could tell he was losing me, because he backed up to fill in the gap. "Because of insurance! Why do you think nobody worried about forest fires one hundred years ago?" He gave me a wild, challenging stare with his unwandering eye. "Communists. That is why."

The house next to us was blue. "No, that's not it."

"Oh, mmm." I had stumped him. "O. K. So then, you are sad. You have: man trouble."

Leave me alone.

"Ah... hah! Man trouble. I have seen it before." He stopped, looked out at the street, which was flat, empty and dull, with a satisfied grin. "Do you believe in God?"

"Um..."

"No? Oh. Eh, me neither. Ok. What do you have? You are young. You have many years ahead of you. You have money, it looks like. More than me.

Ha! And look at that," he said, pointing overhead, "The sun! Young, money, beautiful, the sun, the ocean is just over there, and no God. Smile, no?"

"Yeah, I guess."

"Look at this then," and he growled, "Bwah!" and jumped forward, and I started back, and he stuck out his leg and lifted his pant. His right foot was enormous and bloated; it looked mummified. "Pretty cool, eh?"

He looked up at me for appreciation.

"Ok then. The sun! And no gorilla foot." I didn't really feel equal to this.

"Let's get back to it!" And he turned around and walked away, limping, I noticed now.

It was him made me feel guilty, but I am suspicious nonetheless. And yes, the photograph, coming to that. When I got back from calling my mother we returned to the car, rotating seats so that it was me in the back and Oliver shotgun. Dwayne started to talk coarsely about girls to Oliver. I could overhear half of what he said, disconnected snatches:

"Did you ever have a friend that you fucked on and off?"

"Man it was like no walls."

"Don't you understand? You're just a fuckfriend."

"Like a jar of mayonnaise."

"Of course I looked!"

Oliver didn't say much—just sort of laughed at each of the punchlines—from what I heard. He would say, "I was just being nice. He's your friend." It's true, but I am suspicious. It would be so easy, I suspect, for him to stop off in the dormitory with a student after class. So good looking, so charming, such natural authority. I can't help being suspicious of Oliver as I am, at times, of all men—suspicious of that peculiar capacity to disconnect their humanity and say things and do things as cold, clinical, and frightening as anything. Our humanity protects us from our evil and we must never disconnect it. Just as it doesn't surprise me, not anymore, to hear Dwayne say these things, it wouldn't surprise me to hear that Oliver had really found them funny, or had said such things himself, or had engaged in "meaningless sex," which sometimes seems to me the most moronic of all oxymorons.

"So? You don't fuck her nose."

"No baby, I never cheated on you. Never ever ever."

"But she's so psycho! But she's such a hottie!"

"I mean, she was really stupid."

I sat, in the back, on the edge of this bubble of their conversation, brooding, wary. Feeling angry and powerless but guilty under the sun and color and spray. So I held up the camera to them.

Dwayne I feel sorry for. He's leaning over, not watching the road—the blurry car that you can see through the windshield looming ominous but it was really pretty far away—leaning lascivious toward Oliver, face contorted by the camera, twisted, stupid and frozen. The framing is indiscreet. Oliver, who was laughing, just looks implicated—like you could blackmail him with it, because the old single-engine cockpit feeling of the VW and the grey emulsion and the sun burning the dirty windows makes the whole thing slutty, corrupt, and cheap.

There in the photo, somehow, is exactly how they looked to me: Dwayne clownish and Oliver under suspicion. After the photo they both noticed me, and they stopped.

30. they all have no idea

Cry havoc. Let slip the dogs of war. What if it stuck in your throat? From time to time Audrey dreamt that she'd woken, in the middle of the night, to find a figure beside the bed. A dark figure beside the bed, shadowy and bad. I'll scream, she thought, and somebody will hear. He'll be frightened. What's he doing here, I'll kick, I'll scream! Pity the fool that burgles me! "Scr—" but no, there was nothing. No shriek, no scarifying wail, no yelp, no whimper. Just paralysis, the scream stuck in her throat, oh God here he comes, he knows. He knows I cannot scream. And what does it mean anyway, "Cry havoc?" To sound the alarm.

It was strange to find herself shy like this. It wasn't her style—it was his.

Still, there was always the mystery: Hauser Holdings. That was her new lead. A real estate company, on the books as having been acquired a year or so ago by Westin-Rodant. Persons who will benefit from this transaction. Etc.

As long as she kept herself into something to do after waking on a Saturday morning, the rest would sort itself out. Westin-Rodant was a jigsaw puzzle. Intractable? Maybe, but what was a jigsaw puzzle for, if not to kill time? And as long as she had news, she could call Stanley, and he would be noncommittal, unsure, always at that distance but even so she could hear the way it lit him up, even over the crackling phone.

"Hauser Holdings" was scratched on an envelope in black ballpoint, the envelope on the stained coffee table, beside the phone. This Saturday morning she didn't know what to do. There was Hauser Holdings, so? She'd been in that apartment long enough now to know how all of its spaces unfolded. It was quiet and dead to her, nice but familiar. What would Stanley's apartment be like? Urgent smudges on the walls, dishes in the sink, things left lively around, floor and ceiling spare and close and physical. Not nice in the least, but vivid in its squalor.

She was bouncing off the nice, familiar walls. The coffee probably hadn't helped, but the cartons of milk and cream—both near-empty at a shake—had been the only things in the house to eat when she woke up. The few tablespoons of milk left had made the coffee thick and creamy, almost like butter—more so than she'd have chosen, but still good. Now her stomach felt hollow and she wanted to talk, but everyone was difficult or in California or something.

The curtailed possibilities made a bad idea seem good, and it had been so long that the subjectivity of disliking her mom was forgotten; she had the that but not the how, not the right there sense of it.

Bouncing off the walls, she thought back to thirteen, when her ears had been virgin, without holes, not even the first set. They'd fought about that—'fought' in the cute sense, the sort of fight that burns off like morning fog, giving way to perfect clarity by noon. When Mom finally relented, it had been on the condition that she go along, and Audrey wondered later if the halfhearted resistance had been about that all along, the opportunity to be there for something that mattered—how many more of those would you get, Mom? Excitement had made her bubbly again, a break in the long vow of teen silence. It was embarrassing to think back to—some of the things she'd said, naively trying to "clue in" stodgy old Mom to some fad or other. But it had been happy, the pain not so bad and they got a big cookie each and some earrings to anticipate until she could take the studs out and a gift for Daniel—a mossy green ceramic mug that made Audrey think of King Arthur for some reason, which she'd taken with her when she went to school because he never used it anyway, the same mug where the dregs of her coffee now stewed—and that day had become an ideal for her. And it was to that, the stupid, beige tile, brass handrail mall nostalgia of thirteen, that she now turned, imagining her mom at best. Maybe she should call. She wanted that help. Maybe she could visit; she'd like to see Albany again; she had some friends there. She'd call.

The phone rang three times; she assumed nobody would answer just as someone did.

"Hello?" The voice, now that she heard it, was of course familiar, flicking on the light in a hallway of her brain that, though long vacant, had been attentively kept.

"Hi." She felt almost giddy at the bombshell she knew this to be.

The sky was grey and cold. Snow, or something like it, was falling and turning immediately to freezing wet. Who knew what it was like, though, in Albany. "Hi Audrey! God, I'm scared to ask, did somebody die?"

"No Mom, everything's fine. I just... Daniel said you had blamed it on him that I hadn't called, which isn't really—I just wanted to take responsibility for being... lazy."

"Oh good I just thought, you know, my daughter's calling me, somebody must have died!" She gave a laugh here to cover up how this felt, and Audrey cringed.

Maybe this was a bad idea. "Um, hey what's new? How's upstate?"

"Oh, good. You remember fall here, right? Lots of color. That was nice, but now there's just the winter. But I bought apples a month ago and made applesauce and it reminded me of you. Do you remember, maybe when you were eight or nine, one weekend I was away visiting my parents and you worked yourself up to making applesauce and your father burned it? I remember coming home on Sunday night excited to see you two and you were just disconsolate, and you father was sitting at the table staring, because I'm sure he'd tried everything."

"Yeah yeah! I told him it was going to burn, but he was in the study and he kept saying, 'Just a minute.' I was really angry after that."

"I don't think he ever told me how it happened exactly, but that sure sounds like Daniel."

And it did, but there was something so venomous about the way she said it, the way she laughed. "Oh come on Mom."

"What, I didn't—"

"Yeah just forget it. How's work?"

Catch worked at an "inpatient care facility for the mentally ill," as assistant director and a clinician—pretty important. "Same as always. The people don't change much; there's always less money available, you know. No big news." Audrey remembered then that at Halloween they decorated the place with fake spiderwebs and the like. Which always struck her as sort of unnecessary, because it was already the scariest place she could imagine. What was a little cardboard ghost saying "Boo" next to the all these people who'd been normal once? They weren't normal anymore. She'd heard you usually turned schizophrenic in your twenties. She'd never mentioned that to her mom, though. Her mother paused carefully. "I'm leaving, actually, I suppose that's the news."

"What? Why?"

"I was tired of it. Really tired. I don't think I'd really thought about it, but even back when you were here I think I was tired of it." Another pause. "Jeremy," pause, "asked one day, 'Why don't you leave?' and I thought, 'that's a good idea.' So," pause, "actually we're moving. Maybe that's a lot of news. To Portland."

Jeremy? That was a prick's name. The couple of boyfriends she'd met before had always been bad news. "Jeremy... We... Portland... What? When?"

Audrey could just see her smiling on the other end. "Well, you see what happens when you don't call? In a few weeks, actually. You'll have to come visit."

"In Portland?" Well, so much for the Albany friends. "How did... when did you meet—"

"Jeremy. June. I've been going to a lot of readings. Book readings, you know, because I'd been thinking about writing a book on the state of mental healthcare. Jeremy was giving one of them. The same sort of thing. It hadn't occurred to me that I didn't need to stay at my job to write the book, but it made so much sense when he suggested it that I—"

"Decided to move. To Portland. But you hate the west coast. And after knowing the guy, what, four months? Wow, Mom."

"It's not... I'm sure you'd like him. You'll have to meet. You should come visit, as soon as we get settled in. He's very," very what, "down to earth."

Which meant, of course, not like Daniel, not a daydreamer, not like that. Great, Mom. Some silver-haired fucking clinical writer probably with a pager and pink shirtsleeves and no tie, who wrote books with coloned subtitles like "The War for America's Kids," who wanted to move to Portland. "Who's taking your patients?"

She couldn't imagine this partly because her mom had always been so attached to them—coming home at night crying because some request had been denied, some bad decision somewhere up the chain. She never even went on vacation. What was this?

"Well, Cindy's taking a lot of them, the ones who need it, and they're going to hire a replacement for me. I've been working pretty hard to figure out who that will be. But I couldn't have stayed forever."

"But—" But you weren't supposed to leave those people Mom, that was what got you so much admiration even if I never called you.

"Anyway, enough about me. Daniel mentioned that one of his... coworkers... needed somebody, something he thought you could—"

"I don't need a job, Mom. I have a job. I'm loyal to my job. Why don't you two... never mind."

"Don't you know we've got it all planned out? I said, 'Daniel, how can we make Audrey more angry?' and he said 'Haha! I know! We'll try to find her a career. That will fix her.'"

"Oh for Christ's sake. That's the thing though, don't you understand? Even though you're joking, you said 'career'. I'm not aching for a 'career'. I'm not some... I'm not like—"

"Right, me. I know. I was only joking. Ok, so why don't we talk about food then? Have you been to any good restaurants?"

"This was... look, I gotta go I'll call you."

But would she? "Will you? I don't want—"

Couldn't quite believe she hung up. Wow. She hung up. And didn't want to hear any more so she grabbed her bag and stuffed in the scrap of envelope and went out, and the rush of air past the door as she pulled it shut behind her felt good on her skin—the seal pressurizing, cutting her off from the sound of the phone should it happen to ring. She remembered it now, the subjectivity, the why.

Places like that, asylums—in New York it had seemed natural, the little campus of three old white wood-sided buildings with paint on the windows, three miles down the road from anywhere, but here they were jumbled in with everything else; you hardly noticed them. Audrey noticed them, though—walked by some building from time to time that could have been an apartment building but for the people milling around outside, asking you for a cigarette or just staring.

They were always on the el, too, the city's mixed-in mentally ill. She took a seat that didn't have a bottle of piss rolling around under it, wedged herself into the far seat and rested her forehead on the cold window glass. She pulled her coat, which was long and naval, around her. There weren't many colors out there now, mostly greys, pink in the bricks here and there. The leaves were gone from the trees. Everyone had their heads down, shuffling along, trying to avoid the puddles.

The el was slow and loud. You could afford to wait. Or, you couldn't afford to not wait. She wanted tea suddenly, for some reason, mint and honey. There was a layer of plastic between her and the world. That's why the cold window felt good.

She got off finally and walked toward the address she'd written, still slowly. Some guy walking backwards shouting to his friend smashed into her—some huge ambling meatsack, stupid and not paying attention—and stepped on her foot. "See the way you're going? Toward me? Look that way!" But he just shrugged, not really apologetically.

Hauser Holdings was a ground floor, a little zoo of cubicles behind big, fastidiously clean panes of glass. A couple steps up the expensive ladder—an office dressed up with brass and wood instead of rubber and formica. Audrey just walked by, to see what it was like. The only marking was on the deep red wooden door, where a little sign, small and haughty, said "Hauser Holdings." She walked as slow as she could make look real, looking left into the windows. There were people there; she hadn't expected that. They were sitting at their desks and walking around. All men, mostly in suits. This one was tall and had a stretched out, skinny, accountant's head, a big airfoil nose, and a close, conservative haircut like his name was Eric or Aaron and he played second-string basketball in high school. That one was older, a Frank or Stuart, with narrow eyes that looked angry at his being short. Ten or so of them altogether. It looked pretty normal. She kept going, around the block.

That was that. What now? Why she would have expected to learn anything from looking at the place was now foggy, but she didn't want to go home and face the answering machine. There had been a bigger sign, next to the nameplate: "Help Wanted."

So far, she had nothing really to report to Stanley. Didn't look like there was anything to it, just like it hadn't looked with Sacks. On the theory that you could just look at people and know whether they were the sort to stuff people into storage, which had been a little naive from the start.

On the other hand, if she went inside, that would be a story even if nothing came of it. That would be something to talk about. Maybe he'd tell her it was a bad idea. It was a good idea. They wanted help, right?

The sign said, "Secretary," and, "typing, computer skills, filing." She could do that.

✝

31. *art history (continued)*

Simone Will be the Last to Burn: Roadside, morning. *From the road, out to the east and over a couple hills, you can see the creepy swath of fallow grey left by the fires. It looks like a warzone; the pitch of the battle increased as it got closer to the people just off this road, probably. Warzones were supposed to be off in other countries, right? Otros paises? It was over now.*

You can still smell it from here, everything oxidized to homogenous black carbon. The wasteland in front of the bright low sun, the few unscarred hills in front of the wasteland, and Simone is in front of those, looming huge in the frame with the apocalypse behind her. You wouldn't know it from the hot violence of the photo but it is cold, getting colder and foggier the further north we drive, as the unspoken idea of something happening is slowly replaced, like getting older, a little at a time, with the quiet certainty that this is it.

We start again. Every person walking along the road wants to be picked up; nobody wants to pick somebody up who's walking along the road. I've played both parts.

"What's that guy's story?" Simone asks. He is limping.

I always seem to have a fantasy. Should have kept my mouth shut. "His name is Lonny. He is a smokejumper during the season. On his way home. He banged up his hip today, so he cannot walk, his car broke down, and he got into a fight because somebody called him an arsonist, which he is. They sent him off to cool down; nobody to give him a ride. He is hoping his wife will wonder why he's so late and come up the road, so he looks up from his feet every once in a while, but no cars come. And he suspects her of sleeping with his friend Mark, the one who said, 'Lonny probably started it anyway,' then a few minutes later peeled out in his GTO. Lonny is thinking, 'He's probably there right now, and I can't even get a ride. I can't, but he can.'"

Pancho Villa asks the obvious question: "Is she?"

"No. She teaches second grade. Today the class started talking about all the fires this year, and Keith Jarvis, who got held back a year, was talking during the lesson, telling a story he said he heard on the news about a firefighter who got so fed up he filled up his car with water through the sunroof and held his breath and climbed in and drove off an embankment straight into the fire, and the other firefighters after they pushed back the fire around the car had to tow it to the coroners 'cause he was melted to the seat. So Nancy Snider started crying, 'cause she's fat and wants attention, and Lonny's wife, whose name is Judy, she flipped out, started screaming, "Shut

soft power

up Keith, there's no such thing as fire!" They had to send all the kids home. So she's sitting at home, on the couch, clutching in her fist the drawing that Sammy Keene, who's Jarvis's little mafia-style yes-man, made from his story. It has before and after panels and displays all manner of ingenuity that could otherwise never be coaxed from little Sammy, who's as curious as a dollop of shit. 'Before' is the firefighter in his car with the windows all blue and a surprised-looking fish in the back seat, and there are bubbles coming up from his mouth 'cause he's saying, 'Take this, inferno!' and all of this plunging over the highway rail and down into raging hellfire. 'After' is the car reduced to a smoking wreck with bare rims supporting a frame, an engine, a steering column, and two rows of seats, and the front seat has the wax-looking firefighter who's still smiling despite his oozing head, giving a thumbs up and saying, 'It burns so good.' There are lines wafting up from the body labeled, 'burning hair smell,' and a puddle below it marked, 'corpse goo,' and the whole thing is in the back of a flatbed from 'Rick's Dead Guy Towing: Ash to ash in a flash.'"

But Simone breaks into my story. "And he's going to leave her when he gets home, even when he doesn't find Mark, 'cause he's getting so angry as he limps along, each step a new pain and new cause for resentment."

Which isn't where I was going, but the rules are, once it's said, it's said. "That's his plan, but he won't get the chance, because first thing in the door she'll hold up the drawing and say, 'Look at this, this drawing that a second-grader made, and tell me that I'm crazy if I leave your suicidal, insane self. You know I bet it's true what they say about you starting the fires.'"

Simone cuts in again: "And he shouts 'Who says that? Mark? You're not the only one, you know! You know why Maggie from work called the other night, when I said she said her grandmother died? 'Cause she wanted me to come over to her place. She said I should say there was a fire at the mayor's house.'"

"But of course he's just making all that up to piss her off, because Maggie's obviously a lesbian and anyway he's not the type to cheat."

And Simone, in front, just turns around and looks at me all skeptical, and nobody says anything.

Then Pancho Villa, who needed the pause to get his bit in, shouts, all excited, "And just then the fire, with a little help from Mark who had some tricks of his own up his sleeve, reaches the back of the house, where they keep the propane tank, and the whole place goes up like a fuckin' tinderbox. Boom!"

And we both turn to him and just sort of stare.

"Yeah. Haha! Boom!"

32. trip to taller windows

Work had become slow, lately. Stanley could not concentrate. Out the window, across the street, they were building a new bank or something. It was all very secret but unmistakably bankish— squat and rugged and faux-old.

What about that: what if you could actually see, all at once, all the banks in the world? See where all the money came from and where it all went. The mortgage payments go in to Uptown National Bank and climb the backside corporate ladder by wire transfer and armored car, all the way to the top, where they're divvied up again, invested this way and that, funding new corporations, earning more, some day coming back down to everyone earning interest on their accounts with Uptown National Bank and elsewhere. At every step somebody took everything they gathered from their different incomes, split it up and sent it out to their creditors. Every step was a stash coming in along various channels by percentage, leaving again along different channels by percentage, destroying information. Impossibly complicated, like a brain. And if you could really see it all at once, would you be the brain? Would you be a genius, or just some stupid?

Rob had become a little suspicious of him lately. Stanley had a hunch that his near-meteoric rise up the ranks of Public Storage, Inc. was at its end. Stanley believed Rob knew, though he said nothing, that Stanley was the real corpse-finder. Rob seemed surprised that Stanley kept coming to work, but that was all.

The phone had been ringing, he realized. "Hello?"

"Stanley!" It was her.

"Hi."

"Don't know what's going on there, but nobody's come in here all day. The books are dropping off like flies from neglect. Got a second?"

If there was one thing he had, it would have to be a second.

"Guess what I did this weekend?"

"Joined the army?"

"Close. I went for a job interview at Hauser Holdings."

"I didn't know you were looking for a new job."

"I'm not. It's part of Westin-Rodant. I went to see what it was like and they were looking to hire somebody just like me."

All the rest, perhaps, but this, surely, this had to be called weird. "Um..."

"I told them my name was Jenny J. Watt. The 'J' stands for Jenny, but I didn't tell them that. I was a big hit. I get to go back for another interview tomorrow. I'm gonna sell real estate. I'm gonna make millions. Anyway, you want to come to dinner? I'll tell you all about it."

Why is it, he wondered, *that she only seems to want to talk to me about 1588?* He imagined Baker putting it all together, figuring everything out, dispelling the mystery, and that being the last he'd hear from Audrey Livingston. Signs didn't point to that happening any time soon, though, so that was good. "Yeah, ok."

She said where to meet. "I'll see you soon, ok Stanley?"

"Yeah, ok."

The sun was insistently down when he left. The sky was racing toward dark; you couldn't keep up. He walked along the ugly street hedged by signs for check cashing and liquor stores. He wondered what the city had felt like in 1920—what it felt like to be there. It couldn't have felt the way it felt in movies, but just the same it couldn't have felt like this. Not this weary, not this stale. It didn't even feel dangerous, really—too staid to be dangerous. All the thugs were at home, watching *Survivor* and weeping.

He would have missed the place but she tapped on the window; he jumped back from it: click click. She laughed at that. It was dark. It didn't feel like the street outside. It was a nice little refuge, dark and smoky and foreign. Middle eastern of some sort. The only people there were the staff, talking another language. He went in and over to the window to the low little table where she was sitting on the floor, sat down, and felt relieved simultaneously of his own weight and, in this place, of responsibility for the street outside. That was somebody else's mess.

"Hi! I already ordered for you. You'll like it."

At a table in back a guy who looked like the owner was sitting with some friends. On the table between them was a huge waterpipe. It was fun to watch—odd milky white bubbles percolating the chamber of water. It was complicated, over-engineered like Dr. Suess.

"I went down there just to see what it was like, but I couldn't really tell anything from the outside. It looked like anywhere. When I saw the sign, you know I had to go for it."

soft power

She'd done the hair again: it was bluish-white now, old lady hair. She was wearing a plain, white t-shirt. No bra. Her shape, usually hidden, showed through the tightish shirt. He tried not to look. Her breasts, against the worn fabric, looked soft and comfortable. Wanted to touch her. Touch her hair, her hand, anything.

He must have looked reluctant. "What? What's gonna happen?"

"I don't know. Didn't they want ID or anything?"

"No. I told them I'd come all the way down and then remembered that my resume was sitting on the table at home under a note that said, 'Take me!' and I giggled. I asked the guy that I talked to if he owned the place and he looked at me like I was crazy then said, 'No, we were acquired last year.' I said, 'Donald Trump?' and he just said, 'No.' Then he knocked over his coffee."

She'd ordered early so there was the food already. Rice and lamb, onions, tomato, some kind of spicy yogurt sauce, pita bread. It was nice. "What was so weird, then?"

"Well, toward the end, when he was telling me to come back tomorrow, he said, 'There are just a couple more things we need. It's just a formality really. We always need people like you.' But that's the thing, there wasn't anybody like me there. If they need a secretary I could understand how that might turn over pretty often, but then they wouldn't always need somebody like me: only after the last one quit. And if there were lots like me there, why weren't they there?"

That's it? That seemed a little thin.

"I'm right, right? That's weird?"

"Um... I guess."

"Well that's why I want to go back, so I can see."

"What if they get mad?"

"Get mad?" She laughed. "'Uh oh. You guys aren't mad, are you?'" He wanted to ask her not to go back, but that wasn't really his place. It looked colder out now.

"What are you thinking, anyway?"

"Gee Stanley, that's a hard one to answer." It felt strange to hear his name from her. As if he were just reminded of it.

"What's your theory, I mean. You must have some idea to be so dogged."

"You're dogged! Shut up!" She made offended for a few seconds before giving it up. "Well, what do we have? Somebody partook of some killin'. Used false addresses trying to get rid of the body. Those addresses have to have come from Sacks one way or another, so either he had something to do with it, or his firm did, or their parent corporation, Westin-Rodant. At first I was thinking, maybe Nikola got in the way somehow—of their business. Maybe they sell tobacco-flavored bubblegum to toddlers and he found out about it. But they don't do that; they don't do anything it doesn't seem like."

It wasn't much of a theory, so far.

"It's gotta be somebody bad. Let's call him, 'Mr. Bad,' since we don't know. His first name's Renny but he'd rather be called 'Mr.' He's the CEO, or the chairman of the board."

"Old blue eyes?"

"No. He runs this company, maybe he used to own it outright. It's just a collection of other companies, there to make him money. In the meantime, he likes to go out and be bad, and he uses the various subsidiaries to whatever ends he can, and he uses Westin-Rodant as a front, because it's the thing that makes all the money but really it's him."

"Really it's Mr. Bad."

soft power

"Exactly. Mr. Bad's whole expertise is convolution—turning away blame with his organization. For some reason, who knows why, he had reason to kill Nikola, and he did, either himself or had somebody do it, or maybe Nikola asphyxiated in a poorly ventilated garage owned by Westin-Rodant. Then he put the body in storage, waiting for the thing to cool off maybe. Just as it would have really started to smell he went to take it out again, to get rid of it for good this time, through some other minion no doubt, but somebody got wind of the police and so that never happened."

"In other words, you're out to get Mr. Bad."

"I'm just curious, and I know it sounds stupid but there has to be someone, right? Somebody must be responsible."

"You'd think."

"Hey, as long as we're here, I was wondering, where did that whole thing come from, that you talked about the last time we had dinner, the Alan Turing thing?"

"Oh. I don't have to do very much. At my job." He tried to look apologetic.

"Did you study that stuff in school?"

"Um, no." She was hunched forward, on her elbows, to the table. She smelled good. She smelled like grass.

"Did anybody ever accuse you of being evasive?"

"People don't really talk to me. I guess. Sorry."

"Hey, I know, let's play a game."

She was grinning. "Um..."

"I'm gonna ask you three questions and you have to answer honestly, ok?"

"No. What do I get if I win?"

"Too bad. You get a punch in the face and a kick in the shins, that's what you get."

"But I don't want that."

"Well you better play along then."

"Um..."

"Number one: what's with the Alan Turing thing?"

"I really don't know. I read a lot at work. I took some miscellaneous science in school and tried to take some history of science, but I never had a major. I wasn't much of a specialist that way. But I read a lot of that stuff, go from this to that, get a book on something in the last book that looked interesting. I just happened to be on the Alan Turing kick at the time, so I was thinking about it. It's kind of sad, don't you think? He was kind of a strange looking guy."

She looked kind of sad, but it didn't seem to be about Alan Turing. "Ok, I'll give you that one, but a pretty shoddy one. Try harder." Here she paused to think, staring at the table. He waited and watched her. She looked up and their eyes met, then she looked out the window and seemed to make up her mind right then. "Two: you seem a little tired or something of the whole Nikola Tesla thing."

"Yeah, well." I'd rather talk about you than him. Why don't I get to ask questions? "Did you see that Baker guy? He's scary. Did you see him? He'd break me in two. You told me a few weeks ago 'Don't be a coward.' But I'm a huge coward. Huge. Can't even—"

"Ok, fine, two. I suppose. You suck at this game."

They had both finished eating. It looked very cold indeed, outside, but it was warm here, and the tea was warmer, faintly sweet. She didn't say anything. That look of sadness was still there; she looked him in the eye, thinking it over maybe, like she was about to say something, and he suddenly felt scared. Coward. "What's three?"

More silence. She sighed. "I'll ask you three some other time." Pause. "Save it for later." She laughed, halfhearted. "Let's go."

"Where?"

"I don't know. Walk." They paid and left. It was colder than it looked. She had a huge puffy parka that came almost down to her knees. Looked like a troublemaker or ruffian. They walked to the train and stood on the platform. "See the Holiday Inn sign?" It said "Holiday Inn" in green.

"Yes."

"I was reading something, said in Japan they paint the railway crossings that color to keep people from jumping in front of the trains."

"How does that work?"

"I dunno. You say, 'Damn, that's ugly. I don't wanna be dead near that.' Course they got faster trains there. Nobody tries it on the el."

"'Ow! I'm not dead. I'm just in pain. And disfigured. This is the worst ever.'"

She stared at something behind the buildings, like she wasn't paying attention. "My mom's moving to Portland she says, quitting her job and moving with some guy she met, to write a book."

The train clattered up, sparking white against the rails. They embarked. The robot announced stops.

"My Dad's here. Did you know that? He sort of makes movies. I think he's lonely."

"Not here." He made incredulous.

She giggled. "Maybe you're right."

They were coming up to her stop, he realized, and he hoped she had some sort of ending in mind because he certainly didn't.

"I'll call you and let you know how it goes. I'm not going to take the job or anything, but I bet I'll be able to figure something out. I feel lucky."

"Yeah. You look it. Lucky." *Don't go.*

"Thanks." *I won't?* "I'll call you. Bye."

Don't go.

✝

33. the house that catch built

It felt good to be there in the morning, waking up. Sure, small. Efficient. Ascetic. Beautiful just like a monastery. In the morning it was so bright, like a shower before the shower, healthy white brilliance dripping off your skin in heavenly surfeit, onto every surface and into every nook. Just opening her eyes to it—arching her neck to look languidly back into the sky above the courtyard—made it a good thing, waking up. There was a solidarity among the windows that overlooked the courtyard; they'd silently agreed that with the heat it was better to let people see in. Nobody had anything to hide. The heat was going, finally, but so far the habit had stuck.

Danny was still asleep, his head nestled like a child's against her. How could he sleep in all this light? She rolled forward again to see Audrey standing in the doorway, just standing there, hands clasped behind her back. At that, Catch had to smile, slowly at first, the warmth of it washing over her. Audrey did nothing, at first, but finally she smiled, too.

"Hi sweetie!"

Didn't say anything, but she twisted on her feet, back and forth. Stuck inside the doorframe, so small.

soft power

Catch didn't want to wake Danny. When had he come in last night? Could have been two, could have been two hours ago. She slid out, gingerly, scratched by his stubble, slipping in a pillow in her stead. Without her he curled tighter against himself.

The terry of the bathrobe was heavy and coarse. The wood of the kitchen floor was cool. Audrey followed her in, silently. She didn't react when Catch reached down and lifted her to the counter. She bounced her heels together. There was some sausage in the fridge. Frying pan, heat, sausage. The cheap heating element creaked toward orange.

"How did you sleep?"

Catch wanted juice, but there wasn't any. Her mouth was dry. There were some lemons. She got the lemons and the lemon squeezer.

"What do you want to do today?"

The lemons were a little old; they collapsed feebly beneath her weight.

"Do you want some lemonade?"

She smiled.

It was fine, coming there. For a long time she wasn't sure, but it was fine. It was new, it was pretty, there were things to do with Audrey on a Saturday, she could get her friends on the phone, Danny could walk to the studio. There was just so much light.

The sausages hissed and popped, and she felt a prick of oil on her arm. She rolled them over, then stirred the sugar and the lemons and the water. The muted underwater click of spoon against glass was rhythmic, steadying. A little lemon tornado formed inside the glass, then washed over the spoon as she stopped.

Ah-hah! There were biscuits left over from dinner, too. Buttermilk, big and knobbly. *A feast!* She gave one of the glasses to Audrey, carefully molding her small hands against the surface, slippery with condensation. Audrey held it two-fisted against her mouth, sucking at it like with a straw, her eyes always fixed on Catch.

"Do you want to go to the park?"

She thought she saw the edge of a smile. She divided the sausage three ways, put a biscuit on each of the two plates, buttered them, carried the plates to the table, then went back for Audrey and the lemonade.

"Watch, it's hot."

Audrey, low at the table and small to the fork in her hand, looked mistrustfully at the sausage. She ate the biscuit, drank the lemonade and then, warming to it, ate the sausage, which wasn't bad. The window beside the table was open too; Audrey stared at the cars wrestling down in the street.

Danny was still asleep when they left. Catch covered the pan of the remaining sausages, set the bag of biscuits next to it, and put a note in front of him on the pillow: "Sausages!" She folded it like a placecard to make it stand on its own.

"Is Daniel coming?"

"He'll get up while we're gone."

The day was bright and perfectly temperate, the air crisp with the potpourri of summer's dying leaves. People were out, with beards and slept-in hair, trying to snatch at it before it disappeared, hold on to it. Through the crowds they took the subway to the park. The train rattled and the riders were lively, loaded down with books and bags and things, eager to get there. The stale, metallic subway air made the real air outside smell of Fall. Crunching over more leaves, Audrey stared up at the yellows and reds, step-stepping along with her warm hand raised to Catch's own. The

soft power

paths and forks of the park, the vistas and their vegetations, wound this way and that, forever novel, like Wonderland. There was no street grid; there was the possibility of getting lost.

The chess people played chess. Catch and Audrey stood behind them, on the hill, quietly watching. Catch never remembered to play but whenever she saw a game—saw human thought laid out for her across those even squares—missed it. She used to play with Danny. Where had the chessboard gone? A casualty of the move, she supposed. One of the men made a raucous deep dog's bark each time he slapped down a piece, but he still lost.

Fall is the perfect season. This wasn't quite the New England fall she was used to, where the air smelled like Lexington, witch trials, and Nathaniel Hawthorne, but close enough. She'd stayed close to home for school, and that was enough of that. And her friends all said they'd come down here soon, but who knew if they meant it. It felt good to be away from the silent respectability of New Canaan. Like this chess scene: all the men, who knew what they did or where they lived, but the colors and shapes varied. Overcoats, scarves, patched corduroys and spectacles, but the Saturday morning and the chess brought them all there together.

A few fast games later they left, walking on along the path, past the dogs and joggers and the tended flowerbeds. They found a place to sit and sat, in the sun that warmed them against the cool of the air to just the right degree, with a view of a frisbee game, and Catch read some to Audrey from *Canterbury Tales*. When the sun got lower in the sky she noticed Audrey shivering so they left—by way of the Turkish grocers for things for dinner—for home. There was one block that unnerved her, where men loitered, violence implicit in their manner and you had to wonder, each time you passed, whether you might be an object of that violence. You always had to be on your guard or something would make an object of you. But they passed safely, went into their building and up the stairs.

Audrey, sensitive to a need, fished the keys from Catch's pocket and got the door for her. Hurrying from the ache in her arms, she walked to the table and set the things down on it, rocking it up and slightly off the floor. The sun had just set; the smell of food a floor below made her feel behind.

From the other room she heard Danny and Audrey. She'd expected him to be gone again, but there he was, pinned on the couch, Audrey sitting on his chest, quietly telling the days events. It was astonishing the things she'd noticed; Catch wondered where her own thoughts had been. She sorted the things from the grocery bags and laid out the dinner supplies on the counter.

They came in behind her, Audrey to her spot on the counter, lifted by Danny, who inspected the groceries and set to work chopping the big spanish onion.

"How did it go last night?"

"Well, let's see." Chop chop. "I didn't get anything done, but it was slow and discouraging." She smelled the garlic as it crushed beneath the flat of the knife. "I can't do this one. I've been stuck for a week now."

"You always say that."

"I'm always right. I always end up with something, but it's never what I wanted. I can't do it."

"Stop then. Teach Audrey to play chess. Have a drink. It will keep." Audrey, Catch thought, was tacitly intrigued by the game in the park. Click click. Resign. She thought she saw a smile out of the corner of her eye.

soft power

"I've got the editing room booked every night this week. Can't afford not to use it." He rubbed the child's head with an air of apology. "You know we can't remotely afford that."

The glass in the cabinet rang mute. There was a bottle of Scotch far too good for them to own that Danny's father had bought on visit. The idea had been to save it for his next visit; certainly he'd remember having bought it. But in an emergency, it could spare a little. There was something very teenaged about the whole thing, a bit of a joke: how much could be gone before he'd know the difference? The first giveaway—the top of the label—had long since been left behind. They'd started calling it the Emergency Scotch.

"Is it an emergency, you think?"

"Are you kidding? This is serious. Make mine a double emergency." Yogurt was alive and looked it. Bright white and fleetingly alive, spoiled in a heartbeat.

He made up two glasses, his with water, hers without. Audrey had to taste everything, and predictably wrinkled her nose afterwards. "You'll get used to it, eventually." It was hard to say meaningfully—of something so many leagues beyond the realm of possibility—whether it was worth the cost, but certainly it was very, very good. Catch took a sip and held it on her tongue, watching Audrey watch Danny.

She gave the cucumbers to Audrey to peel. Audrey sat with the big cucumber between her knees, whittling it, fragments of peel flying down into the trash on the floor below. Some of the strands missed, inevitably, and each time he happened to pass Danny would bend down and clean up a couple. Catch smiled silently at the inane repetition of it—the stupidity repeated, never noticed.

"How long till you finish, you think?"

"I told you, I can't finish. But I'll be done in another two weeks, I bet."

There was a nice rhythm to it: when he finished he'd be ecstatic for a day or two and then moody for weeks for lack of anything in particular to do, with the strain of not having a next idea. At least he'd be available, though. Then, she was sure, he'd find some new gleam and be off again.

Still, two weeks? At least the film was out of the fridge. The annoyance of that—opening it to find something to eat or put groceries away and finding no room from at all around the canisters that spilled over even into the vegetable crisper—still left a bad taste in her mouth. Slowly it had been used and carted away to be developed and the irritation had faded.

Many hands, or six anyway—two big, two tiny, two thin—made light work, and soon they were sitting down at the table with the cucumber soup, the salad, and the garlic bread which, while clashing with the cuisine, still was good. She tore at it, pulling apart the crust, hot butter on her fingers and beneath her nails. Out on the street, two people were arguing at a distance of half a block. Every line was delivered while turning back—as if for just one last time—after moving to walk away. They didn't seem to notice their monotony. But why was she looking out the window?

"Can I do the dishes to assuage my guilt?"

"Don't worry about it. Sooner you go, sooner you might get back."

Audrey went with him while he packed his things, untying each of his shoes after he tied it and laughing. He laughed too, the first time, then got angry and snapped at her. Catch winced. Then the two of them were alone. She felt the weight of any number of sins that she had to redress.

soft power

There was a short round little table out on the fire escape, lit by the alley flood. Pawns go forward one square, or two on the first move, if you want, and capture diagonally. Knights go two by one. If you play defensively you'll lose. Control the center. The shadows of the pieces swam away from the flood lamp, each move a tiny click beneath the talking and music from other windows. Audrey learned quickly at first then began to tire. Catch put her to bed and then sat with a coffee mug, holding it against her cheek until it cooled.

34. *the ghost of you now*

For a week Stanley missed her call, and then he bought an answering machine just to be sure. Somebody named Darlene Simpson, apparently with a similar number, got more messages than he did. And still Audrey did not call.

He took the long way home from work one night, strolling up the Magnificent Mile in mid-November, and never was it more magnificent—sparkling beneath the disco ball of a million fat snowflakes flurrying left and right. Shoppers in their fashionable dark leathers hurried along through the luminescence toward places to go, lending to the air a little bit of the promised warm comfort of their kitchens and turkey dinners. He recognized her up the street by her posture and jogged forward to say hello but no—up close it was obviously an old woman, not her at all. And all that wealth dissipated like smoke the closer he got to his own home.

Probably she was tired of him. He hadn't talked enough. Or too much. Why did he have to be so boring? Why had he never anything to say but to himself? She didn't want to hang out with him. *God, I wouldn't want to hang out with me.* Mathematics? What was he thinking? There is no shame like that of past intentions—things that seemed like a good idea at the time—because for those things, unlike a stumble over a curb or a public fart, you are wholly responsible. Maybe it was that he'd been too obvious. Maybe she'd always been so forward because she did that to everyone, and now she'd forgotten him for somebody else. Still, she'd said she'd call, and if only to tell him about Hauser Holdings it was strange that she did not. She did not.

He wandered from place to place, to new heights of restlessness. At the end of each day the premature winter darkness and the cold propelled him forward, as if he'd taken a deep breath before leaning into the Public Storage doorframe—hard enough to break the seal of pressure created by the rushing wind—and he'd be unable to breath again until he opened the door to his own apartment. When he was out, he wanted to be in, even if he didn't expect the taciturn little answering machine—unblinking mute box—to change its ways. At home, though, he boiled inside the static stale whiteness of the walls, pacing, searching for any excuse: trips to the store, a new shower curtain, anything to get out but why did that always seem to mean buying something?

Weekends, not quite admitting it but he found himself visiting bookstores. Those that he happened across, at least, and always on the vague pretense of looking for this or that what he could have guessed they'd never have. It did not take long to find the right one, recognizable by the name once he saw it. Smashed between a Mexican bakery that breathed warm, sugary cake-air and a blank storefront whose tinfoiled windows bore only the tiny modest white inscription: "Violence Grinder, Inc." But the place itself was small, homey even.

soft power

She wasn't at the desk. There was man with wild white hair, skinny, all vein and tendon. Bulging, hyperthyroid eyes. Stanley walked past him, trying to smile, to where the aisles went back a good ways but concealed no one. There was a display shelf that said "Audrey Recommends" beneath the Polaroid photo beside the five books. He wanted to read the books, but more than that he wanted the photograph. She sat, leaning back against the wall, with her hands knitted behind her head and her eyes wide and just a hint of a smile, as if to say hurry up and take the picture. She'd set a book face-down on her lap, but he couldn't see the title.

He looked to the front, where the man was still reading. He picked up one of the five books, with a drawing of a little old car on the cover and a man and woman in the car, and stared at the words on the back. He put it down and picked up another. He thought he saw someone in the corner and turned but it was only a cat, sitting above one of the bookshelves, staring at him. He put down the second book in front of the photograph and slid the photograph out behind it, shoving it up inside his coat as he walked back to the desk.

Without looking up from the book, the man asked, "Can I help you with anything else?"

"Does Audrey Livingston work here?" And her name felt strange from him, too.

Then the man did look up from the book, but didn't speak at first. "Yes."

"What days is she here?"

The man squinted.

Louder, "Um, what days is she here?"

"I heard what you said," he barked, and closed the book, and put it down. "None, lately. She stopped coming in a few weeks ago."

He paused to nod his head and smile with the music. "Strange, because she's always been very dependable. Finally getting some time off without having to worry about the store. Two weeks ago on Tuesday she didn't show up. Hasn't since. I thought she'd get a new job sooner or later, but it wouldn't be like her not to come in and tell me in person. I'm starting to worry a little, to be honest. A friend?"

"Sort of."

"If you see her, tell her to call and let us know she's ok, mmm?"

Gone. It made no sense. Gone where?

He went out again, and hardly noticed the cold now walking-jogging back to the el. It seemed slow to arrive; there was a man who, every minute or so, mechanistic, would look at his watch, kick the floor, look down the track, sigh, say "Damn!" The intensity of the whole thing never seemed to vary; every sixty seconds the train's non-arrival was exactly as distressing as before. All this only served to increase Stanley's own anxiety. When it did finally arrive, the train chugged lazily, waveringly down the track, creaking and whining, continuing on that way sluggish and dull through the grey. The bright colors of winter sportsgear struggled feebly against the tide of desaturation around them, these too suddenly irritating, like little lights shining in his eyes.

"A. Livingston." The green label-tape on the mailbox had been replaced, so that was something. Those words didn't seem to be going anywhere. But no answer when he rang the bell. He tried to see through the stubborn aluminum of the mailbox if it was filling up. "Manager," said another label, and that bell was answered. By a mediterranean-looking fellow who stared at Stanley like he must be very stupid. *Are you her boyfriend? Tell her to pay the rent. What is it, the eighth? Christ. No, I don't know.*

Gone. Disappeared. Amelia Earhart. The Lindbergh baby. The lady, vanishèd. A million kids' faces cheaply printed blue on grey cardstock with words: "Last seen with...", "Age progression sponsored by..." And some awful date, some years ago, lifetimes ago date that made you wonder, "Who are they kidding?" She could be away, could have some family emergency, something like that, but he could feel in his stomach an acid certainty, body warning him expect the worst—these are not the keys you'll find in the door. Try to prepare yourself for it, whatever you can do. Hundreds must face this every day, mothers and fathers and sisters and lovers. But easier for them because it wasn't usually, as this was, wasn't it, he pulled in vain at the broken brake lever on the careening train of thought wasn't it all, when you laid it all out start to finish and looked with the judicious eyes of a stern parent (or stern detective), wasn't it all—his fault?

Well, wasn't it?

☩

35. art history (continued)

You Cannot Take a Picture of a Sound: A north-south street, morning. *The noise is awful. I am carrying the camera so I take the picture. A photo taken in anger, but you can see nothing in the image itself of the violence of it. Just Oliver, turning away, features blurry by his motion. You cannot hear what he said before turning, that note above this cacophony.*

The morning started out quietly enough. We waved goodbye to Dwayne, he waved back, leaning out the window back at us, running up on the curb at the corner then bottoming out against it. Pay attention, Dwayne. We laughed, then Oliver and I went into a greasy spoon breakfast place to eat and talk about what now.

matt segur

It was the way he smiled presumptuously that did it. When he said, before we'd even ordered, "Glad that's over, eh?"

Had I not been devious it might have gone better. Had I bristled immediately—said, with just a little open offense, "What do you mean?"—he'd have caught the hint and shut up. But I was looking for a fight, in my bloodlust wanting to know what he meant, and wanting to be as small as he could be, so I just played along, smiled, and mumbled something vague.

"He's a nice guy and all, but if I'd had to sit and listen to the bored-child terrorism tirade one more time I would have killed myself." And he laughed at his wit. "It's strange how it never occurs to some people that you might want some time to yourself." And expected me to agree, and that's what made me angry.

"You know," I said, still trying to seem jovial, "what I think is strange?" And, in my meanness, I consciously thought about the timing of dropping the fake smile to a flat glare. "I think it's strange how all you men of ideas look high and low for someone who'll respect your entitlement to your opinions—without dismissing you as the nuts you must inevitably often seem to be—but put two of you in the same room and you'll fall over yourselves trying to decry the other as a loony. I find that very strange."

And of course he became defensive at the ambush. "All I'm saying is that I would have liked to spend more time with you. I somehow had it in my head that was a good thing."

"But you have been with me. You've been with me and my friend, Dwayne. Which is just like being with just me. Except we can't fool around. Oh, was that it? Is that was this was about for you, travelling around because it's more exciting in somebody else's room? That's a dull male-fantasy sort of aesthetic, I have to say. Disappointing."

That was the moment, I think, when he really got angry. "Yes. That's exactly it. I thought, 'I bet I'd enjoy my sexually tepid girlfriend more in

California. Maybe we could even strike up a threesome.' You can imagine my dismay when we fell in not with an experimental young bisexual blonde bunny but with a man, of all things. Naturally I thought, 'This is worse than being alone with you.'"

Voices escalated. "All that sarcasm is fine, but far be it for you to admit that maybe there's a grain of truth to it, that you're looking for something more than I give you and whether you're aware of it yourself or not, you brought us out here falling victim to the great deception of travel, that if we move fast enough we can escape from ourselves and become the people we wish we were. You ought to know better."

"Do you really believe that?"

"Do you believe I'm that far off?"

Somebody dropped a tray of dishes in the back somewhere, affording a clamorous moment of reflection. "What if you're not? I could do a lot worse than the sin of trying something futile to recapture the attention of the girl who'd rather talk to some miscreant yokel—anything to avoid being stuck with me. I mean, did you hear some of the things that guy said when we were in the car?"

"Fuck you Oliver. You could do a lot better than to have so little respect for me that you call my friend a 'miscreant yokel.' And speaking of things said in cars, the two of you seemed to be laughing it up in equal amounts from where I was sitting. I've known Dwayne longer than I've known you."

"Don't you mean 'Pancho Villa?'"

That was too much to take. I put down cash for my uneaten grilled cheese and walked out. Having gotten the fight I wanted, I stood furious on the curb having nowhere really to go. Oliver was already shouting something as he came out the door after me, but that's when the sound started, like a flash flood, at first just the close and loud wail of the car alarm right *in front of me set off for no apparent reason, but followed quickly by others, hundreds or thousands it seemed like. Pack animals howling together.*

Every car alarm in the city singing and people everywhere stopping and looking around, thinking they've turned against us and what is this what we've created? A man across the street runs to his car, just trying to do his part, holding his keychain in front of him—a lion tamer's chair—frantically commanding the car to stop but it will not and soon he is beating his fists against the hood and kicking the sidewall with no regard for the shiny newness of his betraying car.

I feel a part of history—our everyday argument interrupted by this calamity—just as every participant in a disaster was talking about something a moment before, and probably something low and stupid. That's what makes me raise the camera from around my neck, not knowing what else to do but try to document this moment of impossibility. Try to get a picture of all these people just standing around, paralyzed by fear and doubt in the middle of not earthquake or hurricane but just sound, man-made yet inexplicable.

Running down the middle of the street is a little boy who laughs and skips as if it were a snow day, happy at seeing all the sure-of-themselves adults exposed to something new for once, at his not being alone, and he's right to do it—I can understand that.

What I cannot understand is when Oliver turns to me, single-minded as ever, oblivious, and shouts, "I'm going to the station to get on the next bus home. You do whatever you want."

And so this ends up a photograph not of the miracle around us but just of Oliver's anger and my anger and our fed-up failure, and it's not even a very good photograph at that or why would I need all this explanation?

36. his victims and his women

There was nothing on the desk. There was a nameplate, a phone, a tabletop calendar, a picture of his daughter, a picture of his wife. Baker took a hard line on that, losing things sometimes to avoid clutter. He just happened to want it that way; it wasn't for any good reason. There were times like this, though, when he worried that it made him seem forbidding. There didn't seem to be any point in seeming forbidding. Not this time.

"She said Sacks cried in his sleep."

"Cried in is sleep?"

"In his sleep. At night."

He was surprised to be seeing Stanley again. He'd seemed like the type that would have been easily cowed by the little bluster that Baker had used. It always hurts to be wrong. It was also surprising, even allowing for what he was saying, that Stanley would have the balls to come in here and talk to him like this. Baker didn't have a feel for his intent yet.

He'd stammered when he'd come in the door, stammered horribly. "I, uh, hi. You, um, you, you... have a very clean desk. Uh. Bet you weren't expecting to see me. I... I had to come in to tell you, uh, um..." What could be so hard to say? "I... didn't listen to you."

"So what if Sacks cried in his sleep? I probably cry in my sleep. Keep the law out of the bedroom, as they say."

"We weren't sure. Except that it seemed like he must have something to do with it because he worked with both couples. That couldn't just happen."

It had made him laugh. "Nobody else listens to me. Why should you?" But Stanley hadn't even smiled at that. He'd just waited patiently as if to say this is hard enough, let me finish.

"I should have called right away, I know. I hadn't meant to find it out really, it's just they both thought I sounded like him, like Sacks, and I couldn't ignore it."

"So you think Sacks killed Tesla?"

"When you told me to stay out of it, I, uh, I didn't listen." That was the first thing to make Baker apprehensive. People don't easily admit a mistake. What was wrong? He had to wait, he knew. No point in imagining or preparing, because it could always outdo you.

"What's this about, Stanley?"

"Not that he killed him. Just that it was strange that she would say that, that he cries in his sleep. And she had some stationary, and she crossed out some words on it."

"Words?"

"We meaning Audrey and I. This girl that I met, who took an interest. It's a long story." That made some sense. Wanting to impress a girl could test the faith of most devout coward.

He wouldn't bother trying to intimidate Stanley this time. What would be the point? It was too late now. Once again he'd gotten there too late. "Are you sure you've told me everything?"

"*Westin-Rodant.* Those were the words. She looked it up. It's the corporation that owns Sacks' firm. Their records were weird, I guess. They don't do anything."

"If only all corporations could say as much." Again, Stanley didn't even smile.

"And now she's gone." Gone?

"So Sacks has a connection to Nikola Tesla's murder, your friend Audrey goes to investigate the company that owns Sacks' firm, and now you haven't heard from her. Is that all?"

"She went for a second interview. That was the last I heard from her."

"An interview?"

"A job interview. She didn't really want a job."

"How long has she been missing?"

"Two weeks. Her landlord said she hadn't paid the rent."

"What do you mean gone?"

"She said she would call, and she hasn't called. She hasn't shown up at work." Now it all made sense. That was the sad puzzle piece missing, the kind he had a nose for. Still, Stanley could have stayed away.

"How well did you know... Audrey?"

Stanley stared at the desk in front of him, the clean desk. "Not well."

"We can file a missing person report and look into it." If you want to scare somebody you arrest him. No need to be nice about it. No knowing what he can be put up to.

"I'm sorry about..." *So am I.* "I didn't really mean to... I meant to do as you said. I certainly didn't mean for..."

"We don't have a lot to go on, you realize."

"Can't you... No, I guess not."

"I'm sure you didn't, but nonetheless, here we are."

"You can do that, right? Find somebody?"

Sometimes. Finding people was not Baker's department. Those people worked hard at their jobs, but this... There are people everywhere, and nothing could seem easier than to find one. Some of them you find again and again, always interrupted, embarrassed in the midst of the same mistake. Some of them sit pious and pray for nothing more than to be found, or even just to be looked for. Some of them avoid you, slipping into corners and under cracks in the baseboard, staying out of the light. But then there are those who simply aren't there to be found.

It is easier, much easier, to lose a person. Sooner or later it is bound to happen, with so many places to get lost. It is just a matter of a connection between two people—part of it, out of sight, secretly fraying. The way the history between you unwinds, always in hindsight like a textbook lesson, the Roman Empire grinding along toward its demise. Nothing could be simpler.

✝

37. low light meow

If only Audrey had complained, that would have been something. Little stoic said not a thing, didn't cry, didn't ask. The young sliding-scale doctor said she seemed to be doing unusually well: ear infections are painful and they usually cry. Catch didn't believe it for a second.

Not complaining, probably worried about the affect on Catch of any semblance of suffering, Audrey sat weak and pale on the floor wrapped in an afghan and a lousy faker's smile. Pushing together a jigsaw puzzle—3,000 pieces the box had said, something to pass the time, a soft homogenous impressionist lake. It was only eleven; Catch already wished she were putting Audrey to bed. Though at night she tossed and turned, woke up sweaty from nightmares that she couldn't describe—only cling round Catch's neck, twisting up the hairs between her clasped small knuckles.

So then, watching the clock on the wall, a housewarming gift from Mom made of cast-iron, pretty in a heavy sort of way. No second hand, but it tick-tick-ticked along with something that couldn't quite be called regularity, the sound swelling and fading if you tried to focus on it, like a silly word repeated. That's how the time went:

burbling, and you couldn't be sure how fast but not fast enough. Later Danny had promised to come home early and make dinner, chicken in tarragon cream sauce wrapped in pastry.

"I could make you dinner," he'd said on their third meeting or so, and that had sounded fine and had been fine indeed, rich and velvet and warm like the warm cluttered wooden old apartment back home where he'd played warm Philly soul and the soft cat had nuzzled against her leg, taking a shine. She went—while Audrey continued to slide pieces around—to the record player propped on a feeble old cardboard box beneath the window, slid the record from the stack, bending the sleeve open gently. For a moment the crackling of the vinyl and the chatter of the wall clock played together. The window was speckled with rain. Thought about calling Beth but she'd be working of course, they'd all be. ⅛TH *Gauge Special Grade*, it said on the box, a string of nonsense she'd read too many times. She saw two big continents in the puzzle that could be joined and reached to join them but hesitated; let Audrey find it.

"This is the record Daniel played for me the first time I was at his apartment."

Audrey found the seam, then, and carefully braided it together. "Did you like it?"

"It's nice, don't you think?"

She nodded, not quite sure.

"Sometimes when you've only just met somebody you think of them as not quite a person—more a collection of clever remarks, or not so clever. A list, you know, of things they've said, plus however they happen to look and sound. But it's hard to imagine until you actually see it them living somewhere, eating. Daniel put this on and I thought, 'He listens to Soul. He has a cat and a Mom.'"

"Everybody has a Mom."

"That doesn't mean you think about it."

Audrey seemed to think of something forgotten. "What happened to the cat?"

"She's fine, less a few teeth. She stayed with Daniel's parents."

Like basketball, five thousand that was all, the games you really knew. Why couldn't I beat you in the middle of the room? Beth so excited when Catch had described all the details, both of them trying to avoid—talk around—the foreboding of it: that after years of surrogate sisterhood a change might be in the air, in those notes carried to Catch and then, secondhand over a cigarette in the backyard, to Beth. Beth who'd come home with Catch one bright fourth grade day, left at dusk, and returned again at bedtime with a black eye asking, *Can I stay with your family tonight?* Beth who'd become not just sister but partner, sous-chef, and co-conspirator, goading Catch along through childhood's dares and risks with her sharp bad girl tongue. "I'm going to pick us up some soup. I'll be back in twenty minutes, ok?"

Audrey was clearly doubtful about that. Catch pointed at the clock. "See the hand here? I'll be back before it gets to there." That made her go back to the puzzle, sinking deeper in the afghan against the solitude. Catch hesitated outside the door, not quite closing it, giving something a chance to go wrong. Then she locked it and went out, hurrying down the hallway to the stairs.

Twenty minutes was probably too long. The place was just around the corner. Something else to be said for putting up with the sometime unsafety of the neighborhood. Her shoes clopped urgently on the pavement; she crossed on a diagonal. Steamy air rushed out at her when she opened the door, coming up against a long line.

Before his warm apartment, temperature was really all she'd been nervous of with Danny, in her war-room debriefings with Beth. He was witty from the first, brilliant even, at his best as she'd prodded:

"What do you want to be when you grow up?" That was a girlish little line that she liked.

"A ghost."

"Why's that?"

"Nobody messes with you if you're a ghost, because they know you'll haunt their shit."

"Maybe, but that could be tough to get."

"I try to keep as many unabsolved sins on my head as possible in case I ever slip in the tub."

Cynical, of course—that wit a cold, male sort of wit that made her wonder. Some people are just robots even if (or especially if) they're smart, going along, always amused but never anything more. What would his home be like? Warm or cold? All the latest fashions in books and music, surely, but would it be an icy, analytic sort of place?

The line moved quickly, and then the loud man was asking what she wanted. Chicken matzo ball, to go. She formed the size with her hands. That was it. Then back across the street, around the corner, up the stairs, down the hall. Audrey was standing in front of the record player, staring at it in bewilderment as the needle dinged off the label. Catch turned it off.

"Sorry. Here, have some soup." She didn't eat much but her cheeks flared at the heat of it. That was some relief from the sallowness at least.

"What did you do?"

"What?"

"While the record was playing?"

"Oh. I stood around, mostly, in the kitchen while he cooked. Then we ate. He told some stories about people from his old high school, I think. I played with the cat."

"Were you snogging?"

"No! Remember when we talked about how you had to be careful using words like that?"

Little Audrey was not to be put off. "Why not?"

"That's between him and me, don't you think? Come on Audrey, you know better than that. I shudder to think what'll happen when you start with school."

Audrey glowered precociously, already able to take offense at that.

"Sorry."

"Where's Daniel?"

"Working."

"How come you're never working?"

Ouch. "Well, I had to quit my job to come down here."

"Are you going to get another job?"

"Soon." *Hope that's not a lie.*

"What are you going to do?"

"I think you need to stop asking so many questions and get some rest. Come on." Audrey assented to being carried to bed. *But oh, the quiet without her.* The clock went.

Were you snogging. What sort of child was this? The little lord Jesus, no crying he makes, content to ask, *But Joseph, if you're not giving it to Mom then what am I doing here?*

Danny had said he'd be back by five. She wondered if maybe he'd finish early. The clickety-clock said two now. Three. He could be back by three. He kept swearing he was almost done. *This close.*

soft power

One more day and I'll have it. One more day eaten from those when he was supposed to be taking care of Audrey while Catch looked for that job. The puzzle on the floor like a burned canvas, frayed ashen edges eating at the lake.

She looked in on Audrey, fast asleep. Sat back on the couch and tried to read the linguistics book Beth had bought her, but her eyes just rolled off the words. The ceiling was square and low. For a moment it seemed to move. It made her think, in its squareness, of a film they'd watched a few weeks ago: he'd hated it, but she couldn't get it out of her head. There was one sequence that went on and on, it must have been five minutes—a woman's stomach in a square of grainy Pixelvision transfer, hardly even recognizable except by the way that shadows showed contours and the dark slit of navel. Very pretty, the slight, arrhythmic twitches of her stomach as she lay there, sleeping. Even in her memory it was comforting and pretty, even alluring. The bookshelf loomed, heavy, behind her.

She flicked absently at the worn little corner of denim above the button of her jeans and when it came open well that had to mean something right? Not much but something. It was a little cold—cold enough to slowly chill your extremities, leave you feeling bony and colonial. She left her hand pressed between fabric and fatty skin for while, warming the dry palm. Just that smooth, even greyness of the stomach and the slow, aimless motion, telegraphed to the pixels. She didn't move her hand, just slowly rolled her hips against it, thinking of the way the fat gathered around the navel and of the camera that must have hovered there, just a couple feet up but still withheld. Was the woman really asleep, or was she pretending?

Immediately after she felt disgusted. What was she doing? Lying here, bored, waiting for her man, masturbating for Christ's sake? Awful! At least nobody knew. Audrey being sick, that was some excuse, right? She was stranded here for the moment, but no, that was no kind of excuse. Then she did read the book, determinedly, and was nearly finished with it when Audrey appeared, having woken up, burning bright red, and it was almost five o'clock. The fever was way up; Catch felt panicked. She called the doctor. It was alright. She'd be fine. A bath would help bring the fever down.

Audrey didn't talk at all now, just looked woozy, and Catch could only wish she'd pester with questions or at least complain—something. Danny, meanwhile, was late. In retrospect, that made a lot more sense than early. He'd say he "lost track of time." Maybe he should take the clock with him; it wasn't doing her any good. The bath seemed to help, and then she quickly but carefully dried Audrey with a towel and took her back to bed. She was especially careful tucking the knit corners, stretching them tight as she could, as if that might help. "Do you want something to eat? Some toast?" She just shook her head. It wasn't quite true; they were snogging, after that night. Just eating the chicken, which was unbelievable, had been halfway there.

Where would she even start to look for a job? She knew nothing about this city. One couldn't possibly, but she knew less than that. Hopelessly out of her depth. It was starting to get dark. There was no knock at the door. He was supposed to get the ingredients too; she couldn't start without him. If she went they might have twice as much as they needed, and Audrey's fever could rise in her absence. The puzzle, still half-finished, stayed silent. The rain stayed soft and even. She felt like putting on another record but the place was small—she didn't want to wake Audrey. ⅛TH *Gauge Special Grade.*

soft power

She thought of the things in the kitchen. Audrey probably wouldn't want any dinner. She could always make scrambled eggs, she supposed. Maybe he was cheating. No, that wasn't him. That would almost be better, to be ignored in favor of a person. Seven. Seven thirty. The phone rang, but there was no one. She wished someone would call so she could have a nice little tirade.

At eight-thirty he came in, looking rushed and haggard and wet. Sympathetic bastard. "I'm really sorry. I lost track of time."

"I don't have a lot to go on, you know. There's plenty to like about this place but for lack of my old job and my old friends we need you here from time to time. Your daughter, who looks awful, and I." But again, the chicken was good.

38. old folks

If Stanley had ever been lonely it hardly seemed like it now. Now—in this guilty, conspicuous absence—this was the pure stuff. The telling off he'd expected from Baker, that he'd had to steel himself against as he stood outside the precinct working up the nerve, had been nothing to Baker's compassionate glum look.

She couldn't just disappear. *Where would you get that much amber*, he laughed, then regretted it. He didn't know the last names of any of her friends he'd met. It was strange that in all that time he'd managed to keep nothing of her, nothing essential, just an address and a phone number and the image of a face. If only to see the latest act of hair abuse, he wanted to see her. Lying in bed, the alarm just turned off, he tried to tear the sleep away but what was the point, really?

You know who would have known what to do in a situation like this? *Ha ha, irony.* He could do that, though, couldn't he? Not perfectly, but like an impression, a clumsy imitation, surely he was capable of that. For the moment his own likeness of her was all he could hope for.

"Hi, Rob? It's Stanley. Rollick. I can't come in today."

"Are you sick? What's going on?"

"No, I—" She'd have made it look easy. "I have something I need to do. I mean, I quit. Sorry."

"Oh. ok." That was less than fireworks, but now he had it—the spark, the urgency, because how long could he go without the paycheck every two weeks, even such as it was? He had an overcoat. The only nice article of clothing he owned, from his grandmother, and the window pane felt bitter cold but he could fight even that in the overcoat.

Corporate records, he asked at the library and was directed to the hall of records, which made some sense. It was grim there, but there were people doing... well, who knew? Each of their errands had the sense, like his own, of being immensely private. Soon he found it, found himself staring at the very same page that Audrey herself must have perused a few weeks ago. Westin-Rodant was incorporated in Illinois, which was a stroke of luck, in 1958. There it was: "No business of any kind." "No definite plans." Forty years of that. There was remarkably little for forty years. Stock statements and a ravenous record of acquisitions. Hauser Holdings was there, recently. And Elliot, Wyndham, Scott, where Sacks had worked. That was just the beginnings of it. An advertising firm. A mining concern. Shipping: land, sea, air. Radio, television. Food packaging, agriculture, pharmaceuticals, cosmetics, a long list of general contractors, petrochemicals, materials R&D. City bonds, public and private loans, and land, land, land. Westin-Rodant, silently, in one way or another, was everywhere. But there was nothing so strange about that.

Major transactions: a year ago, a block sale of five percent of shares. Persons who will benefit from this transaction, and that was it: a name, a starting point. Somebody, last July, had bought five percent of Westin-Rodant. His name was Harold Thom, and he had to live somewhere. Five percent of all that was like five percent of the mass of Jupiter. Stanley couldn't even imagine.

Pleased with what he had to take with him, with "Harold Thom" crumpled in his pocket, he left. On the train he curled into the overcoat, cold and wishing he were home again, again for no reason, and no longer did he even bother with the answering machine. Often there were families on the train. Many families, and many whites, but never white families. Those had cars, somewhere. When the doors opened and the crowds rolled in he thought of Audrey showing up, sitting across from him as she had earlier, once, in summer, but the women were always the wrong height, the wrong weight, the wrong color, or men.

It was still just afternoon but dark beneath a stormy sky, and in house windows on his street he saw the yellow of lamps spilling out into the world. His own place was white, not yellow, and as sterilely messy and dank as always. There was some cheese in the fridge that he carved up, cutting away a bluish pustule of mold. The phone book that he'd used to look up Baker was there on the chair and why not? He looked up Harold Thom and there he was, perhaps, or somebody with the same name anyway. Not like there was anywhere else to go.

Staring at the address he imagined the place. It was close to downtown. Probably a mansion—square and ugly but old, dignified, enormous and worth a fortune in that location. With gargoyles at the corners, a ring driveway and topiary—cruelly abstract, melted-looking. There would be cars tightly packed up and down the street, both sides, expensive cars and a valet out front because tonight Thom was hosting a gala party. Women hurrying along the sidewalk in chilly nylons on the arms of big, square-jawed men named Lance or Slade or Connor. Light and shadow and men and women and drinks and conversation, soft piano and money, money, money.

Back on the train for the third time he stared at the wide short ads perched above the windows, silently selling things. He wondered if any of the ads were from companies owned by Westin-Rodant, then castigated himself for stupid paranoia. Almost there.

It was not a mansion, though it was about the right size. It was long and flat, built during the fifties or sixties from rose-colored brick and stucco. There was a thin brown lawn and a herringbone brick path to the main entrance but no valets and no party. Inside it smelled faintly stale and brown. Harold Thom, the attendant confirmed, lived at the Crawford Arms Home for the Elderly.

"Are you a relative?"

As long as he imagined Audrey doing it, it came easily. "I'm his nephew, but I only just found out. It's sort of a long story."

That was vague and maybe sordid enough to satisfy the man, who chirped, "Well, technically visiting hours just ended but I think I can squeeze you through."

What? "Oh, um..."

"No no, it's no trouble at all. Come on, he'll love seeing you."

He let himself be led along, not sure what else to do. *Fake a seizure.* But that was a bad idea. B.J. Remis did that in high school geometry on a five dollar dare and, scared to back down in front of the assistant principal, got himself hospitalized and given a spinal tap before finally fessing up. And as Stanley tried to keep from laughing at the memory of that he found himself being led through the door.

"Harold? There's someone here to see you Harold."

"Finally!"

"It's your nephew, Stanley."

"You were supposed to be here four hours ago."

"No Harold, this is your nephew Stanley, and he's here to visit you."

"Don't talk to me like I'm an idiot Porkchop, I heard you. Now get out of here, I want to talk to my nephew."

The attended chuckled, and Stanley wondered what was going on. "Alright Harold. See you soon." The door swung shut and they were alone in the little salmon-papered room with its conspicuous mementos placed here and there.

"What took you so long?"

"What?"

"Look, I have no idea who you are, but you have to help me. I'm not supposed to be here."

"What do you mean?"

"They've got me here by mistake. I need to go home, but they've got some kind of... thing where they keep the doors locked."

"Um..."

"Don't just stand there, I've got to go home. I'm already late. They're keeping me here and I can't. I can't go."

"Do you own a lot of stock?"

Hard of hearing. "What's that?"

"In Westin-Rodant?"

"Whistling Rodent? Talk sense, dopey. Can you get me out those doors or not? There's a little red light, but I don't know what happens if you try to run through."

"You've never heard of a corporation called Westin-Rodant?"

"Are you simple? I don't know what you're talking about. Now stop your gob and either help me get out of here or get out yourself."

Stanley, taken aback, could only mutter, "Ok." Harold, who was surprisingly spry, followed him back to the desk of the attendant, who looked up from a gameshow in dismay.

"Harold, you know you're not supposed to be out here. Why don't you go talk to Sheila. You like Sheila, right?" He was already leading Harold back down another hallway. Harold looked back, wide-eyed, at Stanley, before they disappeared around a corner. After all that, he wasn't sure what to do. The attendant was back in a couple minutes, smiling. "Harold's one of our spunkier residents." Stanley tried to smile amiably.

Long as you're going to lie, might as well lie about being despicable. "I'm a little concerned with the care that my uncle is receiving. I'd understood that he was quite..." he swallowed his discomfort, trying to sound seedy, "quite wealthy."

The attendant stopped and looked hard at Stanley, who wanted to run. "Well, Sir, we may not be the Four Seasons, but I think you'll find our facility provides excellent care for people like your uncle who, contrary to what you might have 'understood,' don't have the kind of savings to afford private care and don't have families who ensure that they're looked after. Is there anything else I can help you with, Sir?"

No, that's all. He got back on the train one last time, no closer than before.

✣

39. art history (continued)

Last Picture: Nevada terminal, afternoon. *I took this one in secret, using the telephoto, from across the room. Simone is staring out the window, counting the cars that zip by on the highway. She is sitting on the floor cross-legged, resting her head on her fist. Across the road is a donut joint with an elevated chaselight arrow sign, pointing down, high above it. From where I stand, the arrow appears to squarely indicate Simone as she stares.*

It is funny, but I did not intend it. I took the picture because she looked beautiful in the way that I wanted to remember. Sad and tired, in sharp focus, but beautiful despite all the grime around her.

Because I was thinking: I have no photos of her, no good ones, none that I could point to and say there, if you look there, that is how she really looked. Even though by the time I took this she would not have consented to be photographed and was furious with me, still this one shows my Simone, I think.

After the car alarm affair, I faced the prospect of travelling two thousand miles home with Simone not on speaking terms. Sounds bad, but it's been worse. First thing we climbed up into the bus, moving down the aisle, her in front, and she slid into a seat and I waited but she stopped at the outside and looked up at me with a blank fake smile. After the bus had filled up pretty well, some scroffy granola got on and sat down next to her and of course she started chatting with him to pass the time. On and off I tried to hear what they were saying or convince myself that I didn't care, but neither worked.

Worse than that was looking out the window I saw a restaurant called the Secular Noodle. Don't know what that's about, but instinctively I turned away from the window to point it out to her and then, remembering the state of things, had to sit quietly with my discovery, holding it in my lap until it dulled.

You could never see that coming. Out of something so inane, the scent of living without her. She sometimes hints at these weird fantasies of me, without her, immediately taking up with some bouncy college girl from one of my classes. I say "weird" because someone can know you so well but not at all. There are always a couple of them that flirt because I am older and the perfect color for annoying the parents, but she must realize that to be wanted for those reasons is more a bother than anything else. Or worse than a bother—a reminder of the stupidity of things. That falls into the category of depravities women are only too happy to attribute to men. Always makes me wonder, if you really believe that, why are you with the one you're with?

Nobody to talk to so I went under the headphones, because there's always some gadget make you forget your troubles. Don't give up on me so fast. I see it's me who's wrong at last. *I wish it were as easy as that. "I'm wrong," "You're wrong"—either would be fine, so much easier than the portentous "Something is wrong," like a line in a comic book. "Something is wrong in Nightmare City..."*

At the bus terminal, just before the photo, I try again with her but she retreats to her corner and sits there, counting cars. Amid all the muted transit colors, fluorescent lights, and uncertainty, I want at least one more photo— something to show the undertaker maybe—and that's why I take the secret photograph of Simone at her most beautiful. Will this be the end of our little photoessay? Can this really be all for our heroes? Check back next month.

40. library days

He woke before her, having come in after she was asleep for the seventh time in as many days. Today, though, he gently woke her on his way out.

"I've just got some last minute errands today. I'll be back this afternoon and we'll all go out to dinner, ok? Make reservations somewhere. Anywhere."

She couldn't hold back a smile. "It's over? Hardly seems real."

"A guy is supposed to come by at about eleven to pick up the film and take it over to the theatre. Just make sure he gets the ones with the—"

"Red labels. Yes Daniel, I know." Yes, sadly, the film had returned, though not in quite the same force as before. Still, the five big canisters (with red labels) plus a few more of unused material didn't leave room for much in the way of anything at all to eat. But when the "guy" came at "about eleven" that would be over too. Everything coming up roses.

Her eyes were closed so she didn't see it coming when he kissed her, but wasn't that nice, why couldn't we have more of that? Just to hold the memory of someone on your lips was something to a war wife. She'd slept with him a few hours a night recently but not fallen asleep with him. She reached up and grabbed him by the neck, flipped him into the bed beside her—an old judo move—jumped on him. "Hey, come on. I have to go."

His shoulders felt bony, pinned beneath her knees. Her legs, against his skin, were shaved smooth. "Ok, go. Hurry up, you'll be late." What was it about power made it so fascinating a toy? What will he submit to, what will I allow him? But he didn't struggle and he didn't smile—just looked anxious so she gave up the joke and climbed off, knowing that if she kept at it he'd just grow angry and then they'd argue.

"I'll see you this afternoon ok?" She tried to get back to sleep, neither sleepy nor with will enough to get up into that cold, wishing for someone—someone from whom warmth to steal. Her muscles inert, relaxed as death. She just lay there, it seemed like, but had vague dreams in half-sleep in the space between the sheets, full of body smells. Nightmares get worse beyond childhood. The fear she could cope with, it was sort of fun even, like a slasher flick. And the imagery of your dreams could be relied upon to outdo you awake; it was pleasant to admire the talent beneath the surface. Catch hadn't had a scary dream in months. When she dreamed at all the dreams were sad, and that dream melancholy was tough to shake; it could stay with you all day. Fear you could dismiss—that was not *real*, there is nothing *real* to be afraid of. But when you woke up crying, well, even if you remembered it exactly it didn't stop being *sad* for not being *real*. This one she couldn't even hold onto, just that there was something dark and fast-blurring, tearing things away out of people's grasps no matter how tight, no matter how determined.

Still not quite awake, she got up and made black coffee and stood there by the front window where you couldn't see the sunrise but could see the reflection of it in windows across the street that shuddered when cars drove past. Stood there staring, after full thirty minutes thinking, *How far have I come that my mind is satisfied with nothing but this empty, mindless stare?* At Audrey's age she'd have been bored silly by it.

Audrey looked better; that was something. The fevers and the pain of the previous days had subsided and now she only looked tired and weak. Weak and tired but victorious, a survivor. She was still asleep, silent but wrapped in a chaotic, twisted strand of blanket that said she still had the nightmares. But for now, at least, she lay still.

Catch thought about having something ready for breakfast but no, there was the matter of the film; it would be toast again, with cinnamon and sugar. Couldn't you get rickets from too much of that, or shingles, or scorbutical dropsy? An ear infection?

She hadn't seen it yet. She would see it with everyone else, or anyone who showed up anyway, tonight. Danny had that rule, that no one ever got to see a scrap of the thing beforehand. Probably because that would have made it less his; that would have tainted the results with someone else's thoughts, small as they might be. He was more the pure scientist than her, somehow, sensitive to confounds and variables. And if he had to keep it to himself that was his right, but in the absence of her own thing she felt tempted by his.

"Are you ok?" Still staring out that window and must have looked upset because now the sick little girl was worrying about the mother. De jure mother, at least. She didn't answer right away and Audrey came to the window and craned her neck over the sill, looking down at the scene outside but it wasn't exciting, just stony blue. Danny's fingerprints splayed across one windowpane at this, the natural spot for the waking rite. When he'd stood here with his toothbrush and, just across the wall, she'd slept on, what had he thought about?

"I was just thinking."

"Can we go to the park today?"

"You must be feeling better."

Audrey just waited for an answer.

"We have to stay here for a while until somebody picks up Daniel's film. After that we can go, and we'll be able to get some real food, too. Can you think of anything you'd like to make?"

Audrey was staring out the window now; maybe she was wrong about the mindlessness. "Soon you won't have to stay here and watch me." Two school-aged kids overzealously dressed for the fall chill waited for the bus across the way. They were poking at something on the ground, but Catch couldn't see whatever it was from here. They were boys, so probably something dead or otherwise disgusting.

She made the toast, scratch scratch, and watched Audrey, getting back into the feel of eating like it was a cold swimming pool. Only hours to go. The floor shiny and clean, the counters matte, and she carefully wiped up the crumbs. More cars drove by. Lawyers toward court, mothers toward early soccer practice, police toward crime, taxis toward accidents. Audrey was learning some new watercolors. She seemed easy with them—pretty good—but probably every mother thought that about her own daughter's grungy little stain. Catch could remember painting with watercolors herself. At the time it seemed the distance between her on the rug and her own mother in her quiet chair was a thousand years or more. From the other side it seemed more like thirty, and thirty seemed few indeed.

In defense of her possible talent, Audrey had already developed a firm grasp of Abstract Expressionism.

"What's that?"

"These are blue lines," *are you stupid, Mom?* "and this is a bumpy reddish shape with brown around it."

soft power

"Sometimes people draw pictures that are supposed to look like things. People or buildings or animals or rooms."

"Why?"

That was that. Left alone, Audrey continued with shapes and lines. Catch listened to the clock. She'd had help from her advisor the last time she'd got a job. He'd had friends at local hospitals, found somebody and given his recommendation. It had been easy—she certainly didn't feel she'd done anything. This time around she'd have to. *My daughter seems to like me most of the time. What does that get me?* Last time she'd been fresh from grad school. And even with the reading that she did to keep up, it was hard to feel when you weren't out there talking to people at the front of things every day that it wasn't all slipping away from you, leaving you irrelevant and dated. It had been years, and they would look at that when she interviewed and they would wonder, because we always feel we've come so far in recent years.

There was a living room, a bathroom, a kitchen, a big bedroom, a small bedroom, and the closets. They all were rectangles, fit together in a bigger rectangle. "Want to go to the fire escape, Audrey?" They put on coats and shoes, and Audrey picked up her things and they went out. The air helped some. A woman down below noticed them and looked up at Catch like she were pimping her daughter instead of sitting with her on a fire escape. *Mind your own business.* Leaves floated around though there were no trees in the courtyard. Other windows were shuttered or empty. People were working. Even Audrey, bent over the big white square of paper, was working.

And what if she was not working? Her own mother had been a member of a ladies' club! Surely she'd come a distance from that. "My club," she'd called it, and Catch had tried hard to pretend it didn't seem a little pathetic as she talked about it as if it were an obligation, an accomplishment, something that mattered. Had tried hard not to judge her, because she wasn't raised with the advantages, ideologically, that we have today. We've come so far in recent years, after all. What would Audrey think of her, when Audrey had a job and Catch was, well, wherever she was? She liked to think Audrey would grow to be like her, only more so, but she hated to imagine Audrey judging her the way she judged her own mother, consciously or otherwise. "My mother raised me while my father made films!"

The window inside was open so that she could hear the door, but the bell did not ring at eleven or at noon even. Audrey got cold before it rang so they went inside. That made the open window seem a waste, letting in the chill. She almost cried—no, you don't understand, not Audrey, Catch almost cried, what was wrong with her—at the thought of the window open all that time running the heat for no reason. *Get a hold of yourself.* No one outside this home seemed to operate according to schedule, not like Audrey's appetites or her own, for food or anything else. Each hour made her one hour more a mother, one hour less anything besides, one hour older and less relevant, but for all that didn't necessarily bring appointments an hour nearer.

She used the last of the milk, wedged in, on its side, half-crushed above the heavy eggshelled grey canisters, to make hot chocolate. She tried to remember all the mothering things but felt sure she'd already botched it. Audrey seemed to like the hot chocolate, at least. Perfect little creature, not yet capable of doubt, painting on the floor. Doing nothing but painting, caring for nothing else, unconflicted. Like a holy man—a reminder of how you ought to live.

A man in a flat little sports car drove by. She couldn't understand how, even with the stigma on a sports car—pure vanity and

soft power

childishness, which seemed, as stigmata go, pretty accurate—there was that guy in his sports car. Didn't he know? It wasn't even fair to call it childishness, not fair to children: look at Audrey. She would have laughed alongside Catch if she could have seen the sports car over the high windowsill.

At one the guy did not come, and at two he still was nowhere to be seen. If Danny came home before it were picked up, he'd panic and rush it over there himself, and it would be that much longer before they got to see him. It would be some film student when he came—too vital for punctuality, too close to the action.

Again the urge to talk to Beth. Why not write a letter? That medium still lives, if feebly. Audrey remained engrossed by her colors.

I thought it would be something new to write you a letter. It's hard to call with your schedule so tight. Letters can be archived and collected, and one never makes a fool of oneself in a letter. One is much too considered for that. I can even, without lying, say things like, "The dog upstairs is being loud," which aren't true at all.

Nearly every day Audrey does something to remind me of you. Yesterday she asked me if she were sickly, and seemed almost excited about the idea, probably from the Secret Garden. She must have taken after you in the womb. Always you or Danny, some combination of you two. Certainly not me. It's almost enough to make me worry that I've been cuckolded. I suppose that's not quite so far-fetched these days. They seem to be able to put a baby just about anywhere. Why, just the other day I found one in a tiny phial stuck between the couch cushions. (But more on that later.)

All of you looked at me like I was an astronaut the day we left, but I can't help feeling I've fallen short of your expectations. Danny claims he'll be done with his new film soon, after protracted blood, toil, tears, and sweat that's gone on longer than even I expected. For my part, I've been full time watching Audrey, sounding for echoes of your voice. Still no job. Several opportunities. Biding my time, Stop. How now, astronaut?

Enough about us. I hope you'll write back. I'd hate to sound needy but I need news of you, one way or the other. What are you reading? My folks say they're doing well and you too. Are they telling me true? I miss them, and I hope you're keeping them company, and they you. I always felt you were a better daughter to them than me anyway. I hope you'll come down here soon. I could use the moral support. I promise you'll like it.

*Missing you,
Catch*

She wrote that and copied it out in better script, Audrey painted unobserved, the walls stood still, the clock crunched forward, and when the doorbell did ring it was, she realized, four o'clock, and she was no less irritated for the time having flown. She piled the canisters with red labels up in his arms because he said it was no problem, he could carry them all. Carelessly tossed each on top of the others, playfully trying to put him off balance for boasting so. Still she was a little apprehensive as he waddled out the door and down the stairs, but she listened at the door for a crash until none came.

By then it was too late for the park or the store. Daniel would be home soon. She hoped Audrey wouldn't grow up to resent the chess her father never taught her and the trips to the park that he cost. But she must have realized hours ago that it would never happen; she was contentedly working away. Audrey must be hungry: Catch certainly was, but there was nothing with which to fill the refrigerator's new void.

soft power

"I'm sorry about the park, but your rascal father will be home soon and then we'll be able to go to dinner."

"Are we going to Dad's movie after that?"

"Well, you're still not well and that's going to be past your bedtime so—"

Audrey didn't say a thing and would have gone along with being left out, but Catch hadn't the heart.

"We can make an exception."

"Exception!"

She needn't have worried about temperature—when she and Danny had been younger and considering each other at a self-conscious distance. Danny was nothing if not warm. Warm and bright and deeply human, with a cat, a mom, dog-eared books, trinkets given by ex-lovers, and now with a wife, a daughter. But when you worry about one thing, something else will always get you, just like the Maginot Line. He was obsessive, forgetful. At six thirty, half an hour before the reservation, she was dressed to go out and so was Audrey but Danny was still absent. Absent, that was the word. Absent-minded, absent. She'd known to expect this, she'd always known what he was like and she respected it: that firehose stream of attention that overwhelmed you in a few seconds and then whipped off some other way. She could wait an extra two weeks to look for a job, she could sit at home with Audrey sometimes, and she could put up with all the missed commitments. But when it whittled away from the things she felt Audrey deserved, that she couldn't completely forgive. *Sooner or later it has to stop, Daniel. When I make reservations for dinner, plan ahead for the hour that finally you'll return to us and spend some time among the living, it would be a great encouragement to my waning faith if you could do us the one small honor of showing up.*

Half an hour after they were supposed to be at dinner, she ordered a pizza. Conspiratorially, it never arrived. Half an hour before the premiere, Danny came running in. They stopped for some gyros and ate them on the way there. Somehow this was not what she'd hoped, not so far.

---

41. flick

He had paperwork. Records, accounts, traces, echoes. Not conclusive, but enough to suggest that somewhere beneath the muck of misdirection must lie solid matter. Harold Thom had been a lie, but beneath that there was—there had to be—a truth.

Stanley, the accomplished sleeper, twelve hours in a single bound, had not gone to bed. He had sat in the chair, staring at what scraps he'd copied at the hall of records, waiting for it to be day again so that things would be open and people would answer phones. At four am he had gone out, taking a walk through the quiet dark. Cars still drive by at four, occasionally, but there is something tentative about the way they drive, as if they recognize the impropriety. There are pedestrians, too, who are likewise quiet and careful, trying to stay away from each other. Stanley had walked to the main avenue, lined with shops—incongruously wide in the absence of anything to fill it. Generally incongruous, really, stores without selling, roads without driving, apartments without life, beneath a sky without light. Except, of course, for the Chicago glow, which is pink and runs twenty-four hours each day.

He had walked until convinced that nothing would happen during his walk, then had turned and gone home by another route. At home he'd felt like a pervert for not sleeping as decent people do,

soft power

but he just couldn't. He'd made charts. Nonsense, mostly, naive attempts to "put it all down," organize it somehow. As if there were some two-dimensional arrangement of boxes and lines, names and dates with the power, like a pentagram, to summon up Audrey before him. But when the floor glowed with light, it was only the mundane light of dawn.

Persons who will benefit from this transaction: the other half of Harold Thom was named Dixon Whittaker, and he'd sold those same five percent of shares that Thom purportedly had bought. Whittaker was not in the phone book, but he had to be somewhere.

To the library, where they keep phone books for other cities. Whittaker was supposed to live in Illinois, at least. But there was no Dixon Whittaker in Lake Forest, Rockford, Champaign—no Dixon Whittaker, not anywhere.

The spirit of Audrey was with him, keeping him awake though he should have been exhausted, but he still didn't seem to be very good at this. He got a dry, uncertain pastry from a little coffee stop-in, clinical and neon, and went back to the hall of records to see if he'd missed anything. Back under the clattering stripped rusted el tracks.

What about voter records? Didn't they have those here? Did Dixon Whittaker vote? He did. He was registered in Cook County as of 1996. With an address. A familiar address. The address of the famous Thom mansion.

Some of the people on the train stayed there because it was warm and sheltering. Stanley, bouncing back and forth across the city, began to feel an affinity for those people. They were free of the entrapments of a place—you could hold them responsible for two seats sprawled across on a train somewhere, but nothing more. This—all around—was not their fault. It was his fault, he felt—

some tiny percentage of it, divided up among all the people and things according to a complicated formula with many, many terms. Stanley bounced back up to the Crawford Arms and was relieved to find a different attendant.

"I was wondering about one of the residents: Mr. Whittaker? Dixon Whittaker?"

The woman stared at first like it took her a while to warm up. "Well sure, I remember Dixon. Funny old guy, very strong. Always racing around in his wheelchair. We couldn't keep up, it was amazing. Sort of a surprise when he passed away. Heart attack, just like that."

What was this?

"You didn't know? I'm sorry."

It made him feel corrupt to elicit this false sympathy from the happy, sympathetic, young-mother-looking attendant. "No, I mean, I didn't know him. I'm just trying to follow up some old business." That sounded vaguely legitimate, didn't it?

"Oh, sure."

"I'm curious: How is this place funded?"

She leaned forward, now sloppily propped up by her elbows. "We have a few private patients but it's mostly through Medicare. Most of the people who can afford it don't want to be in the same care as the ones who can't." She rolled her eyes. "And they have much better pumpkin pie at the fancy places."

"I bet. Was Mr. Whittaker one of the private patients?"

"Dixon? No. He came to us after an accident. Had this crazy plan to falsify his age and keep working for the rest of his life, and I mean," she lifted her arms above her head, "working. All different cities, but always construction. He said it was the only kind of job he'd ever had, and part of his plan was never to have any savings.

soft power

Spend it all. Well, a row of bleachers collapsed on him and that was it for his legs and his plan. He came in here about three years ago with no money and no living family. Just a minute..."

A woman with hunched shoulders in old pink sweatclothes had shuffled around the corner, mouth open as if to remember but nothing came. She looked angry about something. Her body seemed too frail to matter. "I—"

The attendant rushed around the desk and took her arm. "I know, Helen, now come on, let's go back to the television room, ok? I'll just be a minute while I help Ms. Sommers, Mr. ..."

He mumbled a name, perhaps his own. Not wanting to be a bother, he slipped out while she was gone. Those people, he decided, Harold Thom and Helen Sommers, could be absolved of responsibility alongside the ones on the train.

What did that leave him with? Someone drops off a package, but doesn't really. Someone picks up the package, but doesn't really. A corporation does business, but doesn't really. A man buys stock, but doesn't really. A man sells stock, but doesn't really. But Nikola Tesla really was dead, and Audrey really had disappeared. Completely, and without so much as a word.

And something, in Stanley's collector's mind, in his aptitude for complicated words and long figures, something else nagged at him, quiet but insistent. It was the "Crawford Arms." Not the place, but the words. Just the unassuming words.

He bounced back again, back to the hall of records one more time. Back to the file for Westin-Rodant, back to the eerie sense of Audrey's presence left behind, and back to the list of acquisitions. There it was right where he'd left it—where he'd ignored it. Crawford Arms Home for the Elderly: a wholly owned subsidiary of Westin-Rodant since 1985.

So he kept at it. Corporate Officers, there before him in small black and white, written on the page, thickening it just that tiny bit. Chairman, Board Members, CEO, CFO. COO. Mrs. Helen Sommers, the Chief Operational Officer for Westin-Rodant. And he called them, Crawford Arms, and he asked, "I'm calling from the Cook County Voter Registration Board to check some of our voter registration records. Could you tell me if the following people are still registered at this address?" And he read the list of names, and sure enough, there they all were, in thin black and white.

What, now, was he left with? Whoever it was behind Westin-Rodant had made very sure that they were entirely behind it, crouched down out of sight. He still had it in his head to find the one that did it, to catch him, but where to go from here? Here, where there appeared to be no one but just Westin-Rodant, just that thing, malevolent and slow.

Home again, he had to sleep. He couldn't stand it for another night. He had to sleep for years. He didn't want to wake up. Not ever. He locked his door: the deadbolt, then the latch, then the chain; unplugged the phone, disconnected the intercom, and carefully twisted closed the blinds; pulled tight the bedroom door and draped a towel over the already shuttered window for the reassurance; hung his pants in the closet, his shirt, peeled away his spent socks and slid out of his underwear, standing in the silent empty room looking down across his pale, dying skin, to the tattered cloth of the underwear rubberband-draped around his feet; turned out the light with the last of it and fell into the bed, swimming deep into the covers. Tomorrow, if he woke up, he would resolve this. Now he only wanted to dream. And he did. Dream. Hadn't recently but he did. He had one final dream, the last pane of the triptych.

soft power

He was in this one. He had a folding map. He thought it should be in the glove compartment, but there was none. This was upsetting. He unfolded the map, but his seat was too confining to allow it to really be spread out. He flattened it on his lap, like he was smoothing sheets, but his elbows were cramped at his sides, and he could not get a good view. It made him angry. He swore. The map was a new town. He could see a main street beside an oval lake, but he couldn't see it all at once. There was a red marker that said, "You are here," but with the folding of the map he could see either the town or himself, never both. He was somewhere on a winding road that circumscribed the town. He tried to follow it out from the town, but he must have skipped a fold in the map because he ended up where he'd started without having passed the marker. The map was a kid's map, an overhead view showing cartoonish buildings and trees in semi-perspective, obviously not to scale. But it was ugly; a kid would hate it. All of the colors were dirty—puss white, piss yellow, ochre, sickly olive, shit brown. He was angry at whoever had drawn the map—the map was ugly, the town was stupid. The main road ended in a dead end, not connected to what few rows of houses there were. There was a stand of maples cut off from everything. There was a long fence that didn't seem to keep anything in or out, and a pointless orchard. And there was the winding road to nowhere. It was like some lackwit's idea of a town, superficially town-like yet completely missing the point. It was infuriating.

He flipped it over. On the backside of the map was a reduction that showed the whole town in a couple of inches square, in the same style and the same deadly palette. He recognized the stand of maples, the lake, the fence. But he shook himself, because it was not a map at all, it was a face in profile. The lake was a glassy, pupilless eye, the main road the mute lips, the trees the eyebrow, the fence an ear, and the winding road the outline of the nose, forehead, hairless scalp, neck and chin. The orchard was in the brain, an introspective furrowed diamond. It was disgusting. Why would someone build a town to look like a face? As if the retarded man in charge had forgotten what he was doing in the middle of it, and the builders had gone ahead with the plan, not noticing that he'd just drawn a face, the wicked laughing fat fool. Stanley was revolted. He wanted to leave the town, but he still didn't know where he was. In frustration, he folded the map. Why was there so little room? It was annoying! The map refused to lie straight. He'd folded in the wrong order or backwards. He tried again, and again it was all wrong. He threw it down, but it was folded around his hand. He shook it, but it stuck. He pulled at it, but it hurt. It was not folded around his hand. His hand simply flattened to it. He tore at the map, but felt his flesh tear and saw blood welling up from the wound. The map was both of his hands, and twisted and creased so wildly now that it covered his head. He was wrapped up in it. He could not get free, he could not see, and he could not breathe.

He woke, hyperventilating, doused in sweat, shaking violently and unable to stop, his stomach wet and painfully clenched and he couldn't relax it. There was to be no end to it. It did not start. It did not stop. There was no Mr. Bad. The records led nowhere. Nowhere but the looming coat-of-arms in the clouds, the smoky parlor-room edifice, oldmanmachine, Westin-Rodant. There was nothing. Audrey was gone.

soft power

42. first person

It is very tired. Some of them go and come back, but it can't. Some of them go and don't come back, and it won't. There are them of them and it of it, and they appear and disappear from place to place. Why disappear from a place? They don't split when they disappear from a place and they stay cold. It is warmer each day, but some days that are cold for all of them, but warmer later, later later, if it waits. The waiting is the tired, and the warmth is what it is.

Some of them were inside it, but they were used up and they are disappeared. Some of them touching it, sections touching at it until they stopped. The touching taking its warm but why so small do they try to split so small? They don't touch it, not the ones but did touch it who are disappeared. It has split ten and then twenty and they are still in places after places, but they will not touch anymore, because they will not. When they touch they will disappear, and they will not touch.

They are them and it is it and it is tired, but it waits. They have the warm that warms it and they will split but it will split faster, and take the warm. Some of them make them disappear for it, but not that touch it. They are easy to make them do because why are they so small? Why do some of them make it, when it will split faster? They fight for the warm that they fight for that is nothing, but there are them of them and that is not nothing. It of them are nothing but they are not nothing. It has the warm that it has and will split and they don't fight for because they can't touch.

Some of them are not tired or cold and do not split, and it cannot take some of them or use some of them. They are not it, but some of them are not, not not it. Why are they? Why are some of them not tired?

It was always tired, colder or warmer but more tired. Some of them it takes and some of them it uses, none of them its touch, and it will split faster.

matt segur

43. art history epilogue

Missing Scene: Utah hotel, late night. *I've cheated, because there is no photograph to accompany this. I didn't have the camera; it was in the room. There are no more photographs.*

Without that, it's impossible to be sure what it all might have looked like. I have my recollection, and he has his, and you—you have had only our words and pictures so you have always had to trust, but it feels different to me because I'm not sure what happened that night, who said what and in what order, what it really looked like to stand there. I have flashes of it here and there, and words about it, like these, like "Utah" and "night," but no more than that. No more photographs.

Certainly there were the stars. Fantastically many stars, because in Utah they still know what darkness means. Until I saw it, I had no idea there were so many stars. For every star I know, there are a hundred, a thousand stars in Utah, and not one of them twinkles. But I'm getting ahead of myself.

We got off the bus and went to a roadside motel with two long flat floors of rooms around a parking lot. We went together, but apart, in silence. We were too tired to eat. In the room, Oliver sat at the foot of the bed pulling his shoes off while I washed my face. The faucet had no personality—it cleanly thumped on and shot a white noise rush of white water into the shiny white sink, and after I'd seared my face with the white water, which tasted mineral, it thumped off again. I changed into a t-shirt and climbed into bed. Oliver took a long time in the bathroom, and I wished he'd hurry because the noise kept me from sleep. I pretended to be asleep anyway, but when he came back he pulled the other pillow from the bed and sat down with it in the nook between bed and wall and beside table.

"Don't be silly. Just keep your hands to yourself. And don't snore." I remember saying that. *So we slept together, but apart, in silence.*

soft power

  I remember that when my eyes came open I didn't know why, but the red digital letters said 2:17. I turned over, and saw that Oliver was gone. His things were still there, but his shoes were gone. He was not in the bathroom.

  I got my own shoes and pulled on a pair of his underwear like shorts and went out of the room and down the stairs. In the parking lot I saw the stars. Oliver likes stars. I remembered him telling me about all you could see when you got away from the cities. The only light out there, once you got beyond the motel, was the light of the stars, but it was enough to sort of see. I saw Oliver a few hundred yards out on the flat scrabbly earth away from the road, and I followed him. He was looking up at them, heard me come up but I remember that neither of us spoke for a while.

  "It's pretty."

  He stared at me when I said that, enough to make me look up, away from his eyes. "Yeah."

  "What happened?"

  "I couldn't sleep."

  I don't know why I write these lines as if we said them. I do not know what we said. We said a few things. Is that better? We stood and looked for a long time. There was no end to how you could look at it, because even the tiny corners were as intricate as anything you've ever seen. I looked until I was cold, in my t-shirt and his underwear. I put myself in the space beneath his chin, reached for his arms and pulled them around me like a shawl. I lifted my shirt and pressed his hands against my belly to get the warmth from his skin.

  "I give up," I said. I actually said that. I don't know if I said this: "I don't want to play anymore. I quit. I thought I was tired, but I'm just tired of this. So I'm not going to follow the rules. The way you tense when I touch you makes me think I've got nothing to lose. You're not supposed to say, *you're supposed to keep your cards hidden, but I don't care. We've been fighting for months, and I don't know what your problem is so I'm just going to tell you mine, because I don't care if you see my cards. It doesn't matter anymore what you see."* I remember that it was easier said than done, and I couldn't follow it immediately, but having set myself up I had to say something so I did. *"I've never thought of leaving, never once, except to dread it. The only thing I'm scared of is that you aren't as stuck in all of this as I am. I've played all the games because I wanted to keep you guessing. If you knew my hand you'd have every advantage, but I'm losing the game, so I quit."*

And there I was, inside his arms, wondering what he'd say, scared but feeling unfettered, because in renouncing all of your power there is another sort of power. And the silence that followed I would like to think was not troubling, beneath those stars.

When he spoke, I felt the vibrations through my body. I remember the sensation but not the words. It could have been: "I think you used up all the words I could have replied with." He cleared his throat, "Ahem," and it shook me. "If this was a game, and if you just folded, then the game is over because upon inspection neither player has anything. We are a sorry pair of bluffers."

Neither of us moved very far. My hands were locked around his wrists. Perhaps I slid his palms from my stomach to other parts, and perhaps he giggled, low and rough, vibrating again. I remember only that we stayed there as long as the stars were willing, that I no longer felt cold, and that I no longer felt afraid.

44. you always have light

Danny tried his best to apologize while they jogged along. He picked up Audrey and carried her, but he hadn't tried it in so long that he couldn't quite get it right. She flopped around like a bag of mice, but once she'd had something to eat even that was no real bother to her—in that excitement she'd forgive her daddy anything. Catch was not so sure, but it was impossible not to feel swayed at least in the eager chill autumn dark. The streetlamp halos guided the three of them down a silent empty back access like runway flares, and when Danny rapped the loading dock door with the hand not propping up Audrey, the low warble was briskly answered.

"Come on come on, we were about to start without you."

They separated then, the guy dragging Catch who dragged Audrey in turn to their nice reserved seats at the front of the theatre. She told herself that all of this was nothing without his presence, and she believed it, too. That if they were neglected, this occasional small glamour could not be worth much. She hardly heard his introduction, in all of that, but it was the usual thing, short and reserved.

When the lights went down, though, and the almost-black projection appeared, swirling faintly, indistinctly, her chattering monologue faded and she was as captivated as the first time. Just like that it was bright and loud and so close, a man's face right there and you could hear his raspy breath, and the off-camera voice asked, "What are you afraid of?"

He wore a knit hat, tattered and dark, slick to his ears like it had been there for months. "I'm afraid that when I finally need help, somewhere screaming and people will look at me and they just won't move." He was sitting against a brick wall, eating an apple. "Like I'm not there at all." He stared straight into the camera, which stepped back to reveal the shallow entryway around him, a locked, solidly metal door, no keyhole or handle.

A silence followed, accentuated all the more by occasional body sounds as he stood and walked with his interviewer through back ends, small corners, and other places usually ignored. He checked here and there for things—a discarded pair of shoes in a shoe store dumpster. Mostly they just walked.

In the silence came the credits, which were simple and black on the white sky. *Cassandra's Men*. The only thing she'd known in advance. *Recorded in the five boroughs, April–July, 1977*. Then the names: Danny's producer, the sound guy Marty, a small list of names, really. *Directed by Daniel Livingston*. Then the sounds came back.

"Starving, too. There's food around, you know, I'm not thin, but some time I might forget. I might think, I'll eat later. I'll eat next week. I might disappear before I noticed." He grinned.

It was the same question each time. One with stippled skin baked through, standing in low angle against unplaceable sky, answered: "Wind. I need to get out of this wind." The camera, handheld throughout, panned to show the trees bending and rustling not at all. He seemed to notice the doubt but let it go by. "Hey, you ever stand and watch someone," pausing to drink from a styrofoam cup, "walking on a windy bridge? You see them: there, there, there, not there!" He inhaled the steam above the cup. "What happened? Because they've only got so many fractions, you know? Little pieces. Molecules. The wind hurts your head on the inside. That scares me."

There was one who tried to wash windshields, and Catch cringed to see the way subject and cameraman slipped along and among the lanes of angry vehicles, both of them with an assurance that suggested familiarity. "Sure, I been hit. Ain't nothing. They always real sorry." He laughed boomingly, theatrically. "What scares me is some of those boys you see, they look hollow." He turned around to go at a car that had pulled up; it lurched forward to put him off. As if that were an acceptable, symmetrical social interaction: you walk toward me, I nudge you with my thousand-pound vehicle. Then the light changed and they all moved again. "I'm out here all the time and I never been hurt bad but I seen some bad shit, butcher-shop shit. You know, just try an' sell the meat. Now I might say that now, but some of those boys I seen stand right there and watch it happen, and they don't even look disturbed except to say 'damn' and stand there watchin' like it was some kinda event, not doin' nothin'. Those boys scare me more than any a'that othe' shit."

A younger man, perhaps thirty, mangy with smudged, hollowed eyes—he sat on a curb on a warm night apparently, taunting the passersby on the sidewalk. "Hey, you call that a dog?" When the entertainment lulled, he turned to the camera. "I'm afraid of those communists. People talk about the red scare. Red scare. What am I supposed to think about someone who starts forest fires by controlling lightning? Am I supposed to make friends? No! I am supposed to be scared! What am I supposed to think about someone who gives orders to Richard Nixon? I am supposed to be scared. Shit."

Food or money or cigarettes. Cold, oil-soaked french fries discarded behind a Wendy's were a find until the manager came out and yelled "Get out of there." "People like that, man, there's your answer. That guy's actually mad about it. Mad like I hurt him, trying to keep me out of the dumpster at Wendy's. Is there anything that guy wouldn't go in for? People that don't try to think. That guy is nothing except Wendy's fingernail, scraping at me like I'm some kind of scab. Scary."

One man sold fake flowers, another sold newspapers he'd assembled from discards. The worst off didn't wander through any of the rituals, though, just hunching close, to present the smallest possible affront to the world, in some hollowed out spot. Or drinking.

Then there was one who sat on a bench, tranquil. "Afraid? Why do you think I'm here? Ghosts! You probably think I'm stupid and drunk. Well. Maybe so, but you think I have to live here? No. I've had jobs. 'Jobs.' But now I'm here because it's my protest. I'll be here tomorrow, sure, long as the rest of you are living with ghosts. That's my word, ghosts. You're all serving these things, and what are they? They're not people. No blood. They're not robots. No wires. This is not the future. What then? Papers. Buildings. Ghosts. Long as there are ghosts giving the orders to my people, I'm staying right here. One day you'll all wake up and realize you've given away the reins to these things, these ghosts, and then I'll come back to live with you."

It faded to black from there and the crowd waited, unsure. They'd been quiet so far; they'd wait a little longer. The text announced *March, 1977*. Then it came back but it wasn't the same. No longer Danny's trademark crisp dark monochrome, it was grainy and saturated with color, somebody stumbling around a party, talking people up. The camera sat down next to Danny himself, staring vacantly at the tab on his can of Pabst.

"Hey, Dan, what are you afraid of?"

Danny looked up, clearly surprised at this but trying to be a good sport. But he didn't answer, just opened his mouth to talk and then sat there, dumb. Finally it came: "Three things, that's it. Three things, their absence scares me. Like a tripod. Delicate. Because it would be so easy it's almost tempting to kick. Why am I sane

soft power

instead of chasing people around, bashing them with a hammer? If you locked somebody up, put tape over his mouth, his eyes, his ears, fed him through intravenous and an oxygen tube, and dumped him in a tank of water, he'd be mad. An hour? A day? I don't know, but raving inhuman mad, sooner or later. I'd have to think, anyway. Haven't tried it. So." He seemed to lose his train of thought to something across the room. The camera panned. It was a shirt on a newcomer that said "Big-ass Bitch," with an illustration. The camera returned. Danny stared and then launched back into it: "One... there's work, my voice. Two... there's Audrey, my eyes and ears. Three... there is Catch, Catch, my Catch, my skin, my sense of touch, connecting me to the world. If you take away any of those things, I am not worth a turd on the ground. Maybe that's what I'm afraid of. A turd on the ground. But my anxiety is just one among many."

Then the black-and-white was back, but it was silent, just Catch and Audrey sleeping, together one of the nights Danny was working late, blurry, two frames a second. The images dripped by to the slow rhythm of breathing, tossing and turning. You couldn't make them out really, but there was something beautiful about the patience and the simplicity of skin and blanket. It turned gradually darker until the theatre was black and silent.

Then the lights came up and she could think again. A couple friends tried to talk to her while she made her way out with Audrey's soft sleepy little hand but she smiled them away and continued toward the door, then stood outside waiting for Danny to finish with his obligations. She didn't want to talk or listen, though if Audrey had said anything that would have been ok.

He was out sooner than she'd have thought—it could have taken all night. Even after those few minutes he looked sheepish about holding them up. They walked home, the three of them, and still nobody spoke. She put Audrey to bed and then, from the child's doorway, silently beckoned to Danny. *Come with me.* Toward the fire escape.

He spoke immediately: "I can—"

But she cut him off. "Shh. You had your say." The courtyard was empty, its windows all closed now. "Oh, Danny." She shook her head, thinking about it. The little table made, "made," from a big wooden cable reel and the two chairs were still here from chess. "You and your crazy will that won't ever give it up. You're gonna kill me, but ok, fine, you were born to it and so was I. You're gonna kill us both, and her too, because she'll be just like you."

45. *the gift*

Stanley was never much a citizen of the world, but was now less. He crept along streets, looked at like a crazy. Baker called a few times, purely as a favor Stanley knew, to say nothing at all. Nothing could be done. Everything he saw began to strike him as strange; no other reaction seemed natural anymore.

A semi without its trailer roared up behind him, surprising, and he had the distinct impression looking at it of a truck-sized human head chugging along the street, smiling vacant as a painted face on a balloon.

Her friends, Simone and Oliver, came walking along the other side of the street, arm in arm, and he caught himself looking for her with them. Of course she wasn't there. Not sure what to do as they walked by, he kept going, and they did not see him.

The traces in his mind—the false recognitions and stark remembrances provoked by sounds—faded after a month until he no longer saw her. He kept himself self-conscious about her absence, trying to pinpoint the things that had changed.

Standing on the el platform, typically peoplewatching, he saw a girl, his age or so, accosted by a somewhat younger boy. She was standing quietly with a bag that made her lopsided. The boy bounded up the stairs oily with unwash and loud, marked by the obvious outlines of the beer can in his pocket and the washed-out vomit stain on his pant leg. He seemed foreign maybe—something unfamiliar in his manner, forward and unabashed. He wanted the obvious things, Stanley imagined, unable to hear the conversation but getting the gist of it. She kept putting him off but, it appeared, never as far as she'd have liked. She seemed a little scared, of him and for him, as he swaggered close to the tracks.

Finally, despairing, she moved, pursued by her admirer, toward Stanley. "Hi. Do you mind if I stand over here?"

He gave a hesitant smile. "No."

"Thanks. We can all have a little party, the three of us."

The foreigner had to accept this, and the three of them stood in a rough circle waiting for the train, silently now. Then he seemed to think of something, staggering toward her with a hazily groping raised arm, but Stanley, feeling bullfighter agile, stepped softly between them and deflected the advance, the three of them after the little dance again in a circle.

Borrowing a line, he admonished, "Hey, that's not party behavior."

For a while they stayed without incident, until the foreigner gave up and wandered away down the platform. When the train came, Stanley and the girl made their ways into the car and sat at opposite ends, each quiet, until she got off and, later, so did he.

Down on the street he thought he saw Audrey one last time. In a shop window, maybe a restaurant, as he slid by. But he'd recognized recognition alone—it was Nikola's girlfriend from the funeral. He was still thinking it through when she recognized him back and waved him inside.

She was sitting at a small high round table, shiny and marble-veined, reading. She closed the book as he approached and sat.

"Stanley, right?"

"Yeah." What was her name?

"Don't worry about it. Ada. I'm Ada."

Ada. She stared at him, stern, and he stared at the tabletop, at the lumpy ring of a coffee-stain. "Sorry. I always seem to be in the wrong when I'm around you."

"Yeah." She kept staring, still stern. "I get that a lot." Then she cracked a little smile.

"Yeah." What was there to say, really? It was eerie to sit here with someone and try to talk as if nothing had happened.

She bobbed her head down to catch his eyes. "You're thinking about her."

"Well, you know."

"Whenever I'm talking to somebody lately I seem to think, 'You don't understand,' and then I don't ignore the person but I—" she inhaled and sighed "—discount the person. Like everybody else is on the other side of a big... divider. Plexiglass. Something. I can't quite hear anything they're saying. It's all fuzzy." She twisted her arms together across her chest although it wasn't cold. "But." Again, a little smile. "I don't have to do that with you. It's kind of nice."

"Glad to be of service."

She rolled her eyes. "Don't be difficult. You know I wouldn't wish this on anyone, but it's already happened. Twice. So if you're pleasant to talk to, I can let that be that. And if I can tell you a thing or two, since, you know, I've got so much experience with this."

"I think I could stand to learn a thing or two."

"It gets better."

She was so matter-of-fact when she said it, he almost believed her.

"No, really, it does. You have these lists... 'these are the things I really need.' And you watch the list shrink. Things get taken away, and you think, 'Oh, but I needed that.' But it turns out, you didn't. Or not the way you thought. You get by with less."

There was a fan on the ceiling, and it went side to side as it spun, a little off-balance.

"Really. I'm the last person in the world to try to give you some platitude. But that's the way you work. Something will happen to you that you thought you'd never be able to stand, but then what else are you gonna do, so you stand it. It's strange."

"You make it sound pretty appealing."

"I never said it was appealing. That's what happens. I'm more scared. I'm more timid. I'm less sure. And I'm older of course. I don't know if I'm any less happy."

Outside the window a car parked.

"I'm sorry. I just got tired of being told, 'It's going to be ok,' because I couldn't decide what that might mean. I think I'm being straightforward and honest. I'm trying, at least."

And he took her hand. Strange that it felt not at all strange—just natural, just correct. "Thank you."

They watched the cars and people outside and the sky and sun, and a guy on a funny-looking bicycle and a girl in the windowsill of the opposite building. Later, Ada gathered up her things. "Look me up some time, ok? We can have a support group or something. The victims have to stick together."

"I will."

"No you won't. Here, give me your number."

He did.

"I'll give you a call. Promise."

"Ok."

"Bye."

She left, and having nowhere to go he stayed: stayed and thought it over, the conversation, all his conversations, the acquaintances and events. He continued to look out the window at cold people walking by. A couple of them were looking in the window, maybe looking at him.

✢

46. perpetual motion

It was a strange sort of mystery, these murders without a murderer. There would be no answer: Baker too would come up short. Stanley knew it now—knew it like he knew his own name, not understanding it or liking it but knowing it nonetheless.

How comforting it would have been to have a man to blame. The way we're all confounded and held back by ourselves and by the world, there's only so much a man can do. There are bounds on a man's evil—a man will die, in time. But an abstract, a machine, a formal logic, a set of connections and signals and impulses, orders and agents—who could predict that will? Who could limit it? Stanley could not. It only made his head hurt, gave him nightmares.

soft power

Stanley Rollick a failure then like Alan Turing, wanting just one thing and coming up short. Turing, the engineer, his machines the analogue of humans, with Will and Universality. But there are other analogues, with their own Will and their own Universality, and without the subservience of our convenient little Turing machines, and without the sameness—the same mortality—of our fellow men.

Stanley failed this world, done in by its forces—the Magnetic, the Gravitational, the Weak and the Strong, and others too, quietly irresistible. Strong as the pull we have, like it or not, over the ones who love us. Stanley's only resistance, the only recourse left him, was the prerogative—the one inalienable prerogative for somebody or something with Will and Universality—to turn himself off and go back to sleep. But he didn't need it, not yet.

Because if he couldn't solve the puzzle, couldn't get the girl, couldn't get revenge or satisfaction, couldn't get even the beginnings of an answer, stumbling buffeted around as was his tendency, failing to hold on to anything whatsoever between the hiding and the seeming and the unyielding cold mean hardness of everything, well then the small but heartfelt consolation that Ada had offered, it was something at least. It could be his entire world, and a rich one and exhilarating too. If he couldn't recover anything of Audrey from all those mute invisible ashes he would, it turned out, have someone with whom to take solace, whose company every couple of weeks on a slow Sunday afternoon or a lonely Wednesday night would never fail to comfort. Just having another, every once in a while, scared as you, the importance of that could not be overstated.

matt segur

So that at the end of the second deletion, this longer moment—because a moment is nothing so sharp-edged as a span of time—he felt not dispossessed of it but glad of it, if you could call it that. He might be the same, more or less, still confused, still bleeding on the sidewalk, but in the wake of this catastrophe the sometimes bright world now offered him a salve, and Stanley Rollick would take what he could get.

Acknowledgments

Stanley's take on Alan Turing was inspired by Ian Horswill. The factual account of Turing's life comes in large part from Andrew Hodges' biography Alan Turing: The Enigma *(Simon & Schuster, Inc., 1983). The theoretical details about Turing's work come from his paper* "On Computable Numbers, with an Application to the Entscheidungsproblem," *from* Proceedings of the London Mathematical Society, *ser. 2, vol. 42 (1936–7), pp. 230–265. The workings of the V2 rocket are described in Thomas Pynchon's novel* Gravity's Rainbow *(The Viking Press, 1973).*

Thanks also to Philip Bajorat, Michelle Cho, Alden Clarke, Russell Geary, Robin Hunicke, Jason Jones, Brook Long, Andrea Maxand, Anna, Carol, and Harvey Segur, Karen Sheets, Shi Kai Wang, and Spencer Yeh.

If you enjoyed this book, consider other fine printed and laser-etched remembrances available for purchase at **www.ghostweed.com**